ChangelingPress.com

Torpedo/Beast Duet
A Bones MC Romance
Marteeka Karland

Torpedo/Beast Duet
A Bones MC Romance
Marteeka Karland

All rights reserved.
Copyright ©2021 **Marteeka Karland**

ISBN: 9798516370007

Publisher:
Changeling Press LLC
315 N. Centre St.
Martinsburg, WV 25404
ChangelingPress.com

Printed in the U.S.A.

Editor: Katriena Knights
Cover Artist: Marteeka Karland

The individual stories in this anthology have been previously released in E-Book format.

No part of this publication may be reproduced or shared by any electronic or mechanical means, including but not limited to reprinting, photocopying, or digital reproduction, without prior written permission from Changeling Press LLC.

This book contains sexually explicit scenes and adult language which some may find offensive and which is not appropriate for a young audience. Changeling Press books are for sale to adults, only, as defined by the laws of the country in which you made your purchase.

Torpedo (Bones MC 7)
Marteeka Karland

Ambrosia -- When I went to the penthouse, I was expecting a playboy. I wasn't even surprised when the playboy in question answered the door stark naked. The gun surprised me, but, hey. I just roll with it because it's a job. Given my present circumstances, work is hard to come by. My crazy ex, Tyler, got put in prison, and his equally crazy father, Richmond, decided it was my fault. He's managed to get me fired from every job and kicked out of every apartment I've landed since. What I need is a hero. Unfortunately, those are in short supply. Until I catch the attention of a crazy, naked man wielding a gun. Sensing a theme here?

Torpedo -- After more than a month on the roof of the world, I'm ready for some sunshine. The last thing I need or expect is another woman vying for my attention. The cute little thing who has the job of being my personal butler while I'm on vacation changes all that. She's professional and courteous, never coming on to me like most women do. Lord knows I gave her reason to, answering the door naked as the day I was born. She runs fast enough when I inform her I was in the middle of a self-pleasuring session, though. Can you see my smirk? Unfortunately, she doesn't need a naked man in her life. She needs a hero. One to slay her demons. Fortunately for her, that man is me.

Table of Contents

Torpedo (Bones MC 7)..............................
    Chapter One..
    Chapter Two ....
    Chapter Three...
    Chapter Four..
    Chapter Five ....
    Chapter Six...
    Chapter Seven ....
    Chapter Eight..
    Chapter Nine ....
    Chapter Ten ....
Beast (Salvation's Bane MC 2) ....
    Chapter One..
    Chapter Two ....
    Chapter Three...
    Chapter Four..
    Chapter Five ....
    Chapter Six..2
    Chapter Seven 2
    Chapter Eight..23
Marteeka Karland...251
Changeling Press E-Books 252

Chapter One

The sun beat down like an everlasting holy light. Torpedo basked in it. Scotch in hand, he sipped the amber liquid, savoring the burn. After a month in the cold of the Himalayas, he needed this respite. He was a big man, and spending so much time at high altitude hadn't been easy. Most mountain climbers are slight and wiry. He was tall and heavily muscled. The guide his client had been with had smirked at him the way only an experienced mountaineer could smirk at an amateur who thought he could play with the big boys.

Well, it hadn't been his Goddamned idea in the first fucking place. Little princess meant to show her daddy she could do whatever the fuck she wanted. Daddy had been determined to have someone baby sit her, given the recent threats to him. Torpedo couldn't blame the man for wanting to protect his daughter, but, honestly, the she'd been a bitch about it. She'd done everything she could to make it hard on Torpedo, Shadow, and Vicious, choosing destinations that would be the hardest on the team of big paramilitary bikers.

Fucking bitch.

Just thinking about the situation now made his hackles rise. Had Bones, or more correctly ExFil, been actually calling the shots like they should have been, they'd have never left the Goddamned country. Hell, they might not have left the fucking *house*. It had cost Shadow and Vicious a lovely case of pulmonary edema for which they were still being treated in the hospital. It had cost Daddy's little princess a busted ass. And not in a good way either. That episode had been both repugnant and satisfying.

Had it been any other woman but the spoiled little rich girl, he'd have gladly given her more. The woman had clearly enjoyed her spanking, but she'd disqualified herself from being fucked by virtue of the fact she was a bitch. *And* her voice got on Torpedo's ever-loving last nerve. She was a whiner. Even doing what she'd chosen to do, she whined the whole time. It was too cold. The sun was too powerful so high up on the mountain, and her fair complexion burned easily. Her feet hurt. The wind burned the delicate skin of her cheeks. No. Really. Where's the bathroom? *Blah, blah, blah.*

When Shadow'd had to be carried down the mountain, Torpedo had turned her around and marched her right behind the caravan to the village where he'd called in a helicopter. He could have done it from the camp where they'd all gathered, but Shadow was too big for the type of chopper that could fly at the high altitude. Torpedo had thought it only fair that she'd have to walk down behind Shadow's stretcher. She'd not only made his team miserable, but she'd damned near gotten two of them killed. He'd lectured her the entire way down the mountain. Even Shadow, the man with infinite patience, had given her a piece of his mind.

When he could breathe well enough to talk, that is. Then Torpedo had continued over the internal headset while they were on the helicopter. When they'd gotten on a plane to go back to the States, he'd lectured her some more. Then all the way from the airport to Miami, where her father was waiting in the limo to take her home. She'd bolted from the plane in tears, and Torpedo flipped her off as she went.

Her daddy hadn't been happy about the hand gesture, but he'd warned them she could be a handful.

Apparently, no one had ever spoken to her harshly in her life. Well, as far as Torpedo was concerned, it had been past time. The really funny thing was she'd texted and called him in the days following his departure, trying to get him to go out with her. Or to simply get together to fuck. His response? "Not if your pussy was the last Goddamned pussy on the motherfucking earth."

Now he sat by the pool, soaking up the gloriously warm sunshine, letting his body heal and looking forward to welcoming his brothers to the little vacation the girl's daddy had funded for them. If all went well, Shadow and Vicious would join him in a few more days. Once they were out, the clock would start. They had a month vacation in the lap of luxury coming once all of them were out of the hospital. He got extra as a reward for not killing the man's daughter.

He was currently relaxing in the Imperial Suite at the Breakers Palm Beach. He had access to all the resort had to offer at no cost, and he was utilizing every last fucking amenity. He'd been assured by Cain that the wealthy client was picking up the tab, so Torpedo could give a fuck how much money he spent. While sitting idle wasn't his thing, there were many things he could do in the city to pass the time. Like hang out with Bones' sister club. Salvation's Bane in Palm Beach was filled with employees of ExFil the same as Bones. As far as Torpedo was concerned, they were all brothers and sisters. Vicious was a member of Salvation's Bane, and Torpedo couldn't have asked for a better man at his back.

Having been in the cold for so many days, Torpedo was thoroughly enjoying the sunshine. Naked. By the private pool on the balcony. Well. It had been a hot tub, but he'd cooled down the water and now it was a pool. Of sorts. Anyway, the point was he was warm and not bundled in layers of high-tech cold-weather gear on top of a fucking mountain where the air was too thin to breathe. Fucking paradise.

The chime that signaled someone was at the door made him want to throw a punch. He'd only been here a couple of hours. Neither Shadow nor Vicious were due for a few more days. Which meant someone he didn't know or want in his private oasis was intruding. So help him, if it was that fucking woman, he was going to shoot her.

Gritting his teeth, he stomped to the door, not bothering to put on his shorts or wrap a towel around himself. Fuck 'em. They didn't wanna see his junk, they could damned well leave him the fuck alone. On the way to the door, he snagged his Sig Sauer.

"Who the fuck goes there?" He chambered a round and flung open the door, holding the gun at his side. His gaze met a pair of champagne colored eyes, belonging to the most extraordinary looking woman he'd ever seen in his life. She was dressed in a conservative pantsuit with sensible pump heels, her inky black hair in some kind of complicated twist away from her face. Her body was compact and small. Stood nearly a foot shorter than him. Even in the pantsuit, she had lush curves and a nipped in waist. Her makeup was understated, applied carefully to enhance her natural beauty, not to cover up flaws or give the illusion she was something she wasn't. There should have been nothing sexy at all about her, but Torpedo thought she was easily the most alluring woman he'd ever imagined.

If his nakedness -- or the gun -- bothered her, she didn't give any outward sign. Her gaze stayed firmly on his, her features serene and friendly. "Good afternoon, Mr. Ferguson. My name is Rose, and I'll be your personal butler while you visit us. I trust your accommodations meet with your needs and approval?"

Torpedo looked at her for long, long moments, trying to decide if she was for real or some prank being played on him by his brothers. It would be just like them to throw him a curve in the form of a luscious female, *Days of Thunder* style. "Butler."

"Yes, sir. Anything you require, all you have to do is pick up the phone." She indicated one on the table across from the elevator in the foyer. "Any landline phone from your room reaches me automatically when you pick it up."

"And what services, exactly, does a butler perform in this hotel?" He crossed his arms over his chest, his gun hand on top at the ready.

"Anything you desire." Her expression didn't change. No color leapt into her cheeks. The pulse at her throat didn't increase. Her breathing was still nice and even. If the thought of sex as a service entered her mind, she wasn't overly excited by it. Torpedo wished he could say the same for himself. His cock had begun to stiffen as he looked his fill at the little beauty dropped at his door. Oh, the possibilities...

"I can think of a few things I need," he said, grinning. Realizing she wasn't impressed by the gun, Torpedo unchambered his round and removed the clip. "Come on in. No use standin' out here when there's sun to be bakin' in."

Without waiting to see if the young woman followed him, Torpedo sauntered back to the pool and the balcony. He plopped down on a lounge chair and draped one leg over the side lazily as he poured himself another Scotch.

"Can I offer you some whisky?" He knew the girl wouldn't take his offer, but it amused him to make it.

"I'm afraid not, Mr. Ferguson." Her smile was gentle. For some reason he expected her to either be flustered or snobbish about the drink, but she was simply matter-of-fact, as if she thought he was offering only because it was socially prudent for him to do so. Torpedo could have told her he could give a flying fuck about social decorum. He just wanted to get her drunk and see if she'd loosen up a little.

He shot his glass, savoring the burn all the way to his cock. "Your loss. It's the good stuff."

"I hope you enjoy it, then." She clasped her hands loosely in front of her. "Now, let's talk about your expectations for your stay. My understanding is that you and two more guests will occupy this suite for the next thirty days. Is that correct?"

"Thirty days from the time they arrive," he qualified. "They're still in the hospital. If they don't get out for another week, then it will be thirty-seven days."

Immediately, her expression took on a concerned mien. "Is everything all right?"

"Hazard of the job," he said, annoyance washing over him once more. "Little piece of advice, honey. If someone is hired to protect you, do what they say and don't deliberately make it difficult for them. I guarantee you, they don't want to babysit you any more than you want them to."

"I see," she said, nodding as if she really did. "I suppose if I thought it necessary to have a bodyguard, I'd be foolish not to follow their advice."

"Exactly!" He sat back on the lounger to relax, closing his eyes and simply basking in the sun. God, it felt good! He couldn't describe how incredibly good the heat felt on his skin. He also knew that, if he pretended not to be aware of her, the girl could look her fill of him. Which made him smile.

For all his faults, Torpedo knew he was a good-looking man. Sure, he was scarred and rough around the edges, but his body was rock hard and ripped with muscle. Women loved looking at him, and he enjoyed the attention.

She cleared her throat delicately. When he opened his eyes, she had the little serene smile on her face again, her soft, golden-brown eyes looking directly into his.

"About your stay here." Torpedo could have groaned. The girl was like a dog with a bone. "Are there any events you'd like to plan? Any activities away from the hotel I can set up for you?"

Torpedo grinned at her before closing his eyes again. "I'd like a woman available to me at all times. I've been on a fuckin' mountain for more than a month in less than desirable conditions. Even if I'd had a woman I cared to fuck, sex wasn't an option. I intend to catch up while I'm on vacation."

"That can certainly be arranged. Will your companions be needing the same?"

His eyes snapped open. Was she serious? "I don't want a hooker, woman. I need a woman who's not only willing but enthusiastic." This wasn't working out like he'd planned. He'd hoped to shock her. Get her sputtering with indignation before she left.

"We have services we use for just such occasions. They're more... companions," she qualified delicately, "but what goes on in private stays there. If you'll just tell me what type of woman you'd be interested in, I'll get to work." The woman actually took out a tablet and stylus and started making notes.

"Look... Rose, is it?" When she nodded, he continued. "I'm in a really bad way here." He waved to his cock, which was at half-mast currently. "I was in the middle of some languid self-pleasuring when you interrupted me, so, unless you intend to take care of this yourself, I suggest you leave. OK?"

Her eyes rounded slightly. Finally! A reaction from her! "I -- I apologize, Mr. Ferguson. I had no intention of being in your way." She stood immediately. "I'll return at a later time. And, again, I'm so sorry!" The girl seemed genuinely distressed, and not about his suggestion she get him off. No. She was worried she'd disturbed him. Gotten in the way, as she'd said. For some reason, that nettled Torpedo. He wanted to get under her skin. Make her angry. Not distress her.

"Stop," he commanded. She'd been about halfway to the door but did as he commanded, standing perfectly still with her head down. With a sigh, he got up from the lounger and snagged a towel, wrapping it around his waist. "I'm sorry," he said as he neared her. Gently, he touched her shoulder and turned her to face him. "I was bein' an ass because I've been in a bad fuckin' mood for a fuckin' month, and I was taking it out on you. That was wrong of me."

Her expression was perfectly blank. Not even a hint remained of that little smile she'd had. "The fault was mine for not taking a hint. I've been met at the door by nude men before who just wanted to shock me."

"That wasn't my primary goal, but once you didn't react, it rapidly moved up the priority list."

She nodded once, acknowledging him before squaring her shoulders once again. "I'll leave you alone," she said. "Would it be all right to return at five o'clock this evening?"

Torpedo almost told her to stay, but there was something in her eyes that made him hesitate. He'd spooked her. Frightening wasn't the same as irritating. Better to start with a clean slate. "Five would be perfect. I'll try to make a better impression," he said wryly.

"Very well." She didn't comment on his last statement, only gave a curt nod and turned to leave. Even in the conservative pantsuit, her ass was a thing of beauty as she strode across the foyer to the elevator. He tilted his head, staring at that perfect ass again until she turned to press the button to take her to her floor. Their eyes met, and he swore he saw the sheen of tears.

Once Rose was gone, Torpedo scrubbed his hand over his face in agitation. Maybe his last assignment had gotten to him more than it should have. This woman certainly didn't deserve his attitude. She was probably worried about being fired. He imagined that, at this hotel, if a guest complained about the staff, especially one in the position she was in where her primary job was to make the stay as smooth as possible, that staff member would no longer have a job.

"Fuck."

He had two hours to get himself into a better mood, showered, shaved, and make himself into a domesticated biker. Laughable. Oh well. There was nothing for it now except to act like he had some sense when she came back.

* * *

Ambrosia was trembling by the time she stepped onto the elevator to take her back down to the basement and her dressing room. All the butlers shared the same space. Which was a little unnerving because she was the only female in the group. The guys weren't cruel or anything, but given her past, it made her decidedly uncomfortable.

She suspected management had no desire for her to be there and had deliberately set her up to fail. She knew she could call them out on it and threaten a lawsuit, but, really. What was the point? She wouldn't be here long. Already her soon-to-be-ex father-in-law was making waves. Probably why she'd been told her dressing room was with the male staff members in the same position, since the role of butler was traditionally given to a male and the hotel hadn't factored in a female wanting the job. Assuming she was in the position longer than a few weeks, they'd put a plan into action to give Rose her own dressing quarters. Which was total bullshit. For now, she used her office to dress.

Each of them had a small office space with a desk, computer, and anything else they needed to make the time each executive guest spent at the Breakers as comfortable and inclusive as they wanted it to be. Some people had meetings and corporate functions they need planned or parties or any number of things. It was her job to see to their every need. She wasn't lying when she'd told Gavin Ferguson, her newest client, she could provide him with an escort. She basically had unlimited resources at her disposal where a guest was concerned.

Now, she went to her office and shut the door, hoping to not be disturbed. She should have known better. Since Richmond Foley had decided it was her fault his son, Tyler, was in prison, hotel management seemed to have a leash shoved up her ass. They wanted to know where she was at all times and, if she wasn't exactly where they thought she should be, they wanted to know why. She was supposed to be having a conference with Mr. Ferguson.

The knock came about thirty seconds after she'd closed the door. It was followed by her boss barging in without waiting for her approval.

"You're supposed to be at the penthouse, Rose. This guest is extremely important to us. If he cancels, you'll be responsible for the lost income."

"He was busy, Mario. I can't make the man talk to me if he doesn't want to that very instant. I'm going back at five, per his instruction."

Mario scowled. "If you did something to put him off, you better come clean now. He complains on you, you're outta here."

"Like I'm not on my way out the door anyway," she muttered.

"What was that?" Mario cocked his head as if daring her to repeat herself.

Taking a breath, Rose lifted her chin. What the hell? She was tired of all the rich people she catered to anyway. Most thought they were better than her and talked down to her in a condescending way she hated. "I said, I'm on the way out the door anyway, so why bother? I know Richmond has been putting the heat on everyone to fire me, just like he has my last three jobs." She shrugged. "Why fight the inevitable?"

"You're right," Mario sneered. "Why fight it? This little act of insubordination was the nail in your coffin, young lady." He drew himself up to his full height, which was still several inches shorter than her. "Rose, your services are no longer required. Your last check will be direct-deposited on the regular pay date. And if the penthouse guest cancels his stay early, the balance of his stay will come out of your check."

"That's more than I make, Mario."

"And that's your problem. You should have thought of that before you pissed him off."

"No one said anything about pissing him off! He wanted me to come back later because he was busy!" She left off the masturbating part because she just couldn't bring herself to say it.

"So you say." He waved his hand toward the door. "Off with you! Anything not belonging to the hotel will be returned to you via UPS. I want you out of here now!"

Had she not been so angry, Rose probably would have cried. This was just like Richmond. His son had beaten and raped thirteen women and somehow it was her fault. The man saw it as his personal mission to ruin her life. She'd been the one to call the police after Tyler had broken the windows out of her car, then given her a black eye and a broken arm after she'd refused to have sex with him. Tyler's father had seen that as the start of all his son's problems.

Turned out the police had just been waiting for the right time to arrest him. It gave them reason to get a few search warrants and a few other things she didn't understand. All Richmond saw was that, once she called the police, all of a sudden his only son and heir had been accused of a horrible crime. He blamed Tyler's conviction on the "#MeToo" movement in general and, more specifically, Rose, because she'd been the one to call the police over a simple "lover's spat." Since there was no way to get even with the movement, Rose took the brunt of Richmond's anger.

Instead of wasting her breath fighting with her boss, Rose just rolled her eyes and left. She knew she could kiss her last paycheck goodbye. Possibly any personal effects she had, too. Thank goodness she hadn't settled in to this new role or she might have had more personal equipment and mementos in her office. She was sure she'd have lost it all if she had.

The bus ride to her apartment was long, thanks to the out-of-city commute. Palm Beach was way too rich for her blood. Doubly so now since she didn't have a job. Depressing though it was, it gave her time to just sit and think.

The rent was paid up for two months. When Richmond had started harassing her at her job, she'd made a point to get as far ahead on the bills as she could. She'd known from the start it was only a matter of time before he got her fired.

By the time she got home it was nearing five o'clock. She wondered if Mr. Ferguson would even notice if she didn't show up when she was supposed to. She was smart enough to know the man didn't want her there. Why he'd told her to come back was beyond Rose. He belonged in that penthouse. She didn't. Rose had grown up dirt poor and had learned to recognize people with money at an early age. This guy might be a little worse for wear, but he would definitely fit in with the type of wealth that frequented the Breakers. She sighed. He'd likely forgotten all about her and that little incident.

In a way, she kind of hoped he hadn't. That he'd be so put out at her no-show that he'd cancel the rest of his trip. She knew it wasn't going to happen, but she could wish. More likely, Mario would have her replacement there already. They were probably deep in negotiations about Mr. Ferguson's entertainment for the evening.

She'd just gotten off the bus at her block when her phone chimed. Glancing at the screen she saw it was from the hotel. Fuck 'em. She turned the thing off and stuffed it back in her purse. It wasn't like she had anyone who'd be calling her, and she damned well didn't want to talk to anyone at the resort. Other than maybe Richmond to gloat or threaten her some more, she had no one who'd be calling her.

On second thought...

She dug the phone out of her purse and tossed it into a nearby trash bin. She'd only been in the city six months. She'd been so focused on rebuilding her life she hadn't had time for a social life, and all her so-called friends had bailed on her when she'd called it off with Tyler via police. She was done being a slave to the nastiness of others. She'd find a job cleaning houses or at a fast-food joint. Save everything she made other than to buy cheap food. Once she had enough money, she'd take a bus to LA or maybe Seattle. Someplace far away from Palm Beach. Far away from a life that no longer agreed with her.

Chapter Two

Five o'clock came and, precisely on time, the bell to Torpedo's suite chimed pleasantly. He'd dressed carefully, wanting to make a better impression on the girl. Mainly because he'd been such an ass before, but also because the few minutes he'd been in her company, he'd liked her. She'd taken everything he'd thrown at her and rolled with it. Right up until he'd sexually harassed her. Any balking she did was more than understandable. He owed her more than an apology.

Torpedo opened the door expecting her serene face only to find a tall, thin male. He wore a uniform much the same as Rose had, only more formal. Probably because it was evening. He had pleasing features, if a bit too pretty for Torpedo's taste. The guy had a shave so close it looked painful. Torpedo disliked him on sight.

"Good afternoon, Mr. Ferguson. I'm Jason, and I'll be your butler for the duration of your stay."

"Rose is my butler," he said. "I have no desire for anyone other than her."

"Rose is indisposed, but I assure you I'll be even more efficient than she was."

Torpedo shut the door in the guy's face. He had a moment to wonder if she'd been angry at him and had requested to have someone else take over, but even if she were pissed at him, it didn't really make much sense. She'd be giving up the penthouse in this hotel, which equaled the biggest tip and likely the largest pay. Which meant it was at least possible she'd been replaced unwillingly. If it was because of him, he'd owe her more than an apology.

Torpedo tried not to jump to conclusions or let his temper get the better of him. Yet. Picking up the phone, he called down to the front desk. It rang exactly once before a male voice answered. Jason. "I'm still outside in the foyer, Mr. Ferguson. We can set your itinerary whenever you're ready."

"I won't work with anyone other than Rose. I'd like to speak to your supervisor."

"Of course, sir. I'll get Mario. Would you prefer he come to your suite?"

"Not unless he brings Rose with him." Torpedo hung up the phone with a bit more force than necessary. A couple minutes later, the phone rang, and Torpedo let it. He knew getting what he wanted depended on making hotel management come to him. Sure, he could be rude and condescending, but he wasn't really that kind of person. He preferred to give an order and force it to be followed. By not answering the phone now, he hoped he could force this Mario bastard to bring Rose to him.

Again, the phone rang. Again, Torpedo let it.

Fifteen minutes later, there was a soft knock at the door, not the soft chime of the doorbell. Torpedo leaned against the bar and poured himself a Scotch. The ice tinkled softly in the glass as he filled it. He waited and, like he knew would happen, there was another knock, louder this time.

Torpedo knew it wasn't Rose. He just had a feeling. So he waited until the doorbell chimed softly. Before setting down his glass, he drained it in a long swallow. Just as the chime came once again, he sauntered to the door. When he opened it, he found Jason with a shorter man.

"Good evening, Mr. Ferguson. I'm head of domestic and concierge services, Mario Salazar. I understand you've had a bad experience with our staff and would like to remedy the situation."

"Bad experience?" Torpedo realized now that Rose might have taken the backlash of more than his bad mood. "If by bad experience you mean Rose wasn't here at five like she said she'd be, then yeah. I've most definitely had a bad experience. Now, if you don't mind, I'd like to get with Rose and see exactly what services this place has to offer someone such as myself."

Torpedo was a biker and a mercenary. Not dropping the F-bomb every other word took effort, but he'd also grown up with some wealth. Enjoyed it still, thanks to his work with Cain and ExFil. He knew angry words and threats of retaliation often worked wonders with hotel staff simply because they wanted to avoid bad publicity. Especially when the guest had booked the fucking penthouse for over a fucking month.

"I do apologize, Mr. Ferguson, but Rose is no longer with us. Call it a disagreement in work ethic."

OK. *That* got his attention. "I see. And exactly when did this... disagreement take place? Because she was here and happily employed two hours ago."

"I'm not at liberty to discuss personnel matters, Mr. Ferguson," Mario said with a smile. "I'm sure you understand. Now, if you'll allow Jason to --"

Torpedo shut the door firmly in the man's face.

Pulling out his cell, he dialed Data. Data was Bones' intelligence man. If there was any information on anyone in any computer system *anywhere*, Data could find it, access it, and pass it on to wherever it was needed.

"Everything all right, Torpedo? No one expected to hear from you for at least a couple of weeks. I heard your charge was the devil incarnate."

"Not talking about it, brother," Torpedo said, a smile tugging at his lips. The only reason Data had brought it up was because all three of the men had complained about her. Daily. Trucker had accused them all of whining as much as they accused her of whining, and Data had gotten in his own digs.

"What do I owe the pleasure of this call then?"

"I need information."

"Oh? Anyone I know?"

"A girl."

"Uh oh. Has the mighty Torpedo finally found his downfall? And here I thought it would be the pretty, spoiled little rich girl."

"Just remember I have a photographic memory. I am keeping track of every single remark, and I *will* retaliate."

Data chuckled. "Truce, brother. What is it you need?"

"Her name is Rose. That's all I know. She worked at the Breakers until about two hours ago. I need a name, address, and phone number."

"Wow. You don't want much, do you?"

"Can you do it or not?" Torpedo wasn't really angry, he just wanted results.

"Relax. I'm already into the hotel's system. Her name is Ambrosia Gataki. She just turned nineteen. Sendin' her last address and phone number to your phone." Torpedo could hear Data's fingers flying over the keyboard of his computer. He could just imagine the intelligence man sitting at the bank of computer monitors he called his command center. The thought was comforting when his stomach felt like it was tied in knots. Until she hadn't shown, Torpedo hadn't realized how much he'd been looking forward to seeing Rose. Possibly sparring with her. She'd seemed so unflappable right up until the end that he relished the idea of pushing her until she snapped at him. "I did a search for her and found some... interestin' things. Sendin' that to you as well. You better be careful with this one, brother. Looks like she's been through a lot. Still goin' through shit."

"What do you mean?" A tingle started at the back of his neck. Never a good sign.

"Just read the articles I sent. I also passed along some court documents. She's been in Palm Beach about six months. Worked at the Breakers for four. All was goin' well until Richmond Foley got involved."

The name wasn't unknown to Torpedo. He was a real estate mogul with a colorful past. Had two kids. Both stayed in trouble. Best he could remember, one recently got into more than even Daddy could handle. "What's he got to do with anything?"

"Read the stuff I sent you. I just skimmed."

He hung up and proceeded to read. Until he saw red.

* * *

The sun set in a fiery orange ball behind the city. Rose loved being on the beach at sunrise and sunset. Her job at the hotel had prevented both for all but the occasional morning and evening since she'd started there four months ago. Now, she was determined she would take full advantage of it while she could. Tomorrow she'd take the day off. One day to enjoy the sun, sand, and sea. The next day, she'd start job hunting. If she couldn't find anything close to her apartment, she'd look closer to the city. She wasn't looking to get rich. Just enough to set money back so she could move before her rent money ran out.

The tide was coming in, but she sat in a beach chair far enough back to enjoy the water without getting inundated. As the waves rolled gently to shore, her feet dug into the sand, letting the water pull the grains back before sliding up the beach once more. If there was a heaven, she hoped it had beautiful beaches like this one.

It was dusky dark before she started back to her apartment. Sitting on the beach always calmed her mind when things became too chaotic. Now was no exception. Rose was always surprised at how much more centered she felt after a few hours just sitting and listening to the waves crash and the gulls cry. It was paradise.

Her sandals dangled from her fingertips as she strolled along the sidewalk, still warm from the day's sun. Nighttime in this part of Florida was lovely. It always amazed her how it was warm at night even this early in the year. Her own home state of Ohio was frigid in winter, even at the beginning of March. It was just one of the reasons she loved it here, though she admitted to missing white Christmases and snow angels. Hell, she might end up back there before everything was over, though she intended to make her next stop Seattle. Richmond might leave her alone if she left the state. At least, that was her hope.

Her apartment wasn't in the best part of town, but it wasn't overrun with crime or anything. She had to lock the doors and watch she didn't leave anything of value out where someone might be tempted to investigate, but it wasn't a bad place. The building was relatively clean and free of the trash or drug paraphernalia some areas were plagued with. It wasn't what Tyler had promised her, but she'd take this over anything that bastard had offered her. Mainly because she knew what to expect. What she had to pay for it.

She had never expected anything from Tyler or Richmond, but once she'd agreed to marry him, it was like her whole world changed. She was suddenly expected to dress a certain way, to have the right friends, to behave the way they deemed appropriate. She'd lost herself in those few months she'd been with him, and she grew to be increasingly distressed in their world. It all culminated with the night Tyler had assaulted her.

No. She wasn't going there. Not tonight.

Rose unlocked both locks to her apartment and turned on a light…

And came face to face with Gavin Ferguson.

He sat in the corner on her couch, scrolling through his phone, a scowl on his face.

"What the hell are you doing here?" Her heart pounded as she demanded her answer. How had he gotten into her apartment? How had he found her in the first place?

"Waiting for you." He turned his phone around to show her the screen. There was an image of her taken the night Tyler had been arrested. She was crying, her face bruised and swollen on one side where he'd hit her. No amount of Photoshopping could fix the genuine distress on her face in that moment. She'd been terrified for her life. "You want to explain this?" The man looked at her like it was her fault.

Rose was taken aback. "No. Not really. Besides, it's none of your business."

"It's my business when the fucker keeps harassing you."

"He's in jail, Mr. Ferguson. He doesn't harass me. And that still doesn't make it your business."

"Oh, really." He stood and stalked toward her, each step more menacing than the last. If she had any sense about her, she'd turn and run as hard and fast as she could. It probably wouldn't do her any good, but she just couldn't make herself. She was tired of being pushed around by men who thought they were better than her. Though Gavin Ferguson hadn't suggested such, why wouldn't he? The man was obviously rich. No one stayed in the penthouse at the Breakers unless they had money. She was a nobody. Not even the hired help since she'd been fired. "His father got you fired today. From your last two jobs and kicked out of one apartment as well."

Rose shut her mouth tight to keep from retorting a denial, but she'd suspected Richmond had had a hand in at least the apartment. Figured about the jobs. He was trying to break her spirit. Shrugging, she replied, "So what if he did? I'm good now. I have this apartment paid for two months. I can get a job in a fast-food restaurant to feed myself and save everything else until I get kicked out of here. By then, I can get a bus ticket to LA or Seattle. Far away from Richmond and Tyler."

"Maybe. Or maybe you'd ride right into trouble. As long as you're by yourself, you're vulnerable."

"OK. Fine. You're right. Still doesn't explain why you broke into my apartment or why you hunted me down in the first place." She crossed her arms. "Kinda looks like I'm in more danger from you than Richmond at the moment."

Unexpectedly, he broke into a grin, chuckling softly. "I'd say you have good instincts, but anyone would come up with that assumption given the circumstances." He came to stand in front of her. So close she could almost feel the heat from his body. She could certainly smell the clean, woodsy scent of his skin. He wore a suit, but didn't look completely comfortable. It was more as if he thought that was what he should wear. It didn't really matter, though. In Rose's mind, he was as naked as the first moment she'd laid eyes on him.

He wasn't conventionally handsome, but there was something about him that made Rose certain he could handle himself in any situation. Also, she got the feeling he saw everything. Those hazel eyes of his seemed to look straight into her soul. It was uncomfortable, but also something of a relief. She didn't have to pretend with him because he would know. There'd be no deceiving him.

Rose considered herself a sensible person. Until Tyler, she'd thought herself a good judge of character. Actually, she still thought she was, because she'd known from the beginning Tyler wasn't a good person. She'd just been caught up in him. The attention of someone as good-looking and rich as him. He could have any woman he wanted, but he'd wanted her. So she'd thought. Though this guy should have come across creepy in the extreme, he didn't. Did she trust him entirely? No. But she was willing to see what happened next.

"You're not my enemy," she said.

He raised one dark brow. "So sure?"

"If you'd wanted to harm me, you could have done it already. You were here waiting on me, and I didn't even notice until I turned on the light." Rose dropped her purse on the chair. "I'm tired, Mr. Ferguson. It's been a bitch of a day. You'll pardon me if I don't feel like company tonight."

"Fine. We'll continue our conversation in the morning." He picked up a beer bottle sitting on her coffee table and took a long pull before crossing the short distance to the kitchenette and disposing of the bottle in the glass recycling container. Instead of leaving, however, he plopped back down on the recliner and raised the footrest, going back to his phone.

"What are you doing?"

He didn't even glance at her. "Settling in for the night. I have some reading on you to catch up on. I imagine I'll have many more questions for you when you wake up."

"You're not staying here tonight. I don't want a strange man in my home while I sleep."

He threw her a quick grin. "Then stay up and talk with me. Then I won't be a stranger to you, and I'll have my answers. We both can rest easy."

Rose was at a loss. She was bone tired, and her head was beginning to ache with all the stress of the day. The man in front of her was anything but safe, but she found she wasn't willing to call the police to have him thrown out. She sighed, resigning herself to a long night. "What do you want from me, Mr. Ferguson?"

He looked at her a long moment before answering her. "I want you to get ready for bed. You need sleep."

She shook her head. "Not happening with you here."

"Your other alternative is to come back to the hotel with me. I'm not leaving without you."

"You have to know they'll kick me out if I even try to go back there."

He grinned. "They can try."

"Will you leave me alone and let me rest if I go with you?" As perverse as it sounded, she kind of hoped they'd run into her boss. She was curious how this man would handle such a situation.

"You have my word."

"Fine. But if you rape and murder me in my sleep, know that I will come back and haunt you."

Rose expected him to laugh at her or, at the very least, scoff at her remark. Instead, he put the footrest down and stood, coming to stand in front of her. He framed her face with his hands and forced her to look him in the eye.

"Understand me, Rose. I'd never do anything to hurt you. Especially not like that. You have a man of means and resources who's fixated on you because his son was taken from him. I happen to believe you're not safe here." He brushed his thumb over her bottom lip gently. "Do I have ulterior motives for wanting to keep you close to me? Unquestionably. You're a beautiful woman. Any man would beg to get you into his bed. I'll rely on my own charm to get what I want and do my best to coax you there, but I'd never take what you didn't freely give me." He was completely sober in his response to her. He wasn't angry and didn't take offense. Instead, he simply addressed what he obviously knew were very real concerns of hers. "Now," he held out his hand to her, "will you come with me?"

Before she could stop herself, Rose placed her hand in his. "I need to get some things."

He shrugged. "Pack it all if you want. I have no intention of ever bringing you back here except to pick up anything else you need."

"Don't push your luck, Mr. Ferguson."

"Gavin," he said smoothly.

"Fine. Gavin."

He grinned at her. "You've got ten minutes, then, if you ain't ready, I'm carrying you out."

Chapter Three

If there was one thing Torpedo hated it was having to wear a suit. The damned thing was hot, and the collar and tie were too tight. He wanted a T-shirt and his colors. The only thing that had stopped him from putting them on to go after that intriguing girl was him not wanting to scare her. At least, not yet. Time enough for that later.

He did as he said. Gave her ten minutes to pack a bag. She wasn't ready, so he made good on his word. Tossed her over his shoulder, picked up her bag, and left her apartment. Thing was too small for her anyway. She was a woman who deserved a large, beautiful house. Not this shitty, overpriced, two-room apartment. Well, he was about to pamper her like she'd never been pampered. Torpedo wasn't sure exactly where he was going with this, but he knew it was something he needed to do. Along the way, he'd slay her dragons just because it pleased him to do so.

"You're an ape, Gavin Ferguson!" She'd fumed all the way to the hotel, her arms crossed under her breasts and her lovely copper eyes flashing like new pennies in the sun. "The whole block probably saw us!"

"Only because you make a hell of a lot of noise when you want to." Torpedo had her in the back seat of the limo provided by the hotel for use by whomever was staying in the penthouse. He grinned and winked at her. "Could be fun."

"Oh! You're such a cad!"

He laughed. "Never said I wasn't." They pulled into the large, circular drive of the hotel. He thought about going in the private entrance but decided against it. If there was anyone who worked in that fucking place, he wanted them to know she was with him. Let 'em come after her. Taking on Richmond Foley wasn't something he could do alone simply because he couldn't kill the man outright, but he could definitely take care of hotel staff. Welcomed it, even.

When he took her hand to help her out of the limo, she tried to ignore him, but he forced the issue with a smirk. "Go ahead. Make a scene."

"You'd probably love it," she bit out. She didn't look put out or angry. On the contrary, she looked like she was expecting someone to jump out and order her off the property. She was fully expecting to be embarrassed and shamed into leaving.

"You know I'm not going to let anyone harm you in any way. Right?" It was important to him for her to know he would protect her. He wanted her confident, like she had been when he'd opened that fucking door naked as the day he was born.

"You probably have a great deal of influence, but if you're right and Richmond wants me gone from here, it's going to take a lot more than a playboy in the penthouse to keep management from calling the law to escort me out."

"You leave that to me, honey." And he meant every single word. There was something inside him that needed to protect Rose. Probably because, as a soldier, that was what he did. He protected.

"Whatever," she groused. She followed him out of the limo and only tugged her hand once when he took it to walk into the hotel.

Torpedo made the walk across the lobby to the private elevator like a leisurely stroll. He wanted someone to call her out because, perversely, he was spoiling for a confrontation. The only things he'd had to fight with for over a month were one spoiled brat he hoped to never see again because he couldn't throw her a beating, and one fucking big-ass mountain. He needed a real fight, even if it was only a good cussing out. Anyone trying to stop Rose from accompanying him would do nicely.

As his gaze shifted around the room, Torpedo caught sight of two security guards on opposite sides. One seemed bored -- the other was flirting with one of the girls at the host desk. No one seemed overly interested in Rose or, more importantly, in preventing her from going with him.

"Torpedo!"

He winced. "Fuuuck," he muttered. He looked around until he found the man who'd called to him. Shadow raised a hand while Vicious just gave him a puzzled look. No doubt the suit was throwing them. Knowing there was about to be more of a scene than he'd originally wanted, and that he couldn't fight anybody or even give a verbal tongue lashing, he gripped Rose's hand tighter and quickened his pace. The two men weren't deterred.

"What the fuck, man?" Shadow sounded both amused and puzzled. "A suit *and* a girl? I thought you had your fill on the fuckin' mountain."

"Shut the fuck up, Shadow," Torpedo bit out.

"Look, the girl I can understand. She's pretty and seems to have a much better disposition than that last bitch, but Cain will never forgive the suit. If he finds out, Arkham or Bohannon will be the next vice president, and I'm not sure any of us would survive them." There was laughter in Shadow's voice. When Torpedo glanced at him, he could see amusement on his face as well.

"Can we not do this here?" Though he could really give two shits about their topic of conversation in the hotel lobby, Rose had started to struggle, trying to get her hand out of his iron grip. "Stop struggling, Rose. Unless you want a repeat of what happened at your apartment."

"You can't make me go with all of you."

"Relax, sweetheart," Shadow said, his voice soft now. "We're just fuckin' with Torpedo. No one's gonna hurt you."

Torpedo herded her into the elevator and stabbed the button to the penthouse. He kept his grip on Rose, keeping her just that little bit behind him. Shadow raised his hands in surrender and moved until his back was against the wall. Vicious rolled his eyes and muttered something Torpedo couldn't catch, but he moved back against the wall as well.

He could feel Rose trembling where he crowded her body, forcing hers to touch his. "It's OK. You're fine. Just take a breath."

"I've never done anything to anybody," she whimpered. "Why do people keep trying to hurt me?"

The door slid open and Torpedo urged her out, letting go of her hand and sliding his arm around her waist as he went. "No one is going to hurt you, Rose. No one's even gonna to *try* to hurt you. You're safe with me." He looked down at her bowed head. If she cried, he might have to kill someone. Starting with Shadow for scaring her. "I've read the police reports and the court documents. I also know Richmond Foley can't accept the fact that he raised a monster and is trying to blame you for his son, Tyler's, incarceration."

She looked up at him, her expression blank. "Why am I here, Mr. Ferguson?"

"Because you need help and I can give it to you."

"How do you know that? And when, exactly, did you find out?" She took a step back. "Who are you?"

"Does it matter?" Torpedo took the two steps separating them and, without him deciding to move, his hand just reached down and brushed an errant curl from her cheek and tucked it behind her ear. "You've got a problem and we can solve it. Why not let us?"

"You kidnapped me from my home. Why should I trust you? For all I know, you could have been sent by Richmond to remove me permanently."

Something inside Torpedo threatened to rip free. It was ugly and violent and so fast and sharp he wasn't sure he could contain it. He must have said or done something to spook Rose, because she gave a little gasp and sank down the wall to the floor.

"Hey, Torpedo." Shadow was at his shoulder, laying a calming hand on him. "Ease up, brother. She's spooked enough. You're always the calm one, and she needs you to be calm."

"If he really kidnapped her, ain't nothin' gonna ease her mind 'bout this," Vicious offered. Torpedo turned his head and saw a little smirk on the other man's face. "No wonder she's spooked."

"You're not helping, Vicious." Torpedo gritted his teeth and backed up a step, out of her personal space. He held out a hand to her, willing her to take it. She didn't, but she did stand. Probably thinking she could bolt. "Guys, back the hell off, OK?" Torpedo turned to Shadow and Vicious. "You're scaring her."

"Really?" Shadow said, massive arms crossed over his equally massive chest. "'Cause I'm pretty sure it was your growly meanie face, little bro." He stepped forward and took Rose's hand. "I'm Shadow," he said, grinning like an ape. The bastard gave him a shit-eating grin over his shoulder as he shook Rose's hand. "Don't pay much attention to Torpedo here. He's one step out of the cave. Cain only lets him out on the weekends."

"They call me Vicious." The man from Salvation's Bane stepped forward to take her hand as well. "No idea why. I'm a real pussycat." He winked at her.

"What are you guys? And why the funky names?"

Great. The whole reason Torpedo had put on the fucking suit was to keep her from knowing he was a biker. She could have that information after she got to know him. He wasn't acknowledging to himself why that had been a priority. The boys would have too much fun over that.

"It's kind of a long story," Torpedo said, trying to cut the guys off. He knew without a doubt he'd get no help there.

"We're bikers." Vicious offered, looking all innocent and shit. "They're Bones MC. I'm Salvation's Bane. My club is here in Palm Beach while these hicks hail from Kentucky." When she just blinked at him like it didn't compute, he continued. "We're also mercenaries. Work for a company called ExFil. We specialize in protection and getting people out of difficult situations. Paramilitary and all that shit." His grin widened. "Real badasses and all."

"Why would you take an interest in my situation?" She still looked confused, but not as scared as she had. "I'm nothing to you."

"Why indeed?" Shadow said with a smirk thrown Torpedo's way. "You'll have to ask that one, little miss. We got the call to break out of jail and come help his sorry ass so here we are."

"Jail?!" Her eyes were wide again, her skin going pale.

"Relax," Vicious said. "He was speaking metaphorically, or some shit. We were in the hospital. Last mission took us to a mountain near Mount Everest, and our charge insisted on trying to summit. She had no business being there, and neither did we." He nodded to Torpedo. "Your savior there was the only one of us to get home without a lengthy hospital stay."

"My savior?"

"Yeah. He's gonna save you from your big bad wolf." Vicious chuckled, obviously enjoying the whole situation. "I thought he was in trouble from... err... a rival club, but instead, we find him with a beautiful woman. Figures he'd need some encouragement from his brothers. He's not got nearly the self-confidence, or the equipment, of me and Shadow here."

Shadow guffawed. In that moment, Torpedo could have happily throttled the younger man.

"Not sure why Data sent you clowns here, but you're definitely not helping," he muttered. Torpedo couldn't be angry at them, though. Rose actually grinned before she could stop herself, and it seemed to break the tension in her. "Look," he said, stepping back even farther, trying his best not to crowd her. "Let's me and you sit down at the table. I'll show you what I've got, and you can fill in the gaps. We'll see what's going on and take care of business. You're safe, Rose. I swear it."

* * *

This was probably the dumbest thing she'd ever done in her life, but Rose knew she was going to stay. She was choosing to believe in a man she didn't know. Correction. *Men* she didn't know. And none of them had given her a reason they'd taken an interest in her.

"So. *Torpedo*. Not Gavin Ferguson?"

He shrugged out of his suit jacket and glanced at her over his shoulder before turning to hang up the jacket. "I'm Gavin, but I may not answer to it. No one calls me Gavin, or Mr. Ferguson. Just call me Torpedo."

"I'd ask how you got that name, but I'm half afraid to."

The others snickered, the bastards.

"Well, it ain't for the size of his dick," Vicious offered. "At least, that's what I heard. Don't wanna see it."

Shadow chuckled, raising his hands as if to surrender. "I'm still new to Bones. Known Torpedo for a few years, but not long enough to know that particular bit of information."

"So, motorcycle clubs." Rose hated sounding so ignorant, but she was so out of her element she had no idea what to say or do.

"Yeah," Torpedo said, approaching her once more. "Let's sit. We've got a lot to discuss."

This time, when he held out his hand to her, Rose took it. He closed his around hers gently but firmly, never looking away from her eyes. Even though she still had reservations, she liked the way his skin felt against her palm. They were the hands of a man. Work-roughened and callused. And so big his nearly swallowed her smaller one. Much like he would a child's hand.

He guided her to the table and held a chair for her. Who did that anymore? Certainly not a biker. At least, that was her perspective. She expected more of what her fears had been from the beginning. That the three of them would try to have their way with her whether or not she wanted it. Rose wasn't a complete innocent. She hadn't had sex, but she'd fooled around a few times in high school. She knew without a doubt anything these men would be into would be so far out of her realm of experience she couldn't even comprehend it. The thing was, neither of the other two had touched her other than to shake her hand and introduce themselves. Mr. Ferguson -- Torpedo -- hadn't been inappropriate. Even though she knew it wasn't the best idea, she wanted to hear what they had to say.

"I've read about Tyler Foley's case. They proved he raped and beat five different women, but there were more like thirteen. According to the reports, he would establish a relationship with the women, then threaten to post videos on the Internet of them having sex if they filed charges against him. Does that sound about right?"

"Yes. At least, that's the way it was with me. Only I never had sex with him. I think that was why he wasn't as careful as he usually was. He got impatient."

"Because he couldn't get you on camera to set up his blackmail scheme."

She shrugged. "I guess. He... liked young women. I was sixteen when he first tried to date me. My parents were older and didn't think a man in his mid-twenties should be dating a girl my age. I was their only child, and both were very protective of me."

"Where are they now?"

"They were in a car accident about a year ago. My father died at the scene, my mother a few days later." Saying it out loud hurt even now, but Rose did her best not to let it show. She got the feeling that showing weakness would be a detriment to her with these men.

"So, is that when you started seeing Foley?"

"I guess. It was a few months later. I admit, I was lonely and scared. I didn't like being on my own. I had to work so school was out as was a social life. My parents owned the house, but I still had all the other bills."

"That here in Florida?"

"No. Ohio. The only reason I moved was to get away from Richmond after Tyler was sentenced. But, apparently, he followed me here."

"He's been keeping tabs on you, honey," Torpedo said, sliding a tablet over to her. "Data, our intel man for both Bones and ExFil, pulled everything on you he could find. Including any hits he got from people looking for you. Richmond has fixated on you."

"He blames me for his son being in prison."

"Any idea why?"

"Because I called the police the night he assaulted me. He hit me, but I ran. Locked myself in my car. I was trying to get it started when he broke the window and yanked me out. He'd managed to rip most of my clothes off when the cops pulled up. I have no idea who called them. I tried to, but he pulled me out before I could say anything."

"Did you leave the line open? Complete the call on your cell but didn't get the chance to say anything?"

"I guess. I heard the lady say '911' but I didn't get to say anything to her before Tyler pulled me out. It's possible they heard the whole thing. I was only in the courtroom during my part of the trial. I tried not to follow it at all. Made me have nightmares."

"They'd have used your cell to track where you were and send help."

"I remember the lawyers saying something like that. Yes."

Torpedo took the tablet from her. When he did, his fingers brushed hers. Rose found herself wanting the contact. This was a man she was beginning to believe only wanted to help her. Still, she had to ask. "Why did you come after me? I know they told you I was fired. Why didn't you just let it go?"

He was silent for so long, Rose wasn't sure he would answer her. Finally, he reached back across the table and took her hand in his and squeezed gently. "I'm not really sure I can answer that. Not sure why my damned self."

"Oh. OK." Could she sound any lamer? What did he expect? He was holding her hand. Instead of it being an aggressive way to get her to come with him, now it just seemed intimate. Besides, the man really was too fine. Though she'd tried to ignore him before, she couldn't help remembering how he looked naked. His friends had it wrong. He did indeed have adequate equipment, and a body that looked like it knew how to use that equipment.

He'd cleaned up nicely after she'd left. Obviously, the suit added to his appearance, but he'd also pulled his hair back. The sides and back had been cut so that he could look neat when his hair was up in a hat, or just pulled to the back of his neck. He had a good deal of stubble, but even that had been trimmed and edged. Though his hair was dark, it was streaked liberally with silver, making him look older than his facial features indicated. What woman wouldn't be attracted?

"Look. I'm sorry about your apartment," he offered. "I just wasn't sure how to get you back here. You obviously weren't coming back to work, so I took the only avenue open to me."

"Why look into my background, though?"

"Why ask me hard questions?" He sounded irritated, but his friends, who had retreated into the other room but were obviously still listening, chuckled at his response. "Just accept my help, and we'll talk about other stuff later. Can you do that?"

"Do I have a choice?"

The laughter from the other room was louder this time.

"If I say yes, will you just go with it?"

That made her giggle before she could stop herself. He looked uncomfortable with the line of questioning, which told her a lot about him. He was interested in her for whatever reason. She might be relatively inexperienced, but she was woman enough to know when a man was attracted. "Fine. But we will revisit this later. It's important to me."

"Believe me, honey, it's important to me, too."

Chapter Four

Could a woman be any more... beguiling? Ambrosia Gataki was the very embodiment of an ancient Greek virgin sacrifice. Which probably made him some kind of hideous monster, because he was keeping the exotic beauty.

They'd talked for an hour about her past. How she'd met Tyler Foley, the "incident," and the subsequent aftermath. There were a couple of times he was sure she was going to break down and cry. Not because he thought the events were overly traumatic, though they were, but because he got the sense she'd held everything inside for so long her emotions were overwhelming her with the need to get out. To her credit -- and his great relief -- she had contained the tears.

At some point, his brothers had returned to them, asking their own questions and exchanging angry glances with him and each other. No doubt they were all in on helping his little beauty.

Finally, he called a halt. They didn't have all the information they needed yet, but she was becoming more and more pale, dark circles appearing under her eyes. Torpedo glanced at his watch to see it was after ten. "We need food," he announced. "It's past my feedin' time."

"Was just thinkin' the same thing, brother." Shadow grinned and went to the phone sitting on the bar. "Anyone got objections to pizza and beer?"

"I just want a Coke, if that's all right." Rose laced her fingers together in front of her, resting her hands on the table. She went by Rose, but he kind of liked the feel of Ambrosia in his mind. He got the feeling that, if he ever had a taste of her, he'd become addicted -- just as mortals were supposed to if they tasted the nectar of the gods.

"You can have whatever you want, baby," Torpedo said, reaching to cover her slim hands with one of his. He tried to give her an encouraging smile, but was afraid it came out wolfish.

She sucked in a breath, her face flushing the second he laid his hand over hers. Torpedo didn't miss the fluttering of her pulse at her throat or the way her breathing quickened. He nearly grinned. Could it be that his little virgin sacrifice was interested in him, too? He wasn't about to bet the farm on it, but, with enough care, he might be able to seduce her.

This could get tricky. And what was his ultimate goal? He was afraid he already knew. Had known from the moment he laid eyes on her.

"Let's sit outside while we wait for the food," he said to Rose. He stood, urging him to come with him. Retaining possession of her hand, he led her to the balcony by the hot tub. The warm night air was relaxing, the breeze coming off the ocean, sublime. The moon shone brightly and, with the subtle ambiance of the hot tub lights sparkling under the water, made a decidedly romantic atmosphere.

They sat on a lounger meant for two. He still held her hand, but other than that, they didn't touch. Torpedo could still feel her slight trembling.

"You know I'm not going to hurt you. Right? Not me or my brothers."

"Do you have any idea how surreal this is? If I had any sense at all, I'd make some excuse to leave and run as far as I could." She spoke softly, but he got the impression she wasn't scared so much as she thought she should be scared. "I had plans to work as many hours as I could until my rent padding ran out then hop a train to Seattle or somewhere on the West Coast. Try to get as far away from the Foleys as I could."

"You don't have to do that now, baby. We're gonna take care of this."

"I don't see how," she said, giving him a little sad smile. "Richmond Foley has more money than God. If he decides he wants someone out of the way, it's as good as done."

"It's been months since his son was convicted. If he had the means, don't you think he would have already removed you from the equation?" Torpedo shifted so he could look her directly in the eyes. "He's not nearly as rich and powerful as you've been led to believe. He's a bully. It's the one thing the man is good at."

"Do you know him? Or are you getting all your information from your friend?"

"We've run into the man on a couple of occasions." Torpedo couldn't divulge much about the work ExFil had done in the past without Cain's approval, but he could tell her enough. "We've worked for him before. He hired us once to do a job that turned out to go against our code. He deceived us into thinking we were doing one thing when we were really doing something else. When he tried to hire us for another job a couple of years later, Cain turned him down flat. He'd already passed the word onto other companies and, apparently, no one would touch him. We know how deceitful and vindictive the man can be. Firsthand."

"So, you believe me? About all of it? Because no one else seems to. They believe everything Richmond has said about me, taking it as the result of the #MeToo movement. He tells everyone that, had it not been for the movement, no one would have believed me. He says all this would have been a footnote that would have been dismissed before it ever got to trial."

"Baby, there is no one in Bones, Salvation's Bane, or ExFil who would believe a thing out of that son of a bitch's mouth. He's a deplorable human being."

"Since we're on the subject, I need you to explain to me why. Why are you doing this? You have to know I can't pay you."

He sighed. He knew this was coming again. He'd just hoped it would be after he'd had a chance to figure it the fuck out himself. "I wish I could answer that for you. I can tell you without hesitation that it's not about money. You're not paying for *anything*. I'm doing this because it's the right thing to do and because…" He trailed off, swallowing and clearing his throat, uncomfortable with the feelings inside him wanting free. "I have to. I *need* to."

"Good God, man!" Shadow wandered out onto the balcony with the pizza. He set the boxes on the big table in the center of the area then tossed Torpedo a beer can before carefully setting an ice bucket with two Coke cans sticking out of the top on the table next to the pizza. "For all your blustering at your brothers for being idiots with their women, you're really fuckin' this to hell and back." Once again, the only thing that saved Shadow from a beating was Rose's soft giggle before she stifled it with a delicate cough behind her hand. "Just tell the woman you want to get to know her better. That you're into her. That you want to go someplace and have passionate sex with her before fuckin' her ever-lovin' brains out. *Anything* but this infuriatin' vagueness! Christ! You'd think you'd never been in the company of a woman you liked before."

"Shadow…" Torpedo leveled his best don't-fuck-with-me look on the other man. "You're about two seconds away from a bloodbath. And I'm the vice president. I can cull your ass in a heartbeat."

Shadow simply shrugged. "Brother, that don't scare me. All I gotta do is tell Bohannon 'bout this little incident and he'll be all up in your shit. Trucker, too. Seem to remember you getting' all up in their shit over their women. They'll protect me from Cain."

"Fucker," he growled.

Torpedo glanced at Rose, half expecting her to insist on leaving. Instead, she went to the table and sat, opening a pizza box and helping herself to a slice. "This is the best pizza I've ever eaten. You guys should dig in or I'll do much more damage than you can repair."

"You heard the lady," Torpedo said, trying his best to recover, knowing his reputation as a badass was blown completely. At least it was for Rose.

As they sat down, Vicious and Shadow on one side, he and Rose on the other, Shadow nodded at him and said softly. "You're welcome, brother."

Torpedo raised an eyebrow, then promptly flipped him off.

They ate and exchanged friendly banter, getting to know one another. Even Vicious managed to behave himself. The more they talked and laughed together, the more Rose seemed to relax. Torpedo was more grateful to his brothers than he could say.

"I'm gettin' more beer," Shadow said. "Anyone else want something?"

Torpedo readily agreed, but Vicious waved him off. "In case we need to make a getaway back to the clubhouse tonight." He shrugged at Shadow's raised eyebrow. "Hey. You never know. One of us might need to be sober."

The group fell into another comfortable conversation over the next hour. Rose asked them questions as they did her. Torpedo found himself falling deeper under her spell as he discovered she had a wry sense of humor and a sarcastic wit. When she told them how she'd met Torpedo earlier that day, she had Vicious laughing so hard he was wiping tears from his eyes, and he did, indeed, drink a beer after that.

"Torpedo, brother," he addressed his friend. "You better hang on to this one. She's one of a kind." Vicious clapped Torpedo on the shoulder. "Miss Ambrosia Gataki, it has been my most sincere pleasure. If you decide to leave the vice president of Bones in the dust, consider Salvation's Bane. There will always be a home for you there."

"You take care of our boy, little Rose," Shadow said, taking her hand in his for a firm handshake. "He needs a good woman on the back of his bike."

As they left, Rose looked to Torpedo, confusion in her lovely golden eyes. "I don't understand. They think we're together?"

He shrugged. "Probably because they can tell I want us to be." He scrubbed a hand over his face. "Look, Rose. I know we didn't get off to a great start. Let me help you with Richmond. I'll prove I can be a good man to you. Give me a chance."

She was silent for a long while, picking at the hem of her shirt. "I suppose it can't hurt to get to know you better." Her smile was soft and lovely. Just like the woman. "I guess it's like meeting someone in a bar. Only this started out with you answering the door naked."

God, she was beautiful! The moonlight seemed to bathe her in a golden light, highlighting the inky blackness of her hair. Blue highlights gleamed with the breeze that stirred her curls. It was all Torpedo could do to keep from threading a finger through one springy curl and tugging. "That's about right. And now you already know what you're gettin'."

Her laughter tinkled merrily at his suggestive comment. "I should go home. I'll call a cab."

"You know, we've got plenty of rooms. You'll be perfectly safe here if you want to stay. The doors lock and everything."

"Somehow, I doubt something as simple as a locked door would keep you out if you truly wanted in."

"OK, I'll give you that." He laughed. "How about if I swear not to disturb you tonight? We can start there."

Rose thought about it a moment before answering. "I suppose it's the best thing to do. Will you be here in the morning? I really like the others, but I'm not as comfortable around them as I seem to be with you." She gave him a shy smile. "I like you, too." She tilted her head and frowned. "Should I call you Torpedo or Gavin?"

"I'm not sure anyone ever calls me Gavin anymore. But you can call me whatever you like."

"I don't want to embarrass you, so I'll call you Torpedo."

"I'm considering calling you Ambrosia. Would you mind?"

"Not sure I'd remember to answer. I've not been called Ambrosia since high school, and only until my teachers figured out I liked to be called Rose."

"You were serious with Tyler Foley. Did he ever kiss you?"

She blinked several times, the question obviously catching her off guard. "I... Yes. We were engaged."

"Did he ever tell you if your kisses were as delicious as your name implied?"

The flush over her face spread like a warm glow, but she frowned a little. Torpedo could see she was both embarrassed and, quite possibly, aroused by his question. "No. I don't think Tyler particularly enjoyed kissing me. In fact, I'm not really sure why he wanted to marry me at all."

Torpedo stood. "So you didn't have sex with him?"

"No. He wanted to. At least, he said he did. I'm beginning to think I represented a conquest to him. Maybe he thought if he asked me to marry him, he could convince me to have sex with him that way. You know. A commitment from him to prove he was serious about me. Nothing else had convinced me. Certainly not his kisses."

Just like that, Torpedo's pulse quickened, and he couldn't get enough air. "Why? Why wouldn't you want to be intimate with the man you were going to marry?" He had to know. Had to know what mistakes the little fucker had made before he'd gone all psycho and shit. He also had to know if, God help him, she was a virgin.

She shrugged. "It just never seemed right. I'm not a prude or anything. I just hadn't gone all the way before I met Tyler and had decided I wouldn't unless I really wanted to. I didn't want my first time to be because the guy I was with expected it. With Tyler, there was never that passion I needed to convince me I really wanted to."

"Fuck... me..." he whispered.

"Mr. Ferguson --"

"Don't start that, Rose." He took her hand and pulled her to her feet. "I'm not going to pounce on you, and I can make you a promise right this second that I will *never* force myself on you. I will never expect you'll just lie down and let me take something from you. In fact, I'll never make a move on you other than to kiss you unless you expressly tell me what you want."

She got an adorable confused expression as she shook her head at him. "I don't understand."

"If what you need to decide to have sex with a man is passion, an intense physical desire to complete the act, then I'll make it my personal mission to give you that. If I can't, then I don't deserve you, anyway."

With one hand, he reached down to cup her cheek and tilt her head where he wanted it. Then Torpedo took gentle possession of her mouth.

Chapter Five

Had Rose wanted passion before she gave herself to a man? She was getting it in spades now. Torpedo's mouth moved over hers in a languid caress. He didn't hurry her, didn't overpower her or dominate her. He coaxed. Cajoled. He seduced her into letting him have what he wanted. Even then, he didn't take anything she didn't willingly surrender. Before she knew it, Rose was clinging to Torpedo, kissing him back and whimpering as his tongue sought and found hers.

Strong arms wrapped around her, caging her in and holding her to him, but making her feel more protected than trapped. He held her body tightly against his, so tight Rose felt his cock mashed between them, throbbing and pulsing into her belly.

Everything Rose had ever wanted was packed into that kiss. She felt... important. Wanted. No one she'd ever been with had ever made her feel this way. Maybe it was just that Torpedo was vastly more experienced than she was, but she didn't think that was the main issue. There was something about the man that just did it for her. His rock-hard body. His rock-hard cock. The way his lips slid over hers and his teeth nipped her gently. All of it was intoxicating to her. Had he not been holding her so tight, Rose was certain she'd have ended up in on the floor of the balcony in a little heap.

He was right, too. Torpedo could definitely make her want him like she'd always craved wanting a man. Even now, she was on the very edge of begging him to take her to bed. One night. Intense passion. She wanted it with every fiber of her being, but had no idea how to express that wish. At least, not now. Maybe the next time he kissed her so passionately. Assuming he cared to do it again.

When Torpedo ended the kiss, nuzzling her chin until she tilted her head back to let him graze his lips over her neck, a long, whimpering sigh escaped her. Her body was trembling almost violently, and she felt like she was wound tighter than a rubber band.

"Well, my little Ambrosia? How do you like *my* kisses?"

"Torpedo..." His name was a sigh on her lips. Even to herself, she sounded needy and wanton.

"Tell me, my little virgin. I need to know."

"I do," she breathed, unable to do much more when he sucked the delicate skin at her neck and shoulder. "I've never -- I've never been kissed like that."

"Kissed how? It's just a sliding of lips against each other. Right?" He sounded slightly amused, but his voice was husky. Not the smooth, rich baritone she'd grown used to over the evening.

"Not when you do it," she confessed.

"Tell me what you like about it, baby."

"Love your taste. The feel of your tongue against mine." She shivered, recalling the sensations. "Why'd you kiss me?"

"To show you what a real kiss is supposed to feel like." He nipped her earlobe. "And because I've been wanting to taste you since I first laid eyes on you." He was sin and sex. Rose could believe him. *Wanted* to believe him. Tyler had never wanted her like that, or maybe he just wasn't as good at this as Torpedo. Scratch that. Tyler was nowhere near as good. Whether he really wanted her or not, Torpedo had thoroughly convinced her he meant every word he'd just said. Maybe he just wanted an easy lay with a virgin, or maybe it was something more. All Rose knew was, in that moment, she'd willingly give him whatever he wanted from her. Without reservation. She'd deal with the aftermath in the morning, but she wouldn't regret a second.

Just as she was about to surrender to him, Torpedo pulled her close and just hugged her to him. Was she imagining things or was his body shuddering around hers?

"Fuck, Rose," he breathed. "Just… fuck."

With one more hard squeeze, he scooped her up and took her back inside the suite to a bedroom. It was spacious and tastefully decorated. The big bed looked inviting, but too lonely after the kiss they'd just shared.

"My room is next to yours," he said as he set her back on her feet, next to the bed. "If you need anything, just tap on the wall. I'll hear and come to you."

Rose looked around, debating her next move. Did she really want to do this? And what exactly was she contemplating? She wanted him in that bed with her, but if he stayed with her, no way they weren't having sex. "Will you stay with me?"

His eyes flashed, a deep lust showing through when the last word left her mouth. His nostrils flared, and he actually took a step closer to her, gripping her shoulders with his hands. "There is nothing more I want than that, baby. I'm just not sure you're ready."

"Oh, I'm ready. If you need to touch me to see for yourself, you're welcome to."

The growl seemed ripped from his chest, and he wrapped his arms around her again, one hand sliding up from her waist to her ribcage to cup her breast and squeeze. "You have no idea how much I want to do just that. In fact, I'd love to undress you and bury my tongue inside your little cunt. I'd make you ready for me even if you weren't already."

A little cry escaped her at his words. Her knees did give out then, and she sagged against him.

Torpedo's grip tightened on her breast, and his fingers pinched the nipple through the material of her shirt. "I bet you'd be sweet and addictive. *Ambrosia…*"

"Please," she whimpered, not really sure where the little plea came from but meaning it all the same.

"I'm not takin' you tonight, baby. Soon, though. But if you want me to stay with you, I will. I can't promise I won't fuck you tomorrow though. Especially if I wake up with you in my arms. So be sure that's what you want."

Was it? Rose wanted to answer an overwhelming yes, but did she really? This was the equivalent of a one-night stand. He might profess to want more, but didn't most men do that? And even if he was lying to her, was she willing to risk the awkwardness afterward to get the experience?

If sex with Torpedo was anything like his kisses, then there was no question she wanted it. "I want you with me. If you still want me in the morning, I'll be more than willing."

"So, I met your passion criteria for sex?"

"Are you teasing me?"

He grinned before kissing her forehead. "Maybe just a little. But not maliciously. I like that you have standards and that they're not bullshit standards. Holding out just to be married isn't a reason. Holding out until you meet someone who makes you really want it is one of the best reasons I've ever heard. You should have passion. Lust. Sex is as much about you as it is your man."

"Then let's go to bed. The quicker I get to sleep, the quicker you can wake me with sex."

He barked a laugh then kissed her again. There was hunger there, a restrained need she wanted to unleash like he'd done with her.

"I'll only stay if we're both naked," he said. "I want to feel your skin against mine all fuckin' night."

He stared into her eyes, not moving until she gave a slight nod. Butterflies seemed to take wing in her stomach, and her body shook with nerves. Even though she'd been engaged to Tyler, he'd never seen her completely naked. No man had. As aroused as she was, Rose wasn't certain she could bring herself to strip in front of Torpedo.

"Will you turn out the light?" The second she said it, Rose wished she could take back the question. Instantly, Torpedo's humor changed. He looked at her with those intense hazel eyes, and they flashed an intense golden green as he held her gaze. She had no choice but to look away.

"No. I won't." There was a short silence. "I want to see that sexy little body of yours."

She took a breath, nerves nearly overwhelming her. Something inside her seemed to know this was the point of no return. As much as she wanted the experience, she was terrified. Not of Torpedo. Had he frightened her on that level she'd never have agreed to this insanity. It wasn't him so much as it was herself.

"I'll be completely honest with you," she said, lifting her chin to look at him once more. "I've never been naked in front of a man before. While I've definitely seen naked men, you're the first man I've seen in the flesh, so to speak." When he opened his mouth, she plowed on. "I'm not entirely sure I can be as confident as you're probably expecting. Not because I don't want to be. I just…"

"Relax, Rose." He placed his hands on her shoulders. "I won't force you. You don't have to do anything you don't want to. Just don't let your fear of the unknown take something away from you. Not because you think I'll be disappointed." He shook his head. "I've got you here with me. I can kiss you to my heart's content. Might even coax your clothes off you by seducing you to do whatever I want. I'm good. *You'll* be disappointed. This is an experience you only get once. Do you want it to be with me? If you want me enough to gift me with your virginity, I can't imagine you don't want to undress in front of me."

"I know," she said, trying to laugh at herself to make light of the situation. "I panicked." Taking a deep breath, Rose lifted her shirt over her head. Her hands didn't seem to want to work the way they should, and she had trouble hanging on to the material. A graceful striptease this was not. Torpedo stepped closer to her, reaching out to rest his hands on her hips. When he nodded at her, she reached behind her to unhook her bra, letting the thing slip to the floor.

She stood there, bare-breasted before him. His nostrils flared as his eyes focused on her chest. Rose could almost feel his gaze on her like a caress.

"Keep going, baby." It was the look in his eyes that gave her the courage to continue. Torpedo looked at her like he wanted to eat her up. The lust shining in those golden-green depths wasn't something she was used to, and Rose found it a heady thing. He was looking like that at *her*. No other woman. She didn't try to fool herself into thinking he'd never looked at another woman this way, but he was looking at her *now*. Maybe that made her naive, but he was right.

She'd regret it for the rest of her life if she didn't have this experience with him.

With trembling fingers, she undid the button of her jeans. Torpedo's hands stayed at her waist, not shoving at her clothes or restraining her in any way, simply holding her steady. Whether he knew it or not, Torpedo was her anchor.

Rose let her jeans and panties slide down her hips to pool at her feet on the floor. Torpedo's fingers dug deeper into her hips, but eased up as if he were only just aware he might have hurt her. "So fuckin' beautiful..." He sounded in awe as his hands slid from her hips to her waist to her breasts. He didn't cover them with his palms. Instead, he just skimmed over the sides, up and down in a gentle stroke. "When I finally take you, my little Ambrosia, I'm gonna make you scream."

Rose gasped. She wanted to touch him like he was touching her but didn't dare. If he rebuffed her, she'd never get her confidence back. Her gaze strayed to his wide, muscled chest, hugged so lovingly by the immaculate shirt he wore.

Torpedo must have seen her gaze drop and read her expression because he grasped her wrist gently and brought her hands to his chest. "Unbutton my shirt, Ambrosia."

Rose's fingers trembled as she did what he asked. She brushed his hair-roughened chest as she parted the edges of his shirt. When she looked up at him, Torpedo nodded, encouraging her to go on. With slow movements, Rose slid her hands up his chest to hook under the material of his shirt at the shoulders. The muscles were firm, his skin scarred in a few places, but she savored every touch of her palms over every inch.

Keeping her eyes on his face was impossible. There was so much to take in! A firm chest and ripped abs, shoulders that were wide and thick, arms roped with muscle that felt so good when they wrapped tightly around her that they were like a beacon to her. She had to see as well as touch every inch she unwrapped.

She stopped when his shirt dropped to the floor in an elegant slide, but Torpedo nodded at her, silently encouraging her to continue. With a deep breath and trembling fingers, Rose unbuttoned his pants. Her fingers brushed his cock, and she nearly jerked her hand back. His breath caught, but he didn't react in any other way, just nodded at her again.

Knowing she'd never have the nerve she needed to do this if she waited much longer, Rose hooked the waist of his pants in her thumbs and shoved. The fine material pooled at his feet, leaving him standing before her in boxer briefs. His cock stood out proudly in the confining material. Rose couldn't seem to lift her gaze, wanting to see more but not daring to finish this.

"Go on, baby," he urged her. "You've come this far."

Rose wasn't certain she wouldn't pass out. She squeezed her eyes shut and took several deep breaths, trying to calm herself. When she opened them, she found her fingers curling into the waistband, lying against his skin just in front of his hips.

Slowly, she tugged until his cock sprang free, bobbing before her riveted gaze. He was long and thick, the flared head an angry purple. Veins roped all around it as he pulsed in time with his heartbeat.

Her gaze ran the length of him, from his feet up to his face. Not only was he muscled, but scarred and tattooed. To Rose, he looked magnificent. What woman *wouldn't* want him? What man wouldn't want to capitalize on looks like his? Was she just fooling herself that she could do this? Granted, it was a little late in the current situation to be second-guessing herself, but there it was. It all came down to what she wanted. Was the cake worth the bake, so to speak. She thought it might be. If for nothing else, it would be worth it for the personal experience. She wanted this with Torpedo. Not because she expected him to keep her, but because he was a man she would never forget.

Summoning every ounce of courage she possessed, Rose stepped back, bumping into the bed. Torpedo's gaze was locked on her, trapping her with its intensity. A flush swept over her, and sweat erupted over every inch of her skin.

"Get in the bed, Ambrosia." The command was soft but undeniable. She couldn't disobey if she'd wanted to. She didn't want to disobey him.

Turning slowly, Rose climbed in and crawled under the covers. Torpedo was right behind her. He pulled her to him before he was even fully settled, wrapping his arms around her and urging her to lay her head on his chest. He pulled her arm across his chest, so she lay with her palm over his heart. Rose didn't know what to do, was almost afraid to move. She loved his warmth around her, the way his scent surrounded her. Her leg was over one of his thighs so that her mound was just scant inches from his hip. It was the most intimate feeling she'd ever experienced. There was a vulnerability for her in this position. She was in his arms, naked. He could do what he wanted, but he'd promised he wouldn't do anything until the morning.

"Nervous?" His voice was soft, but rough. Had his heart not been pounding beneath her hand, Rose might have thought he was making fun of her.

"I'd be lying if I said no."

"I'd be lying if I said I wasn't either."

"I can't imagine you being nervous about sex."

"Never have been," he confirmed. "Never mattered to me."

"What didn't matter?"

"Sex. It was fun, but it was up to her to tell me if she needed something. I think any woman I took to bed always enjoyed herself, but it wasn't through any effort on my part."

"Oh." It seemed like such a mundane thing to say, but Rose had no idea where he was going with this, or what to say in response.

"This time, Ambrosia, it matters."

Rose couldn't help herself. She gripped him tighter, wanting something she knew she could never have. "I don't think you'll have to worry," she said. "I'm sure I'll have a great time."

"I know you will. I intend to make sure of it."

She shivered, clutching at him again. Torpedo tightened his hold on her, nuzzling the top of her head and placing a kiss there.

"If I forget to tell you," she said softly, cuddling more securely into his side. "Thank you."

He chuckled. "If you forget the first time, you can remember the next time."

Rose said nothing after that. She tried to stay still and will herself to sleep, but it didn't work. When she became uncomfortable, needing to move, Torpedo urged her to roll to her side. He kept her in his embrace, letting her rest her head on one arm while he curled the other around her. His cock found a home nestled between her butt cheeks and, when he bent the arm her head lay on, he palmed a breast. Surprisingly, he didn't play with her nipples or in any other way try to sexually stimulate her. Which was its own stimulant by the simple fact she wanted it and he didn't provide it.

"This is more than a little frustrating," she muttered.

His warm chuckle vibrated through her body like a caress. "I know, baby."

"Then why put us both through it?" She looked back over her shoulder at him. "You know I'm willing."

"I know. Believe me, I'd love to. But I told you I wouldn't take you tonight. One thing you'll learn about me is that, while I'm a bastard, and I skirt the law from time to time as a biker, I'm a man of my word. I never go back on it, and I won't lie to you. No matter how tempting." He dropped his lips to her neck and scraped his teeth over the tender skin. "And, believe me, you are so very tempting."

"God…"

"Just relax, baby. Try to sleep. Tomorrow, I'll show you something spectacular."

It took another hour before Rose felt her eyelids grow heavy. She closed them and allowed herself to drift. Finally, with Torpedo's arms solidly around her, Rose passed out.

* * *

The room was still dark when Rose was lifted gently from the bed. She gasped awake, her eyes landing on Torpedo's face. It was difficult not to panic at first, but when he grinned down at her, Rose settled, slipping her arms around his neck lightly.

"Good morning, Ambrosia." He nuzzled her cheek, kissing it lightly.

"Where are we going?" She sounded breathless even to herself, but there was no help for it. This was it, and she was anxious beyond belief. Her heart was *pounding*.

"To the bathtub. I thought you might want to wash the sleep from your body. Besides, it's a great way to get to know each other."

"And sleeping beside each other naked wasn't?"

His chuckle warmed her insides and vibrated through her entire body. "You can't get to know someone when you're asleep."

"I might give you that. I'm not sure I slept much so the jury is still out."

Torpedo laughed then, setting her on her feet in front of the sink. "You're a treasure, Ambrosia. You know that?" He kissed the end of her nose. "Now, do any morning rituals you need to do and get in that big tub. I'll be back in ten minutes." There was pure seduction in his voice. In his gaze. A promise of so much to come Rose nearly whimpered. Instead, she nodded and did as he told her.

When he returned, she was sitting in the big garden tub, bubbles fizzing around her with the jets. It took all her willpower not to cross her arms over her chest, but she was determined to see this through. Acting shy -- even if she was -- wasn't even an option.

Torpedo's gaze focused intently on her as he stalked across the room. He seemed to make each movement slow and deliberate, as if afraid she'd bolt.

"I'm not backing out," she said, hoping she'd read his thoughts correctly. "I'm not saying you should jump on me or anything, but you don't have to be so careful not so scare me."

"Good," he said, not denying it. "Don't want you to ever be scared of me."

When he sat back on the opposite end, Rose was puzzled. She'd expected him to take her in his arms and begin this, kind of like he had the night before. Instead, he sat with his arms draped lazily over the sides of the tub as if he had no plans to move any time soon.

Raising a quizzical eyebrow, he looked at her as if to say, "What are you gonna to do now, honey?"

She thought for a minute. He'd said this was so they could get to know each other. Apparently, he wanted her to make the first move. Well. She could do that. She might be a little inexperienced, but she knew a little about pleasuring a man, and she'd certainly visited PornHub more than once.

Rose moved to him, laying her hands on his chest and settling herself between his legs. Very slowly, she leaned into him until her lips met his. He didn't move, but he returned her kiss with a fiery passion using nothing but his lips, tongue, and occasionally, his teeth. As before, Rose was swept away. Her hands caressed his shoulders and chest, trying to memorize every muscle she touched. His thighs on either side of her pinned her between them, letting her know she was exactly where he wanted her to be. Still, his arms lay passively over the edge of the tub. If she wanted to be free of him, it was totally in her hands.

Sliding her hands up the sides of his face, she threaded her fingers through his hair, continuing to kiss him, needing more and more of him. Her heart pounded and she began to tremble. God, the man could kiss! When the first whimper escaped her, Torpedo's arms snaked around her, and he moved them to the other side, pressing her body firmly against his.

He urged her legs around his waist, and Rose could feel his cock pulsing between them where it mashed pleasantly against her belly. Instinct took over for Rose and the next thing she knew, her arms had slid down his chest, around his sides to grip his ass. When he flexed against her, sliding his cock between them, she gasped and dug her nails into the muscled cheeks.

"That's it, baby," he whispered at her ear. "Stake your claim."

Was she? She thought she was playing grab-ass. When he said it like that, though, she liked the way it sounded. When he looked into her eyes, Rose loved the possessiveness she saw there sometimes. She'd known him a day -- less than -- but she'd seen that look more than once since he'd met her at the door naked.

Rose pulled his mouth to hers, needing the contact. He obliged with those same drugging kisses, driving Rose nearly out of her mind. She'd never been kissed like this man was doing. She acknowledged she was a rank novice at sex, but there was a realization that he was way out of her league, and she was just along for the ride.

Chapter Six

Torpedo had no intention of being a passive lover, but he was terrified of scaring Rose. Mainly because nothing had ever taken over him quite so much as this small woman. When her body was pressed so tightly against him, he could think of nothing else but being inside her. He tried to let her lead this to get a feel for what she needed, but the more she rubbed herself against him and gripped his ass, digging in her little nails to hold on to him, the more the predator inside him wanted free.

It was in this moment, Torpedo realized what his brothers had gone through. Cain, Bohannon, Sword, Viper, Arkham, Trucker... all of them had felt this overwhelming need to secure their women to them. He understood why all of them had done anything they'd had to, no matter how reckless or brash, to keep the woman they knew in their soul was theirs. Some had fought it. Some not. He wasn't sure which category he fit into. Probably the one that was too damned much for such an innocent. She was nineteen. He was thirty-six. Nearly twice her age! But Torpedo knew he'd never let her go. Taking her virginity tonight was just the beginning. He was going to bind her to him, make her want to stay with him. Once that was accomplished, he was going to beat the living fuck out of Richmond Foley. The man would never even breathe Rose's name again without fear of the Holy Ghost raining down on him.

He grunted when he felt her pussy make contact with the length of his cock, her little lips folding around him in a most intimate blanket. He knew Rose had no idea how to lead their mating, but he wanted her to be just desperate enough to try.

Their bodies, slick with water and the soap bubbles, moved together in a sinuous glide. The experience shouldn't have been a particularly moving one for Torpedo. Maybe it was Rose's unrestrained reactions, the trembling of her body that told him how much she really wanted this. Maybe it was the woman herself. She was strong. A fighter, no matter what she thought. She'd fought back against her enemy the only way she could. By not giving up. She hadn't rolled over and wallowed in self-pity when she'd gotten fired from her job, hadn't whined and complained when she'd gotten kicked out of her apartment. She'd picked up and moved on. Even this time, she had a plan in place. She'd paid her rent in advance and given herself enough of a padding she could work low-income jobs to save up for a move away from Foley. For some reason, Torpedo found her tenacity at making a life for herself sexy as hell. She wasn't asking for help from anyone. She was simply doing what needed to be done. He'd slay her demons for her and, hopefully, prove to her he was worthy of her strength.

Rose did something with her hips, circling them and stroking his dick with her pussy. Lightning seemed to streak up his balls, painful and burning with the need to sink into her immediately. He lifted his head and groaned. She arched against him, crying out herself in the grip of her own sensation. When she began to thrash beneath him, nipping his lips, neck, and shoulder and becoming bolder in her demands, Torpedo knew it was time.

Abruptly he stood, water sluicing off their bodies in a rush. Starting this seduction in the bath suddenly seemed like a really dumb idea. He snagged a couple of towels and tried to get as much of the water beaded on their bodies dried as he could between kisses and touches. It was a halfhearted attempt at best, but it'd have to be good enough. Because, when his mouth found her breast, his little Rose lost her Goddamned mind.

With a shriek, she couldn't seem to decide if she wanted to push him away or hold her to him. Her body moved against him like a dream, a woman doing the most exotic dance over his body. Torpedo greedily moved to the other breast, lavishing as much attention on it as he had the other.

Finally, Rose pushed him away and launched herself at him, wrapping her arms and legs around him in what felt like sheer desperation on her part. Hell, he was just as desperate to be inside her. Somehow, he got them back to the bed, planted a knee on the mattress, and laid her down. When he tried to pull her arms from around his neck, however, she was having none of it.

"No! I need you!" She sounded almost in pain, sobbing her little demand.

"God, I need you, too, baby, but you've got to let me prepare you."

"I'm ready," she panted. "Just do it!"

"I don't want to hurt you," he practically bit out, trying to free himself from her embrace. "I'm still gonna make you feel good."

She sobbed as she let go of him. Tears streaked from her lovely eyes down her temples to wet her hair. "Please don't leave me like this, Torpedo. Please! I'll do anything!" The whispered plea nearly broke his resolve. How could any man be cruel to this woman? She was so naturally sensual, so giving of herself. To think Tyler Foley had been *engaged* to her yet had tried to sexually assault her was completely unthinkable. All the man would have had to do was put a little effort into pleasing her. Which made Torpedo see red. That little fuck would pay in ways he couldn't possibly imagine, simply because he was a stupid shit. And this haze of anger gave Torpedo the control to do what he knew needed to be done rather than what his Ambrosia obviously wanted.

"Never, Ambrosia. I'll always satisfy you. You've just got to trust me."

Instead of waiting for her to acknowledge him, Torpedo shoved her legs apart as he scooted down the bed to lie between her spread thighs. Before she could utter a cry, he dipped his head and latched on to her little pussy.

Rose gasped, nearly sitting up in the bed. One hand went to his head and gripped his hair hard. Torpedo wasn't sure if she was pulling him to her or pushing him away. He doubted if she knew. Her hips seemed to mirror her hands, not knowing whether to thrust at him or squirm from his mouth. Finally, she just gave up and screamed.

He felt her quivering beneath his tongue, a delightful orgasm to start their morning. And it had taken *seconds* to bring her off. She was a passionate little thing. Untried, yes, but teaching her, taking all her firsts, would be the greatest pleasure of his life.

* * *

Rose couldn't move. Pleasure still tingled throughout her body, lulling her into a kind of catharsis. The resulting aftermath of that explosive orgasm had become its own climatic event. She was changed because of it. She didn't know exactly how, but knew she was. Vaguely, she knew Torpedo had moved up her body, but she was still floating, her mind and body not working together at the moment.

When she could finally focus again, Torpedo's weight was a secure anchor pressing her into the bed. She loved the feel of him more than she ever thought possible. What was about to happen was a complete unknown to her, but Rose was ready. This was what she'd been begging for since he'd gotten her alone in the room.

She was vaguely aware of him ripping open a packet and rolling on the condom, but the only thing that mattered to her was when he pressed the head of his cock against her entrance. Rose cried out at the touch of him against her, but he didn't slide inside. Instead, he held himself still, his body above her on stiffened arms. Once she realized he wasn't going anywhere, the haze of lust dissipated enough for her to focus on his face. "What's wrong? Why'd you stop?"

"Just making sure you were still with me." Had he grinned at her, Rose was certain she'd have lost her nerve. Instead, the strain on his face looked as bad as she felt.

"I'm with you," she whispered, nodding several times. "Please don't stop."

He nodded once before pressing into her. The second he did, Rose sucked in a breath, her eyes going wide. There was discomfort. Not pain, exactly, but a stretching she wasn't used to. It burned slightly. There was still a tremendous amount of pleasure, but it was tempered.

"I don't want you to hurt, baby," Torpedo said. Sweat dripped from his nose onto her chest. "But I want you to experience every second of this. The pleasure, but also the slight pain. It won't last long, and it's part of the experience."

"You *want* me to hurt?" Rose was shocked at that. There was a sense he was betraying her, but she wanted to hear his answer.

"Yes. I want you to know you're no longer a virgin." He looked into her eyes, his gaze intense and penetrating. "And I want you to remember it was me you gave this honor." With that, he sank into her, taking her innocence with him. Rose yelped, gasping for breath. The pain was sharp for a few seconds. She could feel the barrier of her innocence tear.

Once he slid inside her until his skin was flush against hers, he again stopped. "Look at me, baby. Keep focused on me."

She blinked several times and reached blindly for his arms. She used her grip to anchor herself and breathe through the discomfort. It took a couple of seconds, but he was right. The pain wasn't that bad and was fleeting. He could have probably distracted her enough she wouldn't have noticed, but she realized he was right. She wanted the whole experience. Everything she could get from it. As to her remembering she'd given him her first time, she wasn't sure how she felt about that. He was definitely her choice, but what would happen after this was over? Torpedo -- Gavin Ferguson -- was a man she'd never forget.

"There you are," he said, lowering his weight so that he rested on his forearms, his body pressing hers into the mattress. "There's my girl. Are you good?"

She nodded. But was she? She'd have to figure that out later. Right now, she wasn't going to let anything, not even her own insecurities and fears over the future, ruin this for her. She'd made it through the pain. Now it was time for the pleasure.

* * *

Torpedo rocked side to side, fitting himself inside Rose to his liking. He brushed over her clit, teasing her back to the fever pitch he'd had her at before he'd deliberately brought her down. When she gasped and whimpered slightly, he knew she was ready, and Torpedo began to move.

In and out. Slow, deliberate strokes eased and coaxed her body into accepting his. He could feel every ripple of her little muscles around his cock as the pleasure built inside her once again. Torpedo knew he'd been a bastard to insist she feel the pain before showing her more of the pleasure he could give her, but he wanted her to think of him every time she thought of sex. This was the first step. Once he'd made her scream her orgasm for the whole hotel to hear, he'd proceed to the next step. Slaying her demons and proving he could protect her in any way she needed him to.

Rose cried out, arching her back and wrapping her arms around him. Her little nails dug into his back this time as she clawed at him. As he sped up his pace, taking care to put as much friction on her clit as he could, she dug more frantically at him. Torpedo welcomed the bite. It kept him focused on his goal instead of allowing him to drown in the sheer pleasure of her hot little body.

It didn't take long for Rose to scream her pleasure. Her little pussy milked his cock in hot, gripping heat. He fought off his own orgasm, not wanting to finish the first round too soon, needing to draw out the experience for both of them as long as he could.

Just as he thought he had a tight grip on his control, Rose leaned up to find his lips with hers. The second she did, she bit down sharply on his lower one.

The shock stripped everything from him, his cock swelling at the unexpectedly aggressive gesture. With a long, hoarse bellow, Torpedo emptied his seed inside the condom. Spurt after pulsing spurt burst from him so forcefully, he vaguely wondered if the condom could contain him. Would he spill inside her? Get her pregnant? In the past, such thoughts had been enough to quell any arousal he had. Now, it only made the experience that much more intense.

For long moments, he lay on top of her, trying to catch his breath. Rose still clung to him, her fingers kneading over and over, her breathing just as ragged as his.

"You good, baby?" Torpedo wasn't sure how he managed to get the words out. Just being with her had tweaked his gray matter beyond repair. Never had a woman affected him like this. Control was something Torpedo prided himself on, and he'd just lost every single ounce of it with Rose.

"Yes," she whispered. "I'm wonderful."

Carefully, he extracted himself from her grip and rose from the bed. He went to the bathroom to clean himself and bring a fresh cloth for her. As he washed himself, he noticed the blood denoting her innocence on the condom and high on one thigh where he'd rubbed against her.

Swearing, he wet another cloth with warm water. She'd be tender. Sore and feeling quite vulnerable. He'd taken her with less finesse than he should have her first time. But, Goddamn, she'd been so fucking passionate! He hadn't expected anything like what she gave him. Every response was real. Every sigh, whimper, moan, and scream. Nothing in his experience with sex could have prepared him for the raw lust she displayed.

No. Lust wasn't the right word. It was more than that. Passion. Uncontrollable hunger for what he was doing to her. She had been more than a simple participant in their lovemaking, too. It hadn't been deliberate on her part -- Torpedo was certain she'd been going on blind instinct. Which made her the most naturally sexual woman he'd ever encountered in his life. This could be a problem, because he could easily come to crave that unbridled hunger in her.

When he cleaned her, she bled, leaving a crimson streak on the insides of both thighs. He pushed her hand away gently when she reached for the cloth to do it herself. With a tender touch, he took great care in getting every smear of blood and her own moisture off her delicate skin before tossing the cloth back into the bathroom and climbing into bed with her.

Torpedo wrapped his body around hers, closing his arms tightly around her. Her body trembled slightly. She clung to him, her head resting on his chest. Normally this was the situation he tried to avoid. He didn't do afterplay or whatever women called this shit. But with Rose, he not only tolerated it, he needed it. In fact, he wasn't entirely sure he didn't need it just as much as she did.

He stroked her back up and down, trying to soothe her, praise her for the wonderful way she'd responded to him. When she continued to tremble, he said, "Talk to me, baby. Tell me what you're feeling."

"That was so wonderful, Torpedo. I never knew."

"I'll always make it good for you. No matter what. Whatever it takes or whatever you need."

There was a long pause, and Torpedo thought she'd drifted off. Hoped it actually, because there were questions about the two of them he needed to really think about. Like the fact that something inside him compelled him to keep her close. It was more than the cuddling. He wanted to wake up with her in his arms before having sex with her. Every single fucking morning of his life. Why now, when he'd never been one to need or even want a woman around the next morning? There was something about Ambrosia that had gotten under his skin. He needed to figure it out before she did and took advantage of him. Because he knew with absolute certainty that he'd give the woman the Goddamned moon if she even hinted that she wanted it. And he'd kill anyone trying to take her from him.

* * *

Had Rose been able to design the morning, she'd never have been able to make a more beautiful one. The sun was warm and bright, the sky deep sapphire blue. The occasional white, puffy cloud drifted lazily along overhead while sea gulls cried from the beach. She was happier than she could ever remember being.

Torpedo had woken her that morning with tender sex, bringing her up gently several times before letting her orgasm. By the time they'd finished, Rose had been mindless with pleasure, clawing and scratching and biting at him to finish her. He'd chuckled, though it had sounded a bit strained, and complied with her wishes. To both their satisfaction.

Now, he had her on the back of his bike, speeding down the highway to a clubhouse. Vicious, one of the two buddies he had with him, was part of Salvation's Bane, a sister club to Torpedo's own biker club. Normally, Rose would have thought twice about jumping on the back of a strange man's motorcycle, but shit. She'd already slept with the man. He hadn't hurt her or done anything she hadn't thoroughly enjoyed. For the first time in a very long time, she actually felt safe. Not safe like she expected to die, and this was the one man who could save her. It was more like Torpedo wasn't going to force her to do anything she didn't want to. She could do whatever she wanted with him and he'd never make her go beyond what she was comfortable with. Rose hadn't felt that from Tyler ever. Felt it even less from his father. Tyler was in jail until Richmond figured a way to get him out. Richmond was on her ass everywhere she went, making her life miserable. Rose got the feeling Torpedo might hinder that endeavor for Richmond.

The trio drove around Palm Springs for over an hour, picking up more and more bikes as they went. Every time they did, someone gave Vicious a wave or a fist bump as they passed. Torpedo and Shadow got a wave or a two-fingered salute. They all nodded to her. All of them joined formation as they rode across town. She noticed they kept her and Torpedo in the center of their band. By design since Torpedo wasn't technically part of their club?

By the time they rolled into the driveway of a huge house, there were at least thirty or forty men riding around them. The noise from the pipes was deafening, especially when they stopped and all of them revved their engines, yelling out their welcome home to their brother.

"Wow," Rose said, yelling to be heard over the roar. "That's something else!"

Torpedo grinned at her. "Sure is, darlin'. Let's get inside. I think Data has been coordinating with Salvation's Bane. They should have all the information they need to help on this end."

"They're not your club. Right? Won't they not want to get involved in a personal matter?"

"Honey, we're all brothers. All of Bones and most of Salvation's Bane works for Cain outside of the biker life. One of us needs help, we all band together. Especially in a situation like this where the problem is outside Bone's territory."

He steadied her as she dismounted the bike, taking a second to get her legs under her after the long ride when she wasn't used to it. Torpedo stood and lashed both helmets to his bike before taking Rose's hand, steering her to the clubhouse.

The heavenly scent of something barbequing hit Rose the second the door opened and had her mouth watering. "Something smells good," she whispered.

"That'd be Tawney's world-famous chicken wings," Vicious said, taking a deep breath through his nose. His eyes were closed in bliss as he inhaled the sharp fragrance. "Woman can make wings like nobody's business." He nodded toward the buffet table the women were setting up. "I suggest you get some before the brothers take them all, Rose."

"Rose?" Torpedo questioned as he narrowed his eyes at Vicious. "What about me."

"You're on your own, Bones. Guests, Salvation's Bane. Then visitin' clubs."

"The fuck you say!"

Vicious laughed as Torpedo urged Rose to the table to grab a plate. Once they had their share of the wings, potato salad, and coleslaw, Torpedo addressed Thorn, the president of Salvation's Bane.

"Cain touch base with you about Rose?"

The other man nodded. "I'm aware of the dynamics of the situation. Sounds like she made some nasty enemies."

"Data's already taken care of things with Tyler, but I'll need help getting to Daddy Foley. I can handle him but getting in and out without being seen can be a problem if you don't know the area."

Thorn waved that away. "It's no problem, brother. Vicious has volunteered to help. He's as good a man as I have. What's your goal? Scare him into leaving the woman alone?"

"Mostly. That and the threat that, if he doesn't, his son will pay the consequences."

Rose gasped, but Torpedo squeezed her leg under the table, hoping she took the hint and didn't say anything.

"Sounds reasonable. He'd be a hard one to cover if you needed to take more drastic measures. Try to keep to your original plan if you can."

"Always, brother," Torpedo said readily. "While I can't deny I'd love to take a more permanent route, it's not appropriate."

Thorn nodded once. "You have my blessing then. How long do you need?"

"A couple days at most. We need to set up a video conference at the pen where Tyler's being kept. Once Data gets that going, I'll be ready."

"We'll keep the doors open for you, brother." Thorn pinned him with a hard stare. "Don't misuse that trust. Vicious will follow your lead. Don't bring more trouble to our door than we can safely handle."

"I'll treat Salvation's Bane as if it were my own club. I wouldn't bring trouble to our door if it could be avoided safely. I'll respect your club the same way."

"Having said that," Thorn continued, "Richmond Foley is a son of a bitch. His son is a bastard of the worst kind. Not gonna lie and say I wouldn't approve if you did take care of that situation permanently."

"The punishment has to fit the crime, Thorn. I know you live by that. Bones does, too."

The president snorted. "Mostly."

Torpedo laughed then, dispelling the tension that had surrounded the men. "Yeah. Mostly."

Chapter Seven

"So, what's the plan?" Rose asked as Torpedo took off his shirt. They'd been given a comfortable room at the Salvation's Bane compound where they could rest. "Rest" as in code for "fuck."

He shrugged. "Waiting on word from Data. Once he establishes what he needs in the prison where Tylor is being held, we'll go have a chat with his daddy."

"Chat? Like really or does 'chat' mean something more sinister?" Rose raised an eyebrow when Torpedo chuckled.

"No, darlin'. I mean chat as in talk. Much as I'd like to throw that man a beating for being a third-class prick, I won't because it would put Bane at risk. I won't take the chance they'll get in trouble when it's not really worth it. Richmond Foley can be controlled."

"Good. I don't want anyone in trouble because of me." She meant it, too. If she was the cause of these good men getting into a fight they couldn't control and win, she'd never forgive herself.

"None of this is because of you, baby. Anything Tyler or Richmond Foley get, they brought on themselves. You're not the only one they hurt. I'm hoping you'll be the last."

She stepped close to Torpedo, her hands going to his chest where she stroked over his shoulders with her palms until she linked her hands around his neck. "So, what do we do in the meantime?"

He gave her a crooked grin. "Oh, I'm sure we'll think of something."

Rose accepted his kiss eagerly when he lowered his head to hers. If she lived to be a hundred, she didn't think she'd ever tire of kissing him. The sweet way he coaxed her and the sometimes-rough aggression seemed to be contradictory, but it was an intoxicating combination. Now, he kissed her tenderly but insistently, taking her into a world of exotic passion. He urged her shirt over her head, leaving her in a lacy bra that pushed her breasts up and together, showing them to their best advantage. She'd worn it for him, hoping he'd get to see her in it. When he growled, her belly fluttered excitedly.

"Have I told you you're fuckin' beautiful?"

She giggled nervously. "I don't know. Can't remember. Probably because when you look at me like you are now, I can't concentrate on anything."

"Well, you're fuckin' beautiful, Ambrosia. So fuckin' beautiful."

"Torpedo..." She sighed his name into her kiss. Nothing was so good as his touch; nothing was so wonderful as when he held her tightly in his arms and told her what to do to please them both. Rose reveled in the power he inspired inside her. Torpedo made her feel like she was a beautiful, desirable woman capable of holding the attention of a virile man like himself. Despite telling him she rarely answered to the name Ambrosia, she loved that he called her than when they had sex. It was like their special thing. His private name for her.

Before she knew it, Torpedo had her naked and his arms wrapped tightly around her. His frame was muscled and large, hers slight and lithe. Rose loved how safe she felt surrounded by him. Even when he was a little rough, she loved everything he did. She also found an answering wildness within herself. She wanted to do everything he demanded, to satisfy his every desire.

He spread her out on the bed, urging her arms above her head so that she grasped the rails on the headboard. "Don't move, Ambrosia. Hold on to the headboard no matter what. Understand?"

When she nodded, he kissed her once more before moving his lips down her body. He lavished kisses over her breasts, sucking on her nipples one at a time. Stubble on his face abraded her skin deliciously, creating an erotic stimulation.

Rose lost herself, letting herself go within the magic Torpedo created. She craved everything he did to her. Still, she was shocked at the sensations when he put his mouth over her sex and sucked, flicking her clit with his tongue. The place was so very sensitive, and Torpedo knew exactly how much pressure to put on her before it became too much.

She cried out, tunneling her fingers through his hair. Whether she was trying to push him away or hold him to her, she didn't know. Everything was too much. Too strong. Yet... perfect!

Torpedo stabbed deep, thrusting his tongue inside her before slipping two fingers to take the place of his tongue. "You taste so delicious." His wicked voice sent shivers through her. An orgasm the likes of which she'd never conceived of was just out of reach. If he'd flick her clit just once more...

"Ah, ah," he said, placing kisses all around her pussy. "None of that, Ambrosia. No coming until I'm ready for you to."

"I -- what?"

He grinned up at her from between her thighs. "You heard me. You don't come this time until I say you can."

"Are you kidding?" Rose couldn't process what he was saying. She couldn't have heard him right.

"I'm dead serious," he said between kisses. "You're not to come until I tell you, or there will be consequences."

She was starting to panic now. No way could he keep this up without her coming. Hell, she was on the verge as they spoke! Somehow, Rose managed to squeak out the question, "Consequences?"

"Oh, yes. Dire consequences."

"Um, what exactly?"

"I'm not certain. I guess you'll have to disobey me to find out." His smile was beyond cocky. He was a man who knew he had the upper hand and intended to use it.

"Oh, God..."

"Indeed."

A third finger entered her as he pumped as deep as he could, occasionally flicking her clit. Rose had managed to back off slightly, but she knew it was only a matter of time. What was she supposed to do? Didn't some men get off on their partners begging them for things?

"Please let me come, Torpedo. I don't think I can stop it." The plea rolled off her lips without a single ounce of hesitation or regret. If he wanted her to beg him for this, she could do it. It was just play, after all.

"No." The answer came immediately, his gaze focused on her like a hawk.

"What?"

"No, Ambrosia. You can't come yet. Not until I say." He kept pumping her cunt with his fingers, his tongue snaking out to tease her clit occasionally. It wasn't long before he had her panting and crying out, her body drenched in sweat.

"I... can't..." She struggled to form words. How to tell him she was coming whether he wanted her to or not? Head thrashing, body trembling, Rose finally gave up the fight. It had been futile anyway. With a scream, Rose let her body fragment. Wave after pulsing wave caught her up in a pleasure so intense it bordered on pain. Her body seized, her hips riding his mouth frantically with nothing more than instinct. Rose knew she couldn't stop her body from moving if she'd wanted to. Nothing in her life had prepared her for the sensations she found with this man. *Nothing*. Never had she dared to dream anything could feel like this.

Finally, the pulsations faded, her body going limp as if tired from a long journey. Perhaps that was exactly what had happened. Torpedo had opened the door to a whole new world of being where sensation ruled, and nothing was as it should be. Perhaps she'd been waiting to give herself to exactly the right man, someone who knew how to do this to her body and enjoyed it as much as she did.

"T-Torpedo..." Rose looked up at him, tears streaming from her eyes she hadn't even known were there. "That was..."

When her eyes finally focused on him, she found him rolling on a condom, his gaze intense and demanding. "Gonna be even better, Ambrosia." His voice was rough and husky, as if maybe he were just as affected as she'd been. Once the condom encased him, he lowered himself to her, probing her entrance carefully before sliding all the way in with one smooth stroke. Rose felt her body open for him, welcoming him inside her. Again, the sensations started building. A firestorm she had no hope of containing.

* * *

The woman in Torpedo's arms was a dream come true. Her responses were genuine and so fucking passionate he could hardly believe it. He knew how to please a woman. He didn't really care if they got off or not, but it was a matter of pride. What man could really call himself a man if he didn't at least try to give as much pleasure as he got? Usually, those matters took care of themselves. The women he was usually with knew what they were doing and how to please both of them. But little Ambrosia was still learning. And, fuck, she was a fast learner!

When he entered her body and settled himself on top of her, she was already thrusting her hips at him, urging him to move inside her the way she needed. She'd even learned how to twist her hips at the end of her movement in such a way that he nearly shot off the second she did it. All of a sudden, his threat to her seemed to ring in his ears. He'd ordered her to hold off her orgasm until he told her to come. What if he couldn't even last long enough to drive her up that high again? That'd be a kick in the nuts.

He shifted to his side, a position he knew would throw her. He needed Rose off balance until he could catch his breath, or he was gonna look like a fool. He pulled one of her thighs over his hip and gripped her ass to keep her close to him. When she tried to roll over to wrap her arms around his neck, he shoved her to her back.

"Stay there, Ambrosia. Squeeze your tits for me while I fuck you."

Her eyes were wild when they met his, her expression stark. Raw. Without hesitation, her hands found her breasts, and she squeezed and rubbed them, looking a little uncomfortable but going at it with gusto.

"Pinch your nipples. Roll them between your fingers. Stretch them out."

She did as he asked and cried out, closing her eyes and arching her back. Torpedo continued to thrust into her, fucking her at a leisurely but steady pace.

"Can you suck them? Can you reach one with your mouth and suck it?"

Again, she whimpered, trying to do what he instructed. She couldn't quite reach, but she licked one ripe peak with the tip of her little pink tongue. The sight was nearly his undoing.

"You look so sexy, Ambrosia," he admitted in a husky voice he could hardly believe was his. "So fuckin' sexy it fuckin' hurts."

He shifted her again. He had to leave her body to get her where he wanted her, which pained him beyond belief. She lay on her back with both legs spread wide and bent at the knee. Torpedo was still on his side as he guided his cock into her again, this time with his lower body under her legs. With her in this position, he had full access to her front and so did she. Once he'd had her start playing with her tits, he found he wanted to watch her do more. He wanted to see just how far he could push her.

"Still feel good, Ambrosia?"

"Yes," she gasped. She looked over at him, a hesitant expression on her face. She hadn't let go of her tits, but had a death grip on both of them. "I don't... what do you want me to do?"

He grinned. "That's exactly the right question, baby." He pumped into her, wanting to get her used to the new position before he played with her.

"It feels different."

Torpedo got the impression she hadn't meant to say that out loud. "Better? Not as good?"

She shook her head. "Just... different."

He grinned, continuing to thrust lazily. He reached for one of her hands and removed it from her breast, replacing it with his own. Rose sighed, arching her back for him, putting herself more fully in his hand. Her breasts were rounded and firm, but small, nearly disappearing into her chest when she lay on her back. Her body was sleek with fine muscle, a young and tempting woman he was fast growing addicted to.

"Stroke your body for me. Rub your hands over your belly and tits."

As he fucked her, Rose did as he asked. Her hands wandered over her body in a light caress. Every time she grazed a nipple, she shivered, and the little nub pebbled prettily. Her hands wandered to just above her mound but never ventured lower. He knew she wanted to. Could tell by the way she hesitated every time she got close.

The next time she went that far, Torpedo snagged her wrist and urged her to continue going lower. "Feel where we're joined, Ambrosia. Stroke your clit if you want. Put your fingers on either side of my cock as I fuck you."

"Oh, God!" She did as he told her, and the second her fingers found her clit, her body spasmed around his, milking him, trying to make him come with her. She screamed, the sound almost agonizing. Torpedo watched in fascination as color flushed Rose's skin a beautiful shade of pink. The fine muscles stood out in her abdomen, rippling with her orgasm. She gripped his cock and her pussy in one small hand, her fingers scissoring around him even as he continued to move in and out of her.

"That's it, baby. Do whatever you need, but get yourself off hard."

She arched her back, finally letting her pussy go and gripping his cock alone. She found his balls when they hit her ass as he continued to fuck her and rolled them in her hand. Torpedo growled, his own body beginning to sweat with the effort to hold back.

"Tell me what to do," she whimpered. "I want you to come, too."

"You want me to come?"

"More than anything!"

He pulled himself out of her, flipping her over to her stomach. With a palm on her back he held her down even as he urged her to her knees with the other hand. With one hard shove, he slammed home, sinking into her wet heat with a hoarse shout.

Torpedo rode her hard. Fast. Her body was a haven he'd never even known he needed until the first time he'd taken her. She was hot and tight, made perfectly for him. The rounded globes of her ass seemed to taunt him with the need to place his mark on her so no one could ever take her from him.

"Oh, I intend to come, Ambrosia. Right after I give you your punishment for coming without permission."

Rose's head whipped around, and she came up on her elbows. "My what?"

Torpedo shoved her back down, stilling his fucking of her. "You heard me. Did you think I was lying when I told you there'd be consequences?"

"I -- I thought you were playing?"

"Oh, my little Ambrosia. You'll find out when it comes to you, I very rarely play. I'm as serious as it gets."

"I don't --"

Before she could really protest, Torpedo brought his hand down on one cheek. The air exploded from her lungs in a startled rush. When he did it again, she gasped. The third time, she... moaned. When she arched up for more with the fourth sharp slap, Torpedo knew he had, indeed, found the perfect woman.

"You like it, don't you?" he bit out, delivering another stinging slap to her ass. "You like your punishment."

"Yes," she cried. "I mean, no! God, I'm so confused!"

"Don't think, Ambrosia," he said at her ear, whispering wickedly. "Just feel."

Torpedo continued to deliver smacks to her ass as he fucked her hard. His handprint was red against the delicate flesh there, marking her as his. The sight, along with her screams and the way she pushed back with every thrust, pushed him headlong into bliss. With a roar, he shoved himself deep inside her, his cock pulsing and straining as he emptied himself into the condom. His body convulsed, jerking with every spurt of his seed. Rose cried out again, her body clamping down on his once again as she found another orgasm. Thank God, because Torpedo knew he couldn't keep going after this cataclysmic release.

He collapsed on top of her, still deep inside her. Rose found his hand with her own and gripped hard, panting just as hard as he was.

"Tell me you're good, baby," he rasped out. His voice was rough after his shouts. Fuck! He must have really lost his shit. He'd been that far gone and couldn't be happier about it.

"I am," she purred. Rose was still out of breath, but she had a death grip on his hand. "Wonderful."

He squeezed her once before disentangling himself from around her body, pulling out and removing the condom. A quick trip to the bathroom to wash and to bring something to wash her, then Torpedo climbed into the bed, pulling Rose into his arms.

Peace filled Torpedo's mind and heart. Pure peace.

A loud thumping came from the door. Someone pounding on the wood. "Goddamn, Torpedo! Keep it the fuck down! Some of us need our fuckin' beauty sleep!"

"Fuck you, Vicious!" Torpedo growled at the man on the other side of the door. A chuckle sounded as Vicious's heavy boots headed back down the hallway. "Sorry," Torpedo muttered to Rose. Thankfully, she giggled, color sweeping up her face, but a beautiful smile did as well.

Yeah. He was fucked.

Chapter Eight

Leaving Rose in bed was the hardest thing Torpedo had ever done. He'd lost count of the number of missions he'd participated in where he'd been convinced he'd never return home. Torpedo was a man who loved living. He was always willing to die for a greater cause, but he'd rather live if at all possible, thank you very much. Even the few situations he'd gone into knowing the chances were great that he wouldn't come back alive were nothing compared to prying his protesting body from her arms. Even standing next to the bed looking down at her, it was hard to turn and leave when everything inside him wanted to crawl back under the covers and continue making love to her.

Fuck.

With a sharp shake of his head, he finished dressing, then headed out, locking the bedroom door so no one would disturb her. If things went the way he planned, he wouldn't be gone more than a few hours anyway. He'd be back inside her before dawn.

Vicious and Shadow were waiting outside his door. All three of them were dressed in black. No club colors to identify them, though Torpedo had no intention of hiding behind anonymity. He wanted that fuck Foley to know who was gunning for him. They all made eye contact, then marched down the hall, Torpedo in the lead.

The ride to Richmond Foley's estate was about thirty minutes, all of it prime beach-front property. The man definitely had means. Why in the world was he picking on a woman like Rose? She was nothing to him. She might represent his son's fall from grace, but she certainly shouldn't be on either Foley's radar. So, what was it?

"It's ego, brother," Shadow said, putting a hand on his shoulder as Torpedo dismounted his bike. They parked under a pier on the beach below Foley's house.

"What?"

"The reason this motherfucker fixated on a sweet girl like Rose. Ego. He can't stand that a nobody took down his family, and it's eating at him."

The moonlight reflected off Shadow's skin, giving him an eerie, otherworldly appearance. Shadow had been a late addition to their crew and club, but he was a fucking good one. The man had insight like no one Torpedo had ever encountered. He could read people to a scary degree.

"When this is done, remind me to thank you for using your powers for good."

Shadow snorted. "Smartass fuck."

Torpedo clapped him on the back. "You're an irreplaceable member, Shadow. Never think we all don't know that."

"Oh, I know. I just didn't know if you knew."

"If you guys need to get a room, there's one that rents by the hour just up the fuckin' street."

"Don't worry, Vicious," Shadow said, punching the other man in the arm. "He loves you too. And for the record, I never rent a room by the hour. Brother needs a good long time to love his woman." He shrugged. "Or guy. Whatever your thing is."

They all three chuckled, the tension easing enough for Torpedo to think clearly instead of how much he wanted to pound that motherfucker, Foley. "Let's get this done. Is Data in position?"

Shadow held up his phone. "On standby. Ready for the… demonstration."

"Good. Tell him ten minutes. Tops."

Shadow sent a quick text and stared at the screen a few seconds before giving a short nod. "He's good. Says you're free to gain the house. South-side entrance. Says to key in the code 218794# when you enter. That will give you thirty minutes of disabled security all the way around. We'll be ghosts in the wind."

Vicious raised an eyebrow. "Good boy you got there."

"Yup. Data's a master at shit like this."

"Hop to it, boys," Shadow said, heading up the stairs, leading the way. "I wanna catch a few Z's before Torpedo and his woman go at it again. Why'd you put me next to those two, Vicious? They're freaks!"

"Fixin' to bust your motherfuckin' head, Shadow," Torpedo groused.

Shadow flipped him off.

Three minutes later, they were at the entrance in question. The place was truly beautiful. The breaker wall was camouflaged by tropical shrubbery and greenery, the pool sculpted into the landscape so that it seemed more like a natural beach than an artificial pool.

"Gotta hand it to the bastard. This place is really something." Torpedo knew he sounded equal parts admiring and grudging.

"No shit. Wouldn't mind havin' me a setup like this. Might make me want to settle down like the rest of you pussies," Shadow said, preparing to open the door that was their goal.

"One of these days, Shadow," Torpedo threatened.

"Yeah," Vicious said. "I can see it now. Some little thing wrapping you around her finger,

Shadow…" He shook his head like he truly regretted Shadow's imaginary situation.

"That's harsh, man. Harsh."

"Cut it out, you clowns." Data's voice came over Shadow's phone. "We're on the clock here."

Shadow opened the door, stepped inside, and keyed the code Data had given them. "We're in."

"OK. Countdown started. Thirty minutes. Get in. Rip it up. Standing by here."

The three men made their way through the house. The intel Data had for them indicated Foley would be in his study, going over the day's reports. Apparently, the man was fastidious in that regard. He always reviewed the day's work before locking it in his safe and going to bed. Tonight was no exception.

"Richmond Foley," Torpedo said as the three men entered the room. Though all were armed, Vicious was the only one with his weapon drawn. Since they were in Bane territory, if shots were fired, it would be Vicious's decision.

"Who's there?" The man didn't sound nearly as afraid as he should. Well, that was about to change.

"My name's Torpedo. I'm here because of my recent acquaintance with a young woman named Ambrosia Gataki. Do you remember her?"

Foley scowled. "It was her lies that put my son in prison," he spat. "I doubt I'll ever forget that little tramp."

Torpedo let the silence drag on as Foley gathered his papers. Probably to put them in the safe before anyone could get a look at them. As if they cared. Once Foley looked back at them, Torpedo caught his gaze and held it. The man still hadn't realized the trouble he was in.

"Whatever you're here for, I don't have it. I'm not giving you money." Still, Torpedo didn't say anything, the two men flanking him still as death. "What?"

"Because you don't have any idea how much Rose means to me, I'll forgive that slight to her. Once. Now you know so there'll be no misunderstanding."

Foley laughed. "How much she means to you? That girl is poison! She'll play you for your money, bleed you dry, then cry foul when she's done with you."

Torpedo took the three steps separating himself and Foley with lightning speed, delivering a slap that spun the older man around so that he fell across his desk. When he reached for his phone, Shadow was there, knocking it out of reach and stomping it on the floor with one heavy-soled bootheel.

"Son of a bitch! Do you have any idea who I am?"

"The better question would be, do I give a flyin' fuck who you are? 'Cause I don't. What I do care about is Rose and how you've made it your personal mission in life to make her miserable. You've followed her all over the country, making sure she has no means of supporting herself. All because you can't admit you raised a fuckin' monster."

"My son was innocent! He didn't rape that girl!"

"If I read the court transcript correctly, she never claimed he raped her. It was the other thirteen women. Rose was just the one to actually call the cops when he tried to beat her senseless. That about right?"

"The evidence was circumstantial at best," Foley argued. "They only convicted him because of who I am. They see him as just another privileged white male thinking he can get away with anything because his father has money. If he'd been of a different background --"

"He'd still have been convicted because he was fuckin' guilty as sin," Torpedo finished. "I'm not here about that, and I don't much care if the man is guilty or not. I'm here about Rose. Now, shut the fuck up and sit down. I have something to show you."

Richmond stood for several seconds, trying his best to stare down Torpedo. When he did sit, he did so behind his desk. Torpedo almost smiled.

"You put your hands anywhere but flat on the top of that desk, and we won't wait to show you what awaits your son if you don't follow my instructions to the letter." Torpedo jerked his head toward Vicious. "He'll put a fuckin' bullet in your brain before I ever give the fuckin' word."

Foley paused, looking startled that Torpedo had called him out. Like he was too stupid to know he had a gun under his desk drawer. Finally, he sat back with a sigh. "What do you want to show me?"

Torpedo grinned. "That's right. Just sit back there and relax." Shadow eased behind Foley, putting a heavy hand on the man's shoulder. With the other hand, he set a tablet in front of the man on the desktop. On the screen was Tyler Foley's smiling, smirking face.

"Son?"

"Hey, Pops. Happy to see me? The boys here said you pulled some strings. Say I'm gonna be free again soon."

"Tyler, who's with you?" Richmond didn't look nearly as confident as his son. Reasonable, since Tyler had no idea who had him. By the look of him, Richmond had a very good idea.

"Three guys. Said you hired 'em." Tyler shrugged, crossing his arms and sitting back in his chair. "They said you wanted a word with me."

"He does, Tyler." Torpedo stepped closer behind Richmond, leaning over the older man's shoulder. "Your daddy is a fierce advocate of yours, you know."

Again, Tyler shrugged. "Always good to have the old man on your side." He winked at the camera.

"So, Tyler, I want us to all get acquainted," Torpedo said, all smiles. Inside, he was dying to blow that smug motherfucker's brains out. "My name's Torpedo."

Tyler barked a short laugh. "Big dick, huh?"

Torpedo smiled. "Yeah. How'd you guess?" He let his grin fade. "My name's Torpedo, but you can call me your worst fuckin' nightmare, you son of a bitch."

A confused look spread over Tyler's face before his eyes widened and a huge fist connected with his jaw. There was a clattering when he fell from his chair. Gruff male voices sounded in the background as someone picked Tyler up bodily while another man put the chair upright. They dumped Tyler back into his seat. He now sported a bloody mouth and wide, terrified eyes.

"What the fuck?" Richmond lunged toward Torpedo, but Shadow reined him in before he even got close.

"That's for being a fuckin' bastard," Torpedo said, nodding at the camera.

"What are you doing? I never hurt nobody!" Tyler's voice was high-pitched and terrified.

Someone slammed a fist into his shoulder. When he stepped back, the hilt of a knife protruded from the joint. Tyler screamed, a horrible, high-pitched wail.

"That's for bein' a fuckin' *lyin'* bastard." Again, Torpedo nodded. Another fist, this time to the other side of his face. "And that's for screamin' like a little girl."

"Stop this!" Richmond demanded. He tried to fight Shadow, but the man simply shoved him back into his chair and gripped the back of his neck so he had to watch the screen.

Fists came at Tyler over and over, giving the man a beating Torpedo was certain Tyler had never imagined. Tyler screamed and screamed until his eyes were swollen shut and his face was covered in blood from his mouth, nose, and several cuts. Someone pulled the knife from his shoulder and slammed it into the other shoulder, yanking it out in one smooth move. They kept it up for a few minutes, Richmond yelling his outrage, Tyler just... yelling. Once Tyler finally stopped all the noise, other than the occasional groan or whimper, Torpedo called a halt.

"Now," he said, his voice congenial. "On to the real business."

"What?" Richmond had become pale as he watched them beat the living shit out of his son. At first, he'd seemed defiant, clearly plotting how he'd get revenge. He probably thought the police would come knocking at Bones' door. Arrest them all and throw them in jail. Throw away the key and all that. The longer the beating continued, the tighter Shadow gripped Richmond's neck. Several times, Vicious had examined his gun, checking the chamber, removing the clip only to slam it back home and chamber a fresh round. All the while, the three bikers kept their gazes glued to Richmond. "What more could you possibly do? Do you plan on killing him?"

"No. At least, not yet." Torpedo took the tablet and gazed at the screen. "That'll be all. My appreciation."

"Anytime, brother." The man on the other end doing most of the beating was a member of Salvation's Bane doing a small stretch for involuntary manslaughter. His time was nearly up, and Torpedo worried this little stunt would extend his time, but the man had assured Data and Thorn he was glad to teach the little bastard a lesson. Apparently, Tyler Foley didn't make friends easily in prison. "I'll have my eye on him. You need him gone, say the word."

Richmond heard every word, his eyes wide and terrified. "Why are you doing this to my son?"

"Cut the fuckin' shit!" Torpedo was losing patience with the bastard. "Your son is a serial rapist and a bully. He hurts women for his own pleasure."

"Look, he might be a little... rough from time to time, but --"

"Be careful what you say, Richmond. I'm not sure little Tyler there can take much more." When Richmond said nothing else, Torpedo continued. "This is about you coming to terms with the monster Tyler became. I have no fuckin' idea what either of your issues are, but you accept responsibility for your part in this and make Tyler understand he has to do the same. You can't do it on your own? I suggest you find some fuckin' help. I'm sure there's a twelve-step program somewhere you can go talk it out. As for Tyler, he drops any appeals he has goin'. He serves his time. More importantly..." Torpedo leaned down to place his hands on the desk and look Richmond Foley straight in the eyes. "You leave Ambrosia Gataki the fuck alone. You don't, Tyler pays the price. You still don't, you'll pay. Is there any part of this you don't fuckin' understand?"

Richmond shook his head, reality finally sinking in. The man looked terrified, no hint of the defiance he'd shown earlier. Good. Torpedo knew it wouldn't last, but he was fully prepared to see to it the Foleys paid for anything they did in the future to harm Rose or either club.

"I want you to remember something, Richmond." Torpedo needed to add one thing so the man could fully understand who and what he was dealing with. "I'm aware you're rich enough to find us and start a war. You'll get some of us, too. Might even get me and Rose, or either of these men with me. But, there's a fuckin' lot of us. You can't get us all. None of our brothers'll hesitate to kill you and Tyler if it comes to that. This is a war you have no fuckin' hope of winning. My advice? Accept the past. Look to the future. Move the fuck on before your past buries you." When Richmond only nodded, Torpedo added, "You need to say the words, Foley."

"I-I understand," he stammered. "I'll leave Rose alone. Once Tyler gets out, he will too."

"Good." He glanced at Vicious and Shadow, nodded, then the three of them left Richmond Foley. The fuck would probably get brave again in a few weeks or months, but he was nothing they couldn't handle. For now, he just wanted to get back to Rose, make love to her, then get the fuck back to Kentucky where he Goddamned belonged.

Chapter Nine

Rose jumped when a male body slipped into the bed and pulled her to him. "Wha --?"

"Shh, baby. I gotcha."

Happiness washed over her like she'd never known. "Torpedo." The only man she'd ever loved. She was sleep-drunk but would know Torpedo anywhere. She'd love to believe he was as attached to her as she was to him. God, she wanted it to be true. The fact, however, was there was no possible way he could be. He was vastly more experienced than her in everything. Especially sex and women. Which meant that there was no way she could keep him satisfied. Once he got bored with her inept attempts to please him, he'd move on. It also meant he would be able to keep his heart separate. Fucking and love were two totally different things, and Rose knew there was no way she could separate the two like Torpedo could.

"I gotcha, baby," he repeated.

"Are you OK? I woke up and you were gone."

"Everything's fine. Just had to take care of some business."

She stilled. "It was about Tyler. Wasn't it?"

"Not gonna lie to you, honey. It was. But It's taken care of."

She struggled to sit up, but Torpedo held her to him, kissing the top of her head. With a sigh, she settled down, wrapping her arm over his chest. "I don't want anything to happen to you because of me. If you hurt someone --"

He stopped her with a kiss and kept kissing her until she sighed, melting into him. No matter how much he did it, Rose could never get used to the way he made her feel. Like she was the only woman who ever mattered to him. The only woman he ever wanted in his life. Thinking like that, believing that, was dangerous to her heart, and the cruelest fiction imaginable.

Raising his head, Torpedo kissed her nose, then her forehead. "Someone got hurt, but nothing that wasn't deserved and not permanently."

"I'm not worried about whoever you hurt, Torpedo. I don't want you or the club to get into trouble because of me. I just…" She looked away from him, her fingers sifting through the hair on his chest to comfort herself. "I just want to be left alone. Live a life with you and not be bothered." That was way more than she should have said, but what else could she say? It was the stark truth.

"Then you have nothing to worry about and everything to look forward to. You can stay with Bones as long as you want. You'll always have a home with us."

She noticed he hadn't said she could always stay with *him*. He'd made it clear she'd have a home with his club, but not necessarily with him. The revelation nearly broke her spirit, to say nothing of her heart.

With nothing else she could say or do, she sat up and put on her shirt. She wanted to put on Torpedo's, but that would be too personal. She had to play this cool or she'd make a fool of herself. Before he could stop or question her, Rose crossed to the bathroom and shut the door. Immediately, tears came. She was so screwed, because she'd gone and fallen in love with a man who would break her heart. He might not want to and certainly wouldn't do it on purpose, but he would still do it. Rose had no one but herself to blame.

Knowing she didn't have much time before Torpedo came looking for her, she relieved herself and washed her hands and face. She couldn't look as if anything was wrong when she went back to him or he'd hound her until she told him what the problem was. It took a little time to get herself under control, but once she did, she slipped back into the room and into Torpedo's bed. He didn't say anything, only pulled her to him and wrapped his arms around her tightly. He nuzzled her face with his, his beard abrading her face. Rose loved the feeling. She had just about dozed off when he finally spoke.

"You gonna tell me what the problem is, baby?"

Immediately, Rose stiffened. No. No, she didn't want to tell him. "Why would you think something was wrong?"

He urged her to look at him. "Rose. Don't start lying to me, and don't pretend everything's fine when it's not." He traced the skin between her eyebrows, evidence she was frowning at him. "Tell me what's going on in that pretty, mixed up head of yours." He smiled tenderly at her. There was a small part of her that wanted to be offended. He was implying she wasn't smart. Or something.

"I think I'm perfectly capable of knowing when everything is fine," she said, knowing it was a non-answer to his question. "I'm not stupid."

"No," he agreed readily. "You're definitely not stupid. But you're young, and I'm quite a bit older than you are. You'd be less than human if you weren't worried about me and my intentions toward you."

"Wow," she said, trying to lighten the mood. "You sound like an old man." She flashed him what she hoped was a cocky grin.

"Yeah," he said, looking more than a bit sheepish. "I know. But it's the truth. I knew you'd have questions and more than a few doubts when I decided to make you mine."

Rose looked away from him and bit her lip. He was a hundred percent right. "Torpedo. Gavin." He raised an eyebrow at her. "I don't even know what that means. Make me yours?"

"Yeah, baby. I knew the first second I was inside you I'd never let you go." He looked away before giving his head a sharp shake then meeting her gaze. The gold in his hazel eyes seeing to flash at her with intent. "No. It was before that even. Fuck! Maybe I knew from the first Goddamned moment I saw you." He looked decidedly uncomfortable. As if just telling her this was somehow more than he could endure. What did that mean? When she shifted in his arms, intending to pull away from him, Torpedo grunted and tightened his grip on her. "No! Don't... Just don't!"

"Torpedo, just because we have sex doesn't mean you have to give me a permanent relationship. Or even a temporary one. We can just have sex."

"No, Ambrosia. We can't." He rolled so that she lay beneath him. She recognized his tone. He needed her. He called her Ambrosia when he fucked her, as if Ambrosia and Rose were two different people.

"Why do you do that?" she asked, needing to distract him before he took her into a world of sensation she had no hope of fighting.

"Do what?"

"Call me Ambrosia just before you fuck me."

He gave her a lopsided grin. "Well, first of all, I'm not about to fuck you, *Ambrosia*." He emphasized her name. "I'm makin' love to you."

"What would your club say about that?"

"Nothin'. Cause you ain't tellin' 'em."

She giggled.

"Second?" Torpedo lowered his head and kissed her gently. "Ambrosia is a fuckin' sexy name. I may not use it where my brothers can hear how much just your fuckin' name affects me, but I'm definitely takin' advantage of it when I show you how much you mean to me."

"You hardly know me. I'm just a passing fad. You'll get tired of how little I know about sex and move on." She had to swallow back tears. Admitting out loud she knew he'd leave her hurt nearly as much as any physical blow. "I'm not certain I'll survive when you do."

He took her mouth then. Slow, drugging kisses. Rose knew she needed to keep control of the conversation, but when he kissed her, there was no way to do anything other than surrender to him.

* * *

Torpedo took his time, enjoying the feel of his mouth on hers. He stroked her tongue with his, coaxing her response so she licked at him with soft, little laps. Rose might not have been experienced with sex, but she learned fast, and she was the most naturally sensual woman he'd ever met. She followed his lead, taking over when he let her. She was never shy about exploring him when he indicated he wanted her to, and she learned from each foray. Torpedo could have told her there was no way he'd ever get bored with her, but he knew she wouldn't believe him. He'd have to show her instead.

With a casual slide of his body, Torpedo rocked inside her. When she gasped and her eyes widened, he kissed her once again.

"Do you think I could ever get tired of the way you respond when I enter you? Even more, do you think you'll ever grow tired of the feeling of me entering your body?"

She blinked up at him, confused. "I don't... I don't understand." He loved that adorable, bewildered look on her face. "I'm sure any woman would love the way you feel."

"No, Ambrosia. Not like you do." He thrust again, picking up an easy rhythm. "Every sensation is new to you. So, I'm asking you right now. How long will it take for you to get used to these sensations? When will you stop lovin' the way I make love to you?"

She shook her head automatically before her lips thinned and she stopped. Then she sighed, looking defeated. "Never, Torpedo. I'll never stop loving this. Not as long as you look at me the way you do." Her breath caught, and she inhaled sharply. "You look at me... like, maybe, I'm the only woman in the world. Like you can't get enough of me."

"That's because I can't, Ambrosia. I'll never get enough of you." He knew it was the Goddamned truth. Rose had gotten under his skin. Wound herself around his heart. He knew she wasn't there yet, but he knew he could get her there. She *wanted* to love him but was afraid. It was OK. He had time.

With a little sob, she wound her arms around him, clinging to Torpedo as he moved inside her. Torpedo kissed her, taking her mouth with a tender sweep of his tongue. She allowed it. Parted her lips to welcome him. Torpedo took her kisses with gratitude, thankful she was giving him a chance. There had never been a time in his life when he'd wanted something as much as he wanted Rose. For such a small woman, she'd swept into his life like a tornado. He'd never known what hit him.

When Rose began to whimper and claw at his shoulders, Torpedo shifted his angle just a little bit, positioning himself to hit her clit just that little bit harder. Immediately, she cried out, screaming sharply. Her body tensed, convulsing around him, trying to take him with her.

"Torpedo!" She gasped out his name, biting down on his shoulder. That little bit of abandoned passion on her part, the little bit of pain she gave was a testament to how lost she was in the pleasure he wanted to desperately to give her.

"That's it, baby. That's it." He was going to come. He knew it and knew he hadn't worn a condom. He'd done it on purpose because he had every intention of tying her to him forever. He wasn't letting her go. If she wasn't convinced to stay with him yet, he'd do everything in his power to convince her he was a man who could love and protect her like no other.

Seconds later, he came deep inside Rose. She clung to him, clutching at his shoulders, digging her heels into his lower back. She seemed to want him in her as much as he needed to be there. His seed bathed her inside, coaxed free by her rippling muscles as her own orgasm continued with strangling intensity.

When it was finally over, when they both lay limp, trying to catch their breath, Rose let out a little sob. She sounded so forlorn it brought Torpedo to his knees. "Baby, talk to me," he urged, lifting his head and kissing her cheek. He tasted her tears, and it gutted him. "Did I hurt you?"

She shook her head but said nothing. He could see she was trying her best to get a rein on her emotions. Still clinging to him, she tried to hide her face in his chest, but Torpedo wouldn't let her.

"You have to talk to me, honey. I can't make it better if I don't know what's wrong."

Finally, Rose looked up at him, fresh tears spilling from her golden eyes. "When you leave, you're going to break my heart."

If she'd slapped him, Torpedo couldn't have been more surprised. He truly thought he'd talked her past her insecurities. "Baby." He stroked her cheek gently with the pad of his thumb. "I'm not going anywhere. Ever. You're staying with me and I'm staying with you."

She shook her head. "No, you won't. You might for a while, but I'm a novelty to you. You've enjoyed teaching me about sex, but once the new wears off, you'll get tired of me and move on. I'm not the type of woman a man like you keeps."

"Rose, you're *exactly* the type of woman a man like me keeps. Do you think I went through all this trouble, getting the Foleys to back off, bringing you home with me, only to let some other man have you? You're one of a kind. When you get your heart involved with someone you throw yourself all in. I want that for myself. I'm not letting any other bastard get his hands on you. Honey, you're mine. Like it or not, I'm not leavin', and I'm not lettin' you go."

She searched his eyes for a long time. Torpedo didn't know how to give her the reassurance she needed. He'd just bared his heart and soul to her -- at least as much as he was capable of. If that didn't convince her, he had no idea what would.

"OK," she finally said. Torpedo knew she wasn't completely convinced. That would take time. Hopefully, he could to that simply by not leaving. By coming home to her every night, by bringing her fully into the circle of his club, maybe he could prove he was telling her the truth. "I'll take your word for it. I'll believe in what we've shared because it's so beautiful and wonderful I have to believe."

"That's all I'm asking, baby. I'll do the rest. You're mine. And I'm yours. Believe that."

She smiled up at him, a genuine, beautiful, gentle smile. "I can do that."

* * *

The ride back to Kentucky was absolutely wonderful. Rose rode behind Torpedo with the wind in her hair and the sun on her face. Once they made it to Tennessee, the weather was a little cooler than was comfortable for her, but Torpedo put a jacket on her, and she was much better. At first, she balked at the thing. "Property of Torpedo" wasn't really her style, but she was honest enough to admit she liked the idea it represented. She wanted to belong to Torpedo. He seemed to see her that way, so, for now, she was rolling with it.

Riding onto the clubhouse property wasn't anything like what Rose was expecting. Actually, she wasn't sure what she expected, but the huge, resort-like building wasn't it. This place was kind of cool. It was spring, and the front entrance was awash in flowers. A sizable garden looked to have been recently planted and the yard freshly mowed. There were several motorcycles parked out front. Three older kids played in the yard, kicking a soccer ball. Two boys and a girl by the looks of it. One overly large man stood at one end, his arms crossed. He looked to be in his late twenties, but it was hard to tell.

As Torpedo pulled alongside the other parked bikes, Rose watched the quartet. The two young men seemed to be on one team, the girl and the older man on the other. The girl squealed and laughed as the boys kicked the ball toward the man, which he easily caught. The girl ran in the other direction, looking back over her shoulder. The big man threw the ball toward her, and she kicked it back down the yard, the two teenagers following hot on her heels. Though they got close to her, they never overtook her, and the girl kicked the ball into what had to be an imaginary goal. She cheered and jeered at the other two, running back to the big man and jumping into his arms. The man glared at the boys over his head before nodding at them, obviously approving of their tactic to let the girl win. Rose realized two things then. The boys were letting her win, and the big man was protective and devoted to the girl. It was plain to see all four of them had a close relationship.

"Is he their father?"

"Stunner? No. But he's same as adopted Suzie. Cliff and Daniel are kind of like her foster brothers. It's a long story, but I'm sure you'll learn it all soon. You'll love Suzie. She's a brilliant little ray of sunshine. The boys are going to be good men. They're as protective of her as Stunner is."

Torpedo got off the bike, and Rose waited. She was excited to meet his club but wasn't sure her legs would hold her, and the last thing she wanted to do was fall on her face first thing. He must have sensed her apprehension because he reached for her hand immediately, assisting her when she gingerly swung the other leg over the seat.

"You good?" He grinned down at her. It wasn't a cruel smile, more like he knew exactly what she was feeling and was remembering the sensations from his first long ride.

"Yeah. Just a little wobbly." She laughed.

"You'll get used to it. You seemed to love the ride. Did I overdo it? Probably should've asked if you wanted to ride with Vicious in the truck."

"No! It was wonderful! I've never felt so free in my life!"

Torpedo put an arm around her, letting her lean on him if she needed. He walked them slowly toward the clubhouse. Shadow and Vicious met them, fist-bumping as they walked up the steps.

"Good ride, brother," Vicious said. "Shame I had to ride in the fuckin' cage."

"Yeah. Sucks to be you." Shadow laughed. "I bet you thought Torpedo's little woman was gonna ride with you when you volunteered to take the chase vehicle. Didn't you?"

Vicious scowled, looking disgruntled. "Might have entered my mind."

"Yeah. Back off." Torpedo sounded dead serious, but Rose saw the twinkle in his eye as he clapped Vicious on the shoulder.

"Shadow!"

Suzie bounded across the yard at full speed, running straight to the big man. His smile was radiant as he knelt to catch the girl and swing her around.

"How's my best girl?"

"Wonderful! Me and Stunner beat Daniel and Cliff at soccer."

The boys followed at a distance, looking appropriately put out at having been beaten by a girl. "You try gettin' a ball past that big monster." Cliff indicated Stunner. "It's impossible!"

"Hey. It's not his fault you can't kick." Suzie laughed, obviously very happy.

"Yeah, well, you've been practicing, and me and Daniel have to finish our schoolwork."

"Maybe if you'd finished it when you were actually in school, you'd have time to practice with her." A woman with silky black hair and laughing blue eyes stood at the top of the steps, hands on her hips as if giving the rambunctious teens what-for. The boys looked down at the ground and sulkily toed the grass, looking all kinds of contrite.

"We tried, Ms. Angel," Cliff said, looking up at the woman. "But it was so pretty out, and Suzie looked like she was lonely. You know we can't stand to see her lonely." Yeah. All kinds of contrite.

"Boy, you know she ain't buyin' it," Shadow said quietly. "She never does."

"Yeah," Suzie chimed in. "You know what she always says. 'If a child's lips are moving about homework, they're usually lying. You gotta check to make sure it's all done.' I bet you tried to tell Mama Angel you were done, didn't you?"

Cliff gave her a withering look, but didn't deny it.

Suzie just laughed and threw her arms around the older boy. "Don't worry," she whispered a little too loudly. "I'll help you with it again."

"Suzie! Don't you dare!" Angel said, skipping down the stairs. "He's supposed to be doing his own homework."

"Huh?" Suzie looked up at Angel with wide, innocent eyes. "He always does his homework himself. I just… uh… check it for him. You know. Make sure it's right."

feeling and was remembering the sensations from his first long ride.

"Yeah. Just a little wobbly." She laughed.

"You'll get used to it. You seemed to love the ride. Did I overdo it? Probably should've asked if you wanted to ride with Vicious in the truck."

"No! It was wonderful! I've never felt so free in my life!"

Torpedo put an arm around her, letting her lean on him if she needed. He walked them slowly toward the clubhouse. Shadow and Vicious met them, fist-bumping as they walked up the steps.

"Good ride, brother," Vicious said. "Shame I had to ride in the fuckin' cage."

"Yeah. Sucks to be you." Shadow laughed. "I bet you thought Torpedo's little woman was gonna ride with you when you volunteered to take the chase vehicle. Didn't you?"

Vicious scowled, looking disgruntled. "Might have entered my mind."

"Yeah. Back off." Torpedo sounded dead serious, but Rose saw the twinkle in his eye as he clapped Vicious on the shoulder.

"Shadow!"

Suzie bounded across the yard at full speed, running straight to the big man. His smile was radiant as he knelt to catch the girl and swing her around.

"How's my best girl?"

"Wonderful! Me and Stunner beat Daniel and Cliff at soccer."

The boys followed at a distance, looking appropriately put out at having been beaten by a girl. "You try gettin' a ball past that big monster." Cliff indicated Stunner. "It's impossible!"

"Hey. It's not his fault you can't kick." Suzie laughed, obviously very happy.

"Yeah, well, you've been practicing, and me and Daniel have to finish our schoolwork."

"Maybe if you'd finished it when you were actually in school, you'd have time to practice with her." A woman with silky black hair and laughing blue eyes stood at the top of the steps, hands on her hips as if giving the rambunctious teens what-for. The boys looked down at the ground and sulkily toed the grass, looking all kinds of contrite.

"We tried, Ms. Angel," Cliff said, looking up at the woman. "But it was so pretty out, and Suzie looked like she was lonely. You know we can't stand to see her lonely." Yeah. All kinds of contrite.

"Boy, you know she ain't buyin' it," Shadow said quietly. "She never does."

"Yeah," Suzie chimed in. "You know what she always says. 'If a child's lips are moving about homework, they're usually lying. You gotta check to make sure it's all done.' I bet you tried to tell Mama Angel you were done, didn't you?"

Cliff gave her a withering look, but didn't deny it.

Suzie just laughed and threw her arms around the older boy. "Don't worry," she whispered a little too loudly. "I'll help you with it again."

"Suzie! Don't you dare!" Angel said, skipping down the stairs. "He's supposed to be doing his own homework."

"Huh?" Suzie looked up at Angel with wide, innocent eyes. "He always does his homework himself. I just... uh... check it for him. You know. Make sure it's right."

"Uh huh," Angel said, clearly not buying it. "You know you're supposed to be several grades behind him. Right?"

"Yeah. But you know I'm a genius. I'm supposed to be smarter than them." She turned her attention to Rose. "I'm Suzie," she said, sticking out her hand, clearly expecting Rose to take it. Naturally, she did.

"My name's Rose. Pleased to meet you, Suzie."

The girl looked from Rose to Torpedo, her face lighting up. "Are you with Torpedo? He's a really nice guy. Bit bossy sometimes, but I'm glad." She wrinkled her nose. "Keeps Pig and Kickstand in line." Apparently, that pair weren't little Suzie's favorite members of Bones.

"Yeah, well, someone has to. They ever want to be patched members they gotta learn to toe the line." Torpedo smiled down at the girl, winking at her.

"They aren't club members?" Rose looked up at Torpedo.

"Not yet. Prospects. You know. Working toward being members."

"I guess I have a lot to learn." Rose didn't like that she was ignorant about such things. Wouldn't she get harassed or something? God forbid she embarrass Torpedo. That would end the fantasy real quick.

"You do," he confirmed. "But it will come. No one expects you to be an expert overnight." Torpedo leaned down and kissed her temple.

Suzie beamed at her. "I'll help you. We can be friends!"

"I'd like that very much." Rose got the feeling there was something off with the girl. She seemed both a young teenager and a child. Like she couldn't make up her mind what she wanted to be. It was obvious everyone she'd met so far adored her. Rose decided right then she needed to know Suzie's story so she didn't inadvertently do or say something to hurt the girl.

"Are you Vicious?" Suzie didn't leave anyone out. It was like she just had to talk to everyone. Almost like she was afraid she'd miss the opportunity to make a friend. "Cain said you'd be coming with Shadow and Torpedo. Did you keep them in line?"

"Tried to, cutie. But you know how our boys are. This one had to be carried down a mountain 'cause he got too lazy to walk, and that one practically got himself hitched. I hear his first meeting with little Rose was a real doozie."

Torpedo nearly choked on his barked laugh. Rose hid her smile with a hand.

"Yes," Angel said, raising an eyebrow at Torpedo. "I heard it was a near disaster."

"Got me the girl, didn't it?" He grinned again, leaning down to kiss the top of Rose's head.

"You can tell me all about it at supper," Suzie said. "I can't wait!"

Rose watched Suzie as she flounced off, taking Stunner by the hand so he followed her. The big man looked at Rose as he passed and nodded his greeting.

"Yeah, Vicious. Can't wait to hear the G-rated version of that story."

Vicious grinned. "Don't worry. It'll be appropriately embarrassing for my brother here."

Angel looked over her shoulder as if she sensed someone approaching. A man emerged from the door before it had closed behind Suzie and Stunner.

"Torpedo," he greeted. He looked grim and maybe a little uncomfortable. "This your woman?"

"She is." Torpedo took two steps, meeting the other man as he descended the stairs. "Rose, this is our president and my boss, Cain. Rose came with us from Florida. We packed up her things for her, but she needs the women to take her shopping."

"We'd love to," Angel said, smiling warmly at Rose. "I'm Cain's wife. I also teach the little punks over there." She stepped close and pulled Rose into a hug. "I'm so happy you joined us."

Rose looked up at Torpedo, unsure of what to do. "I'm lucky," she said softly. "So very lucky to have someone take me in the way he has."

"You can tell us all about it when we shop. It's much less intimidating that way." Angel sounded like she might understand what Rose had gone through. Maybe not the exact circumstances, but that Rose had baggage. God, she hoped she wasn't the only one. While she didn't wish anything bad on any of these people, she didn't want to come across as high maintenance or anything. She was simply a victim of circumstances. With very bad judgment in men.

"Angel, why not take Rose around back and show her the pool and stuff? Torpedo can join her there as soon as he's reported in."

Something about his tone made the hair on the back of Rose's neck stand up. She looked up at Torpedo, and that feeling intensified. They were keeping something from her. Wanting her out of the way for some reason. Rose wanted to protest, wanted to cling to Torpedo, but he patted her shoulder absently, his face unreadable. "Go on, baby. I'll be there in a bit."

"It's OK," Angel said as she guided Rose down the sidewalk around the sidewalk. "You know men. Have to get their club secrets out away from us chicks."

Rose said nothing, but she could practically feel Torpedo pulling away from her. Something wasn't right, and she needed to find out. Now. She couldn't shake the feeling that this was it. The end of her wonderful fairytale fantasy. If it was, what was she going to do?

She turned just in time to see a tall, slender woman with platinum-blonde hair burst out of the clubhouse and literally launch herself from the top of the stairs straight into Torpedo's arms. He wrapped his arms around her, and she wrapped her legs around him. Rose thought she might be sick.

"I missed you so much, Torpedo!" The woman cupped his face in her hands and rained kisses over him. "So much!"

Torpedo didn't say anything, but then the woman didn't really give him a chance. For her part, Rose couldn't move. She stood frozen to the spot, tears welling in her eyes. When the woman fused her mouth to Torpedo's, Rose's legs gave out, and she sat right down in the grass, the fiction she'd managed to weave for herself unraveling right before her eyes.

Chapter Ten

"What the fuck?" Torpedo turned his head this way and that trying to shake Mercedes Collins off him. The woman was like a fucking octopus, all arms and legs, and she had them wrapped around him so tight he could barely breathe. He struggled to find Cain around the woman trying to slowly strangle him to death. Why in the world would Cain let this bitch into the club? "I looked for you! Needed to find you!"

"Mercedes, get the fuck off me!" He tried to extract himself, to shove her off him, but there was no way to do it without hurting her. While he didn't have a problem taking a bitch out if he had to, she wasn't trying to hurt him or any member of his team, and she didn't even know about Rose yet. It wouldn't bother him in the least, but Rose might see him differently if he actually hurt a woman.

"You don't mean that, Torpedo," she purred. "I know you don't. You running from me was just a ploy to make me realize how much I really wanted you." She put her face right next to his, her lips brushing against his ear. "You want a submissive, don't you? A woman to beg for your attention." She sucked on his earlobe even as Torpedo still tried to pry her arms from around him. "I'm that woman, baby. I'm the woman who can please you in everything sexual you can imagine. I'll fuck you right here, in front of your club. I'll do anything."

"Would someone please get this bitch the fuck offa me?" Torpedo was getting desperate. He just knew Angel hadn't gotten Rose away from the drama.

Cain and Shadow set to work prying the woman off him, but she wouldn't budge. Like him, they didn't want to hurt a woman who wasn't trying to hurt them or their families. It just went against everything they believed as men.

"Mercedes, if you don't get off me --"

She covered his mouth with hers again, cutting off his words.

Enough was enough. Torpedo jabbed his thumbs into her armpits. It wouldn't do permanent damage but would hurt like a mother. As expected, she gave a shriek, loosening her grip on him enough for him to shove her away from him. Luckily, Cain and Shadow were there to keep her from falling on her ass, though Torpedo noted Shadow helped catch her out of reflex. He immediately let her go. He even went so far as to shove his hands behind his back and step away so he didn't have to touch her again. Likely he was remembering his trek down the mountain being carried by two Sherpas. All because this woman was a first-class bitch.

"Ouch! Why the fuck'd you do that?"

Torpedo leveled a look on her. "You touch me again, I won't be so nice. Now, what the fuck are you doing here? Your daddy know you're here?" He put a sneer in his voice, letting the woman know he had no respect for her whatsoever.

"Of course Daddy knows. He said I'd be safe here."

"What the fuck, Cain?" If looks could kill, Torpedo knew Cain would be dead. Torpedo had never felt so murderous in his life. "Why's this little bitch here? Were you going to just give her room and board until she actually figured out a way to kill me, Shadow and Vicious?"

Cain held up a placating hand. "She got here maybe an hour ago. Started to send her off, but knew you were on your way back. Figured if you wanted her gone, you should be the one to say so. Didn't figure she'd get the message any other way." Cain shrugged. "She ain't exactly the brightest bulb in the box, brother."

"Goddamnit," Torpedo muttered. "Congratulations on your bad fuckin' timing award."

Cain turned to address Mercedes. "Daddy ain't payin' for your protection this time, Mercedes. We don't do freebies."

She waved that away. "It's not as if I'm like a job or anything." She smiled brightly. "I'm Torpedo's woman. You biker types take care of your own. Right?"

"Just how many women do you have, Torpedo?" Rose's quiet voice seemed to ring out loudly for Torpedo.

He turned his head and spat on the ground before wiping his mouth on his arm. "One, Ambrosia. And that'd be you." He didn't waste his time telling her to come to him. Torpedo went to her, pulling her into his arms. Her body was stiff and unwelcoming, but she didn't pull away. He framed her face in his hands. Looking down into the tears glistening in her eyes nearly gutted him. "You listen to me, Ambrosia. You're mine. I'm yours. The end. Remember when we first met, and I told you I'd been in a bad mood for a month? She's the reason why."

"The woman you were hired to protect?"

"Yes, sweetheart. The very same."

Rose glanced at the woman arguing with Cain and Shadow. Mercedes tried to stomp in Torpedo's direction, but Cain snagged her arm and held her there.

"Did you sleep with her?"

"I don't sleep with clients. Ever. Even if I did, I wouldn't have fucked her. Nothing is worth that kind of grief."

Again, she studied the other woman. Rose appeared more composed, though a single tear dripped from her lashes and she batted it away impatiently. "I'm still yours? You don't want anyone else right now?"

"Ambrosia, I don't want anyone else *ever*. You're it for me. I don't share, and I don't expect you to, either."

He only ever called her Ambrosia when they were having sex. It was an intimate thing to him because her name was so exotic. She'd said no one ever called her by her full name, and he was glad. It was for him. No one else.

His answer seemed to satisfy Rose. She nodded her head crisply then straightened her shoulders and put her head back. Surprising him, Rose stood on her toes and brushed a kiss over his lips. He was about to snag her close, but she twisted away from him and walked back to where the group was watching them. Torpedo followed her, not about to let her out of reach.

"I'm sorry, Torpedo," Angel said softly. "I nearly had her away. Once she saw what was going on…"

"I know. It's not your fault. Thanks for trying to help."

"She seems like a sweet girl. You sure you're up to handling her?"

Torpedo gave her the side-eye, but Angel just giggled, completely unintimidated. "If I say yes will you believe me?"

"No." She threaded her arm through his, looking up at him with a smile. "But I know you'll do your best."

Torpedo kissed the top of her head before squeezing her hand as he extracted himself. He had to hurry to catch up with Rose. When he did, she approached Mercedes, sticking out her hand in greeting.

"I'm Rose. Are you part of the club? Bones?"

Mercedes didn't miss a beat. "Of course I am," she snapped. "I'm Torpedo's woman so stay away from him, bitch."

Rose didn't say a word. She just turned and slid her arms around Torpedo's neck, standing on her tiptoes so she could nuzzle his neck. "Gavin," she said, using his real name the way he'd used hers. It sounded like the sweetest invitation in her impossibly innocent voice. "Do you want me to stay away from you? Because I will if you want me to." She kissed his chin before settling back into the crook of his neck.

"You know I don't want you to stay away, Ambrosia. Ain't nobody got a claim on me but you."

"Then will you please have someone take out the trash? It's starting to smell bad, putting me out of the mood."

Oh, yeah. This woman was *perfect* for him.

"You know..." Vicious said from beside Shadow. The man had stood there with his arms crossed the whole fucking time. Torpedo was certain he'd have laughed his ass off if Mercedes had fallen. He damned sure wouldn't have helped her. "...if you feel the need to cap a bitch, we all know how to get rid of a body."

Mercedes turned to scoff at Vicious, then saw the expression on his face. The woman paled, then backed up two steps straight into Shadow. She whipped around to be faced with the massive African American man, who had an equal look of death in his eyes.

Shadow held her gaze for several seconds before speaking. "If you'd been a man, I'd have killed you on that fuckin' mountain instead of letting the mountain almost kill me and Vicious. Had your daddy not thought enough of you to hire us to protect you, or had we not taken our job seriously, we'd've left your ass." He sniffed at her. "Lady, you ain't worth it."

Cain cleared his throat. "You should probably move along. Mr. Collins isn't paying for our services any longer. This is private property, and you're clearly not welcome here."

Mercedes looked like she'd been slapped. She looked scared and hurt and angry. At any other time in his life, Torpedo would have felt bad. Now, he just wanted to flip her off. Shadow was right, though. She wasn't worth even that bit of attention.

Scooping up his woman, Torpedo took her inside and up to his rooms. After the long ride and the showdown just now, he needed to be inside her. She was his, and he was going to convince her to stay with him for a very, very long time indeed.

* * *

When they reached Torpedo's room, he tossed her on the bed and Rose knew he would have followed her, but the second she landed on the mattress, Rose rolled off the other side. "Oh, no you don't."

Torpedo got an adorably confused and hurt look on his face. Kind of like she'd just taken away his ice cream cone. "What the hell, baby?"

"Don't you 'baby' me, you jackass!" Rose wasn't really mad, but she knew if she was doing this, she was doing it right. Better he figured out now just how serious she was about him rather than accuse her of clinging to him when he didn't want her to. "If I wanted to smell another woman, I'd fuck her myself." She crossed her arms under her breasts. "You want me? You need to wash *her* off first!" She pointed to the bathroom, giving him her sternest look.

Torpedo hung his head, grumbling like a little kid. "It wasn't my fault. It's not like I made her jump on me. And I couldn't just let her fall and hurt herself."

"You know, you almost had me. Right up until that last statement. Tell me exactly *why* you couldn't let her fall on her ass when she jumped at you? She's a grown-ass woman. *She* launched herself at *you*. Why did you catch her? You could have stepped away from her. If she'd hurt herself, it would've been her own damned fault! Vicious didn't offer to help her. Neither did Shadow."

He opened his mouth, then shut it. "You're right," he conceded. Then he got a wicked look in his eye. "You're absolutely right. It all happened so fast, though, I can't even remember where she got me." He hiked a thumb over his shoulder, indicating the bathroom. "I'll just head to the shower. You won't leave, will you?"

"I suppose that depends on if you come out of that shower still smelling like another woman."

"Good point. *Great* point! You know I really want you to be here when I get out. Maybe it would be in both our best interests if you, you know, helped me. Make sure I get her all off."

Rose nearly laughed out loud. He even looked contrite and like he really needed the help in order to do a good job. Instead she managed a scowl long enough to reply. "You're so full of shit."

With a sigh, she led the way to the bathroom, undressing along the way. She didn't bother to see if he followed, just stepped inside the shower and turned on the water. Of course, he was hot on her heels, pulling her back against him as he adjusted the water.

Torpedo reached for the shower gel and handed it to her, raising an eyebrow. Rose tried to hide the way her hands shook and her body trembled as she took the soap from him, squirting a generous amount into her hand. She rubbed her hands together, lathering the gel slightly before putting her hands on his chest and running them lightly over his skin.

"Wash me good, Ambrosia," he said, his voice husky. "I don't want another woman's scent on me to offend you."

"You're lucky I didn't nail your balls to the wall," she muttered, still trying to act put out when she was thrilled to get to run her hands all over him. Even though she had no desire to make him feel guilty -- it truly hadn't been his fault, and he'd rectified the situation as soon as he could -- Rose needed him to know how it had hurt her to see another woman in his arms. "It nearly tore my heart out when she kissed you." Her voice was soft. Try as she might, once she'd uttered the words, there was no way to keep the tears from her voice.

Torpedo pulled her into his hard body, every muscle imprinting itself on her. He was so big and strong. In his arms, she felt safe and protected beyond anything she'd ever known. What she felt for Torpedo wasn't like anything else in her life. No one had ever mattered so much to her. He'd proven himself loyal and caring. He'd slain her demons with the help of his brothers. He gave her pleasure beyond her wildest dreams every day he was with her.

He was her man. Hers.

"I hope you know you're the only woman I'll ever want in my life. I'd never be unfaithful to you. I'm yours. And you're all mine."

"I know." It was true. She did know. "It still hurt, but once I took a couple deep breaths, I knew you didn't want or welcome her advances."

"Damned straight," he muttered before taking her mouth with his.

Rose loved the way he kissed her. Torpedo was capable of such tenderness, but it was always edged with a fierceness that took her breath. Now, as he held her tightly against him, Rose let him sweep her away into their own private world of sensation and lust.

And love.

She knew she loved him. It was there in her chest. The way she felt when she looked at him. When she touched him. When they lay together into the night just talking, right before they made love. He was never impatient with her, even when she didn't seem to know what to do to please him. Torpedo always showed her or told her what he wanted her to do. He guided her, giving her the desire and courage to take over. He praised her with both words and actions. When he came, he always got this surprised look on his face, like he hadn't expected for it to happen when it did. Rose knew she'd get him to answer every single question she had because Torpedo went out of his way to please her. If she wanted a piece of his past, of his feelings, she knew he'd give it to her.

Sliding down his body, Rose knelt on the floor of the shower and glided her fingers over his cock. His sharp, indrawn breath made her smile, as did the way his abdominal muscles rippled with each jerk of his cock in her hand. Taking him between her lips seemed like the most natural thing in the world, his taste like an elixir of life. She slid up and down, moving with him as he thrust helplessly into her mouth.

Rose gripped the front of his thighs, rubbing her hands up and down, letting the coarse hair abrade her palms. She loved the feel of him all over. His body was rough and strong, just like the man.

"Ah, God! That's good, Ambrosia. So fuckin' good!"

His fingers fisted in her hair, and Rose reveled in the slight bite of pain. She let him lead, paying attention to what he liked. What made his shaft pulse in her mouth. Rose was going into this with her whole heart. This was her man. She'd do everything in her power to please him. Anything he wanted, Rose wanted to give him.

After one particularly sharp yell form Torpedo, he pulled her to her feet. She loved the little bite of pain, knowing he had to be nearly at his limit. As she let his cock slide out of her mouth, she caught a little bead of pre-cum from the head and moaned.

"Stand up, baby. I need to be inside you." His voice was gruff, full of need and dark promises. She got a little thrill from his tone, the grip he had on her hair, then her hips when she stood. He spun her around and pulled her against him, wrapping an arm over her breasts and another around her waist. For several seconds, he just squeezed her to him hard. Rose could feel his body trembling around her, and she reveled in it. This was a man who wanted her. She'd driven him to this. Not anyone else. Her. Ambrosia Gataki.

A moment later, he used a hand to guide himself to her entrance and thrust forward in a slow, languorous slide. Rose let her head fall back against his chest as Torpedo's arms came around her once again.

He bent his head to kiss her temple, his breath hot at her ear. "You're so fuckin' sexy, Ambrosia. Sexy and brave. You're my woman."

"And you're my man," she said in a timid voice.

Torpedo immediately caught her chin and lifted her face to him, a hard expression on his face. "I *am* your man. Don't be afraid to claim me. Not to me or anyone else. Something makes you uncomfortable, you tell me. We belong to each other. No one else. You get me?"

She smiled. "I *do* get you. I can see it in your eyes." She reached over her shoulder and cupped his face. Torpedo closed his eyes and rubbed his cheek into her palm as if just her touch alone was bliss. "I can't promise I won't feel just a little bit inadequate or get worried around a beautiful woman who decides to crawl all over you," she said that last in a wry tone, "but, given enough time, I'll be fine." She smiled at him. "I love you, Gavin. I know it in my heart."

"You can't imagine how happy that makes me, baby." He caught her lips in a lingering kiss, his tongue slipping easily into her mouth. "I love you, too."

"Now, show me what it means to be your woman. Make love to me. Make love to me until we both collapse onto the shower floor."

"Now, how can I resist such a command?"

Torpedo buried his face in her neck and gripped her hips as he surged through her slick folds. Rose tunneled her fingers through his hair, thrusting her breasts up.

"So beautiful," he rasped against her skin, his beard tickling her with every word and enhancing her pleasure. "I love the way you look when I fuck you." Her breath came in ragged gasps, punctuated by every thrust of his cock and his body slamming into hers.

"You're my little virgin wanton. So fuckin' sensual it fuckin' hurts."

Rose loved the little hitch in his voice. He fucked her at his leisure, but his fingers bit into her hips, betraying the fact he wanted to go faster. Harder.

"Give it to me, Gavin," she whispered. "Fuck me hard. Like you've never done before."

"Fuck, Ambrosia. Do you know what you're askin'?"

"No. I want you to show me."

He shuddered around her, one arm going around her body to clamp her to him. "You're temptin' the beast, baby. I don't want to hurt you."

"If you do, I'll tell you. Then you can kiss it better." Rose knew she was playing with fire, but Goddamnit, she wanted this. She wanted Torpedo at his most raw. "Do it!" She hissed the command as forcefully as she could, meaning it.

"Fuck!" Torpedo picked her up, his cock never leaving her body. He set her on the floor in front of the long bench at the back of the shower and pushed her forward. "Put your hands down. Use them to balance." She did. The second she braced herself, he adjusted his grip on her waist and *pounded* into her.

Rose gasped, the new sensations overwhelming her in an instant. She cried out but spread her legs wider to hold herself up better. She had to go up on her toes to accommodate his height, but she loved the helpless feeling. She was in his hands to do with as he pleased, and Rose wasn't ashamed to admit it was exhilarating.

"Oh, God, yes! Fuck me," she gasped. "Oh, God!"

"So good," he bit out. "Hot and tight. Sweet little cunt! Gonna make me come!"

"Do it, Gavin. Do it! Come inside me. Do that for me."

"Fuck," he bit out. "Just... fuck!"

He pounded into her, their skin slapping out a staccato rhythm echoing in the room. Her grunts and cries, his snarls and growls accompanied the beat like the sweetest music Rose had ever heard. Seconds later, she felt him swelling inside her. His cock pulsed, splashing her pussy with his seed. His orgasm triggered her own, and she threw her head back, screaming her ecstasy.

Torpedo collapsed on top of her, as he'd done several times before. Rose had found she loved his weight on her, loved the feel of his sweat-slickened body weighing her down.

"You good, baby?"

"Better than good," she said, glancing back at him with a smile.

He rolled over, gently extracting himself from her and pulling her limp body against his. "I love you, Ambrosia. So fuckin' much."

"I love you, too, Gavin."

"Stay with me. I'll keep you safe and happy as long as I live."

"I know you will. 'Cause if you don't, I'll tell Suzie. I have a feeling she has some pull around this place."

Torpedo laughed, the sound the best thing Rose had ever heard. "Point taken, honey."

This wasn't her happy ever after yet, but Rose was certain she was on her way. Torpedo was the man. Bones was the family. She wasn't at home yet, but she'd get there. For now, she'd accept the gift she'd been given and treasure it. Keep it close.

For now. For always.

Beast (Salvation's Bane MC 2)
Marteeka Karland

Fleur: Never in a million years would I have expected a woman I considered a friend to betray me in the worst possible way. Yet it happened. Drugged and in the back room of a BDSM club, I was about to be used in a brutal way. Until *he* exploded to my rescue.

Beast: I'm Salvation's Bane's enforcer. My job is to protect. So when I notice something amiss in the BDSM club Bane owns, I'm there to shut that shit down. What I find is a woman who ignites passions inside me better left alone. What will she think when she finds out the lengths I'll go to protect what's mine? I come by my name honestly. When it comes to protecting my club, or my woman, I'm the most ferocious beast you could ever imagine.

Chapter One

The second Fleur stepped into the darkened interior of the Playground club, she knew she'd made a huge mistake. At first, the fact that she'd been ushered to the head of the line... No. Ushered wasn't the word for it. A big man had grabbed her upper arm and *dragged* her from her place halfway back and to the front. From there she'd been passed off from one person to another -- most of the time she wasn't sure if a man or woman had her -- until she'd been shoved up to the bar inside the most infamous club in Palm Beach.

The bass from the music thumped through her body like a massive shockwave. She wasn't used to the club life. Had never been to a club in her life. It was like her ears were stunned and she couldn't actually hear the bass, but she could feel it as it threatened to pulverize her insides.

"What will the lovely little pretty-pretty have?"

The bartender was tall and slender. Like most everyone at the club, he wore an elaborate mask to cover his face. His voice was a grating tenor in an over-the-top English accent. His creepy tone made Fleur shiver. No. This definitely wasn't the place for her. Why had she let Debbie talk her into coming here? Because she was a pushover. That's why. Fleur wanted to please. If that meant she did things she didn't really want to do, she sucked it up and did them. Unfortunately, Debbie was still waiting halfway down the line to get in. Fleur was on her own.

"Uh, just water, please," she said softly, knowing the bartender probably wouldn't hear her. The noise was unlike anything she'd ever experienced. With the music and the shrieks as women were spanked, whipped, caned, and/or fucked, it was hard to hear herself think, much less carry on a conversation, no matter how brief.

"Of course, my pretty-pretty." The smile the bartender gave her was as evil as they came. At least, to Fleur it was. There was probably nothing sinister about it, but she was already creeped out. It seemed that everywhere she looked there were people leering at her. It was probably her imagination, but she felt like a bug under a microscope.

The bartender set a tall glass of ice water in front of her. "Drink up, pretty-pretty. It gets hot in here." He gave her a lascivious wink. Even through the mask she could make out a sort of disturbing interest. Like he was already doing things to her that were unmentionable. The thought nearly made her heave in disgust. She needed to get the hell out of there. Fast.

"Thanks," she all but whispered, her eyes downcast as she picked up her drink and sipped. It was cold, but not refreshing at all. In fact, she tasted something else. Something… sour?

As if reading her mind, the bartender smiled. His eyes through the mask were practically gleaming. "It's lemon, my pretty-pretty. Lemon with a dash of lime. The lemon in the water helps prevent dehydration. You'll need it in here." He nodded to her glass. "Drink up, pretty-pretty."

The way he said "pretty-pretty" gave her a decidedly uneasy feeling. She tried to tell herself that was just his culture. He was obviously not native to America, given his accent. Perhaps it was just a term of endearment she wasn't used to. True to form, unwilling to make someone else uncomfortable or risk hurting another's feelings, she simply smiled and drank the water. She didn't like it, preferring plain, cold water, but she drank anyway.

Once she'd finished the glass, he smiled at her. The gleam in his eyes now positively fevered. "That's a good little pretty-pretty."

She turned to leave, but the movement caused a slight wave of dizziness. She tried not to be obvious about it, but she held on to the bar a few seconds until the feeling passed. Once she was sure it was just the quick movement, she headed through the crowd back to the door.

At least, she thought that was the way she was headed. Somehow, Fleur must have gotten turned around, because the next thing she knew she was standing not ten feet away from a raised dais where a man was having sex with a woman on her hands and knees. The woman had a black collar buckled around her throat, attached to a chain held by the man. He was on one knee, the other leg bent. One hand gripped her hip while the other pulled on the chain to force her head back and her back to arch. He pounded into her with such force Fleur winced.

She felt the room spin again, this time more pronouncedly than at the bar. It was the shock of seeing such a blatant display. Had to be. Both the man and woman were covered in sweat, the lights beating down on them for all to see their show. Several people surrounded the dais, urging them on. A couple of assertive men even reached under the woman to tweak her nipples, to her obvious delight. To Fleur's utter shock, another man stepped in front of the woman and unfastened his pants, pulling out an impressive-looking cock. He gripped the woman's hair, leaning down to say something to her. The woman nodded and immediately opened her mouth wide to accept him. Her ruby-red lips closed around his member and she began to bob her head, sucking him with abandon.

Fleur couldn't seem to look away no matter how much she wanted to. The sight both fascinated and repulsed her. This was so not the place for her. Debbie kept telling Fleur she was a submissive, that she would enjoy the Playground if she'd just give it a try. Maybe even find a Dom to take her in hand and show her the darker side of sex, but Fleur knew this wasn't for her.

She whirled around...

And nearly hit the ground as her knees buckled. She found herself pulled against a man's hard body. Silver buckles holding together leather straps over his chest dug into her skin painfully. He was lean, but not overly muscled, his chest and arms free of hair and oiled so that she could feel the vile stuff on her face where she touched his skin.

"There, there," he soothed, pulling her more firmly against him. "Did you see something that shocked you, pretty little thing?"

"I -- yes. Pleas..." She pushed against him slightly, suddenly unable to struggle. "I need... I need to go. This isn't for me."

"But you've only just arrived. Come with me. I'll show you around, and you can get more comfortable. I believe you'd be perfect for the Playground. A perfect little plaything."

"No! I-I don't want to be here." Fleur was becoming desperate. She shouldn't be there.

"Nonsense. You'll love it." The man's breath was hot on her face. His scent, while not unpleasant, was strong with cologne. With the body heat around her and the increasing dizziness, it nauseated her.

"I think I'm going to be sick," Fleur whimpered, trying to get away. She had no idea where the bathroom might be, but knew she couldn't stay where she was. If she could make it to a wall, at least she wouldn't vomit in the middle of the floor.

"Come with me, pretty thing. I'll make sure you're taken care of."

That was what she wanted to hear. What she needed to hear. Fleur had been waiting to hear those words forever. At least it seemed that way. She'd been on her own since she was thirteen and knew she didn't want to go on like this. A man to take care of her was her deepest, most fervent dream. At least, that was what she thought. Right? It was all so fuzzy. But this man would take care of her. Right?

"That's right, love." He picked her up and carried her out of the main room. "I'm going to take such good care of you."

Fleur whimpered. She wanted to believe. Wanted the fairytale. But something in the back of her mind told her this wasn't the man for her. She needed to get away, but her body betrayed her, going limp against him. She had no strength left to resist. Her mind was telling her this was what she wanted, but her instincts were telling her something altogether different. With a strangled cry, Fleur let the blackness -- and the strange man -- have her.

* * *

Her mind in a fog, her mouth dry as dust, Fleur tried to open her eyes. They felt like someone had thrown sand into them. When she moved her hand to try to rub her eyes, she couldn't. Something held her down, prevented her from moving her arms or legs. Fleur knew she should panic, that something was very, very wrong, but she couldn't seem to force her brain to work. The room spun. Any movement of her head made the sensation worse. She tried to speak, but there was something in her mouth. A cloth? Struggling was out of the question, but the adrenaline surge seemed to focus things around her. Not clearly, but at least she could take stock of her body.

She was lying on her front, head turned to the side. A large, soft pillow cradled her head, but it was so deep it nearly covered her nose. With the cloth in her mouth, the fear of smothering was starting to kick in.

Smothering was one of Fleur's worst fears. She'd been trapped once as a child in an old, discarded freezer, the top locked. She could remember how the air had grown stale and it had been hot. She remembered thinking she couldn't breathe. It had been terrifying. And an experience she had avoided repeating at all costs.

Then, as now, she had to fight for the next breath. Even though Fleur tried to raise her head, she was just too weak. She tried turning slightly on her side, but her arms had been stretched in a V over her head.

"Ah, the pretty little submissive is awake at last." The voice was familiar. So was the scent. Sickly sweet cologne. Something trailed over her shoulders... Was she naked?

"Oh, God." Her voice was muffled, and she remembered the gag.

"Just relax. I've given you a little something to help you fly, my pretty little toy. I promise you'll enjoy everything I do to you. Eventually."

The first strike hit without warning, taking her breath. Pain exploded over her buttocks. A second strike got her right upper thigh, just at the skin where her buttocks started. Fleur wanted to scream, but the gag held in most of the noise. She was still dizzy, but it wasn't enough for her to just pass out, much as she wanted to. She knew what was about to happen and wanted with everything in her not to experience it.

Tears formed, but the pillow soaked them up. The next strike hit vertically down the left side of her back. Then the right. The sting was unimaginable. She'd had beatings before, but nothing like this. She was certain the man had drawn blood. Her skin would be shredded.

All Fleur could do was tense up. Screams tried to emerge from her throat, but the gag muffled them. The more she struggled, the harder he beat her. The sound of his sadistic chuckle was sinister and loud in the small room. And still her head spun. Had she not been in so much pain and shock, she might have simply passed out. For some reason, she couldn't. Her mind remained stubbornly at the fore, taking all the man had to give and refusing to give her the blissful darkness she desperately needed.

Fleur sobbed, closing her eyes tightly against the pain. She bit down on her gag until her jaw and teeth hurt. She tried to make noise. *Any* noise. Anything that would hopefully bring someone to help. But then, who in this place would aid her? And exactly how were they supposed to distinguish any noise she made from the normal atmosphere if they did choose to help? No. She was on her own. Which meant she was well and truly fucked.

* * *

The Playground was hopping tonight. Gideon "Beast" Leigh sat at a bar on the far end of the club, watching the various scenes play out before him. He drank a cup of black coffee because he refused to drink a Coke unless it was liberally laced with Jack. Since they didn't serve alcohol at the club -- alcohol and BDSM didn't mix well -- he made do with the coffee.

Beast had seen several women he'd considered introducing himself to, but his heart just wasn't in it. Most of the time, he loved getting bouncer duty at the Playground, but tonight wasn't one of them. His mind kept drifting back to an incident that had happened earlier in the day. One that had left him speechless and more than a little unnerved.

Besides the Playground, Salvation's Bane owned a couple of gyms in Palm Beach as well as a strip club. All but Playground were more for money laundering if they needed it, but all had to be monitored and policed. Last thing they wanted was to give the fuzz a reason to look at them too closely. Beast was at the gym, running diagnostics on their security system and generally scoping out the place. He always liked to keep tabs on their members and know who were regulars and who were fading on their New Year's resolutions. He was just about to go for his own workout when he saw... *her*.

This petite little thing with curly chestnut hair pulled back in a knot on top of her head. With unusual silver-green eyes and pale, thin limbs, she looked like she belonged in high school instead of the fucking gym. Which made Beast more than a little uncomfortable.

Instead of being on a treadmill or something light to go with her frame and lack of musculature, the girl was on the bench press, her friend spotting her with only the bar. Which was still too fucking heavy for her. She was obviously struggling, but her friend, though encouraging her to push it up, wasn't watching her. She was watching a group of young men in the corner. Watching... intently.

Beast focused on the girl. The more she strained to push up the bar over and over, the more she wiggled, giving everyone a good view when her gym shorts gaped. Normally, he'd have thought her "friend" was letting the jocks across the room look their fill at her expense, making fun of her behind her back, but none of them pointed or laughed. Instead, they looked intently, speaking in low tones. When one of them nodded, the girl's friend called it, praising her for a job well done as she helped her put the bar back in the rack.

"I can't believe they load those heavy bars down with weights," she panted. "I can barely lift it as it is."

"You'll get used to it, Fleur." Her friend patted Fleur on the shoulder as the girl sat up, obviously winded from her efforts. "We both will." She smiled at Fleur before taking her own place on the bench. Fleur seemed oblivious to the men in the corner talking and continuing to watch her.

Beast sensed a trap, and he always trusted his instincts. Something was off about the whole situation. So he did what any self-respecting enforcer would do. He made a big deal about flexing his muscles as he moved to the free weights stationed between the two groups. Beast could be intimidating when he wanted to be. Just then, he wanted to be.

The boys had tried to hold his gaze, thinking themselves safe in a group. Once Beast began curling an insanely heavy dumbbell, they decided against confronting him. Then Beast shifted his gaze to Debbie, not a veiled threat but a notice that he was on to her. The girl had the good sense to realize she was in trouble. If they were setting the young woman up for something nefarious, they weren't going to do it in his fucking gym.

Once the immediate threat was contained, he pulled the gym roster up and looked everyone up. The girl was Fleur Durand, guest of her friend, Debbie Johnson. Debbie's mother and father worked for Argent Tech way the fuck up in Rockwell. Debbie had recently moved to their residence in Palm Springs, apparently so her parties didn't inconvenience her parents. The men were Ben and Jeremy Hay, brothers and sons of Jeremiah Hay, the president of a local bank, big in local politics, and their crony, Greg Kinson. While Greg's parents were affluent, they weren't as well off or as well-known as Jerimiah Hay. All three boys were prone to getting into trouble their parents were continually having to bail them out of. Once, Greg's father had refused to bond him out of jail. The Hay brothers, however, had bailed him out once they'd posted their own bond, and the lesson was never learned.

Beast knew that, one day, all three would go too far. He was afraid that time was close, and it had everything to do with little Miss Fleur Durant. Which left only Fleur. There wasn't much on her. Her last address was in Tennessee, but she'd apparently moved. If she'd made Palm Beach her home, she hadn't secured any kind of residence in her name. It was possible she was staying with Miss Johnson.

As he thought back to that moment in the gym, Beast pulled out his phone, which was linked with the security camera feeds for the club. Something was still nagging him, tickling the back of his neck, as it were. Maybe it was just the girl. She'd been... lovely. Fragile. Not normally the type of woman he went for, but she called to everything protective inside of him and he'd somehow latched onto the memory.

Reviewing the feeds, he didn't see anything out of the ordinary. There were camera feeds even in the private rooms paid for by members who wanted to have private sessions with subs they'd met or brought with them. No place, not even the bathrooms, was off limits. Salvation's Bane had no desire to gain the reputation of a club where rape could happen. Every room was monitored closely with video and audio surveillance, against the law or not. Since the club was owned by the men in Salvation's Bane, they had complete control over the footage they recorded and who had access to it. Bane themselves would take care of any assholes using their club to assault women. No need to get the police involved.

Not getting what he needed on his phone, he decided to have a closer look in his office. He had larger monitors and greater control over what he saw from there.

At first glance, nothing looked amiss. There was some kinky play going on all over the damned place, but nothing out of the ordinary. Most of the couples going at it were ones familiar to him. A few were newcomers, but, still, nothing that raised any red flags. Everyone was behaving themselves. More or less.

Then he turned to the private rooms. Still nothing… until he came to one with people in it he didn't recognize. *Fucking masks.* The room was normally rented by Azriel Ivanovich, part of the Shadow Demons in Rockwell, Illinois. According to the key card, Azriel was the occupant. Beast made it his business to know every member of the Playground and who they regularly brought with them. Most took the hint and introduced him to new partners. The two men currently in Ivanovich's room were most decidedly *not* Azriel Ivanovich. With the masks on, he couldn't positively identify either. The girl they'd brought to the room hadn't moved since he'd started watching. Which was a huge red flag. So he backed up the feed...

"Goddamn motherfuckers!" Beast snagged a radio as he shoved away from the console, headed straight to the room in question. "I need anyone not actively engaged in a security issue to suite 2187." Three guards answered immediately. "And bring the Goddamned tasers." Two more security responded moments later. Something he made a mental note of.

Less than a minute later, he was outside the door in question at almost the same time as Lock and Grease. Only a couple seconds later, Ripper was at his side with a case of tasers. Beast snagged one as he gave a solid kick hard enough not only to break the door frame, but to splinter the door off the hinges.

Without further instructions, he tased one of the guys who'd been ready to thrust inside the woman tied to the bed. She gave a sharp yelp and turned her head to the side. Her eyes were wild and wet with tears. How she was breathing, he had no idea. She had a cloth gag stuffed in her mouth, and the pillow was thick and molded to her head. He could barely see one silver-green eye above the pillow.

This time Beast didn't bother with the taser. He was too furious. Grabbing the nearest man by the hair as the guy turned around, he yanked, smashing his fist into the side of the guy's head once before flinging him out of the way. At the same time, Ripper shot the other guy with his taser. The bastard froze, his body tensing as the current ripped through him until he collapsed on the floor. It was all over in a matter of seconds. The men were slammed against the floor, their hands zip-tied behind their backs, and the girl freed.

That didn't satisfy Beast. Nothing would, except blood and more than a little of it.

"Take those motherfuckers to my office," he snapped. "They're gettin' ready to learn a lesson they'll never fuckin' forget."

"You can't touch us!" The one who'd been tased was starting to fight again. "My dad's lawyer will eat you for breakfast!"

Beast took the two steps separating them and backhanded him so hard it spun him around. Blood flew from the younger man's mouth, painting a bright spatter across the wall.

"Ain't no fuckin' lawyer in the whole Goddamned world can get your ass outta this one, kid. You're gonna get a beatin' like you ain't never imagined."

"Easy, dude! He ain't kiddin' 'bout his old man."

Beast slowly turned his gaze to the security guy who'd spoken. The man was fresh out of the Marines. Good service record. Beast had thought the kid would be a good fit for ExFil, but he was starting to rethink that assumption.

"You know what's goin' on here?" His voice was soft, but anyone who knew him would be able to tell he was riding the edge of eruption.

"They're havin' a good time. It's why people come here, Gideon." The kid's name was Darrin Montgomery, but Beast just called him New Kid. Because he was new. And because of shit like this.

"You and I will be havin' a talk later, New Kid. In the meantime, let me make it clear to you that your job is not to make decisions. Your job is to do what I fuckin' tell you. I'm the one who makes the fuckin' decisions. I have all the information. What was going on here was not play."

Beast turned back to the bed. Ripper and Lock had untied the girl and turned her to her side. Her back was a mass of welts and shallow cuts he'd have to get Doc to look at. Her eyes were wide and terrified, the pupils dilated. He'd bet his last fucking dollar the girl had been drugged. Hell, from what he'd seen on the feed they'd practically dragged her into the room, one of her arms over each of their shoulders as they'd entered.

"Ripper, once she's settled away from here, follow her movements backwards on the feeds. I want to know exactly what happened from the second she set foot on the property and who else I need to kill before tonight's over."

As he'd hoped, both the young men in custody and New Kid looked decidedly nervous. Also, as he'd hoped, none of them said a fucking word. Good. He'd made an impression.

With swift, angry movements, Beast ripped the masks off first one man, then the other. "You've got to be fuckin' kiddin' me!" Currently in his custody were fucking Jeremy Hay and Greg Kinson. "God *fuckin'* dammit!" He turned to Ripper. "Change of plan. That one," he pointed to Jeremy, "has a brother in here somewhere. Wherever he is there's bound to be another girl in trouble." He got on the radio. "Priority One," he said. "Be on the lookout for a man named Ben Hay and a young woman, Debbie Johnson. Ripper will send pics to your phones. Take the masks off every motherfucker in the whole Goddamned place. Find them and bring them to my office ASAP. Notify me if there is a girl in need of assistance."

He looked up at Lock. The other man met his gaze with a grim one. "If she's not been drugged, I'll turn in my resignation."

"Keep your Goddamned resignation. You're right." Beast nodded curtly. "Take her to a private room in the Cooling Station. Make her comfortable and wait with her until I get there. Call Doc, too. We'll need him." The Cooling Station was on the top floor of the three-story building. It was a place Doms could bring their subs after play to rest, rehydrate, and bring down as softly as he felt she need.

"I'll see if there's anyone she wants me to call for her." Lock was a good choice for this. He'd make sure she was kept comfortable and safe.

Beast knelt down in front of the girl beside the bed. He hadn't recognized her at first because her hair was down and her eyes weren't that startling silver-green he'd noticed at the gym, but it was the same girl. Where before he'd admired her, now everything protective in him powered its way to the front, demanding he take care of her. Well, he could do that. Just not in the normal sense of the word. He was about to open Hell's gates on her attackers.

God have mercy on their souls.

Chapter Two

Everything sounded like it was coming from inside a deep well. Fleur couldn't get her bearings, but she knew she wasn't safe. There was a sharp prick at the bend of her elbow, and she tried to pull away. Gentle hands prevented it and the pain was fleeting so she settled, her mind not wanting to focus, but she still couldn't make herself pass out. She whimpered, trying to ask where she was but unable to form the words.

"Everything's gonna be OK, girl." The voice was gruff, but not unpleasant. In fact, it was oddly reassuring. Fleur had learned early in life she couldn't trust just anybody, but she thought that voice cast some kind of spell that made her *want* to trust him. "We stopped it and we'll protect you until you feel better. Just rest for me. Can you do that?"

Could she? Fleur didn't know. She wanted to, but her mind refused to take even that little command and just surrender.

"Where'm I?" Her voice was slurred. No wonder, either, because her mouth was as dry as cotton.

"The Playground. I've got you in a safe room where you can rest."

At the mention of the club Debbie had pushed her into going to, Fleur's eyes snapped open. Her mind tried to think, to figure out how to get her out of there, but the room spun and everything was fuzzy and distorted. Kind of like she imagined a bad trip on acid or something would be.

"Easy now. Don't go gettin' all upset. I told you. We're gonna protect you."

Fleur shook her head, trying to clear it. When she looked up at him, she was surprised to recognize the man the voice belonged to. "You were at the gym this morning."

"That's right. Good. You've got your wits about you."

"Why're you here when you were there?" Her words were still slurring, but she had to know. She had the feeling something had been very wrong at the gym.

"Honey, my club owns both the gym and the Playground."

"Oh, no!" She'd been right. Somehow, she'd been set up. Was this guy her enemy? Was he with the men who'd taken her to that horrible room, tied her down, and beaten her? Just thinking about it made her realize her back was on *fire*. It was a testament to just how drugged she was that she hadn't noticed it before now. "Please don' hur' me anymore..." Fleur hated how weak and pitiful she sounded, but there was no way she could defend herself in this condition. Hot tears spilled down her cheeks. Begging was all she had. If this man chose to hurt her anyway, there was absolutely nothing she could do.

"Hey, hey. Take a breath." A big and rough, but gentle, hand stroked hair back from her face as well as the tears away. "You're safe. No one's gonna hurt you again. I swear it. Doc here is giving you fluids so you're not so dehydrated. If you can answer some questions, he'd like to give you some medicine to help your back. Is there anyone you need us to call for you? Someone to come be with you?"

God, she wanted to believe him! How long had she wanted to hear -- and believe -- she was safe? Too damned long to actually believe this guy.

"I just need to get up." She tried sitting, but gentle hands pushed her back, not letting her lie on her back, but urging her to stay on her side. Had it not been for the pillow earlier, making her feel like she was going to smother, she'd have wanted to be on her belly.

"You're too sick right now." That was another voice, presumably Doc. "Just rest. Let us call someone for you."

She let out a little whimper before answering him. "Debbie Johnson. Her number is in my phone." Fleur tried with everything in her to focus her eyes on either of the two men. She thought one of them grunted at her preference of who to call, but she couldn't be sure. The first one was nearest her, the one she recognized from the gym. Just as she'd feared, he was a big as she'd remembered. She'd heard people call him Beast and remembered thinking how much it fit. He was absolutely *huge*. Arms much bigger than her thighs, powerful shoulders, a chest that seemed to go on for miles... Yes. He was aptly named.

"There you are," he said. The smile he gave her was more a baring of teeth, but it was somehow reassuring. Like he was just waiting for someone to mess with her so he could prove he meant what he said. "I like it when you look at me." When she said nothing, he continued. "You see me, girl? Know I mean what I say?"

Oh, yeah. She saw him. He definitely meant what he said. "Yes," she whispered. She thought it alarming he didn't acknowledge her about Debbie. She had a bad feeling the woman she'd called friend wasn't really her friend.

"Good. Doc here's gonna patch you up so we can move you someplace more comfortable. I'm gonna find out what drug you were given so Doc knows what to expect with you. You're safe with us. No one's gonna hurt you."

He kept saying that, but Fleur was glad of it. She felt like the more she heard it, the more likely she was to believe it. She must have truly believed him, because she nodded her head and closed her eyes. The second she did, oblivion claimed her.

* * *

Beast knew the woman slept when her eyes closed. Doc gave him a curt nod and went back to work on her hurts. Those little motherfuckers were getting ready to pay. Big time.

"Don't forget to find out what she was drugged with before you beat someone unconscious," Doc warned. "If it's something too powerful, I might have to take her to the hospital."

"Noted," he said. Normally, he'd be offended by Doc's reminder, but if he were perfectly honest, his main goal at that very moment was to pound the living fuck out of the two men currently waiting with Lock and Grease in his office.

He stood, unable to resist brushing the hair from Fleur's forehead. One of his fingers found its way through a curl and tugged. Her eyes opened slightly, still a little dazed. Then her lips curled into a soft smile, and he was torn between melting for her or wanting to punch whatever motherfucker she thought she was smiling at other than him. In all his life, Beast could never remember a woman affecting him like this. He hadn't even seen her as a desirable woman. God help him if he ever did, because the lass was definitely lovely.

She had a little pixie face with delicate, high cheeks. Her brows were a light golden brown and her eyelashes a slightly darker shade of brown. Her little bow of a mouth, he knew, made the loveliest smile he'd ever seen. But it was her eyes that were so startling. A mesmerizing silver-green, they didn't look real. Almost like contacts, but he knew Doc would have removed them if that were the case. No. Beast would bet his life that everything about Fleur Durand was real. She was a true natural beauty. And too Goddamned trusting for her own good.

"You need to get a handle on this, Beast," Doc said, giving him an amused glance. "Otherwise, we're gonna have dead bodies all over the fuckin' place, and we can't bring that kind of attention to ourselves."

Beast shot him an annoyed glance but said nothing. What was the point? Doc was right. It'd be touch and go as it was with the Hay boys. Once Ripper got the footage and information he needed, he was going to give the young men a choice. If they chose poorly? Well, he'd choose for them.

The walk to his office only angered him more. He kept seeing Fleur in the gym as she'd looked at the woman she'd considered a friend. It was hard to reconcile that face with the one on the woman lying in the bed two floors up. That woman was nearly broken, and with good reason. Her back hadn't exactly been shredded, but much more of what those boys had dished out to her and it would have been. The more he thought about it, the madder Beast got.

No. *Mad* or *angry* were too insipid for what he was feeling. *Enraged* was a better word. Beast was Salvation's Bane's enforcer. He not only enforced the rules that kept them all safe, but he punished those who didn't follow the rules, and he protected the people he was responsible for. That included the clubs. Early in their venture, more than one person had learned exactly how serious he was about his responsibilities. It was why people rarely put a toe out of line in any of their clubs or gyms. Or the MC. He ran a tight ship. What had happened tonight was a serious breach of everything he held sacred.

The door opened at his approach and Ripper poked his head out. "Thought you were outside," he said. Instead of the ready smile, he met Beast with a grim expression on his face. "Found the other Hay boy and the woman. Woman keeps saying she got separated from Fleur and that she's never seen the boys before tonight."

Beast snorted. "Of course she hasn't. Did you get the feed from the gym?"

"Yeah. When you texted I wasn't sure exactly what I was looking for, but I found it soon enough. They were careful. Only time they had contact was right before Fleur got there. They all stood together chatting. After Fleur left, the boys gave little Debbie an envelope. Can't confirm there was money inside, but it sure as hell proves she's lying."

Clenching his teeth until his jaw ached, Beast took a deep breath before entering the office. As much as he wanted to let his temper loose, now wasn't the time. He'd save that for the gym.

Inside, the Hay brothers sat with their arms crossed, smug expressions on their faces like they were above anything Beast thought to thrust at them. The Kinson boy had a similar look on his face, but he wasn't as confident. It was probably more for the benefit of his friends so he didn't lose face. The Johnson girl looked appropriately concerned and outraged, sitting well away from the guys.

He didn't take the usual seat behind his desk, but went straight to the bank of monitors on the far side where he knew Ripper had his findings ready for him. Glancing at the stills for a moment, he backed up the feeds and watched for himself. None of his "guests" could see what he was watching. The guys were muttering amongst themselves, their outrage and belief that Beast could do nothing to them at odds with the nervous glances they shot his way. By the time he stood and moved to his desk, the guys had worked up their courage.

"We demand you let us go or we're calling our lawyer." That was from Jeremy Hay, the eldest of the Hay brothers.

Beast didn't rise to his remarks, simply sitting there staring at them.

"I don't even know why you attacked us in the first place," Ben said, snorting as though it were all some kind of big joke. "We weren't doing anything everyone else wasn't doing. It's why people come here in the first damned place."

"Besides," Jeremy continued. "Even if you wanted to kick us out, you had no right to assault us." He put his chin up. "I'm gonna sue your fucking ass. When I'm done, I'll own this fucking shithole."

"Look, I just want out of here." Ah, finally little Debbie spoke. So far, the only one to keep quiet was Greg Kinson. All he'd done was murmur his agreement with the Hay brothers. "I need to find Fleur. She was depending on me being with her. Without me, she's probably more than a little nervous."

The girl was good. Playing the part of concerned buddy right up to the end. Had he been less angry, Beast might have been impressed with all their cool under fire, but he was past that. Way fucking past.

He wanted to backhand every one of them, Debbie especially. The guys deserved to be beaten to a bloody pulp for what they'd done to Fleur. Debbie… deserved far, far worse.

Unfortunately, no matter how much he wanted to make the woman suffer, Beast didn't ever lay a hand on a woman. He was too big and strong to risk actually hitting a woman, even in a sparring match. If he did to this woman what he wanted to do to her, if he fought her the way he needed to, he'd kill her and wouldn't lose a moment's sleep. But if he did that, how could he convince Fleur he was different than she was? And why did he care in the first fucking place?

With a sharp shake of his head, Beast picked up his phone and sent a text to Venus. The woman was slight and fragile looking but built with sinewy muscle and subtle strength. She was short and wiry, but Beast considered her one of the scariest people he'd ever met. Probably because she'd been trained somewhere in Russia to do things only Thorn and Cain knew about, and that was fine by him. Thorn knew because he was their president. Cain because he was their boss at ExFil. Venus was the only female patched member of Salvation's Bane, and her membership was well earned. Beast had learned to trust her over the couple of years they'd worked together and had become rather fond of the woman, considering her just one of the guys, no matter how sexist it sounded. In fact, the only thing he didn't like about the woman was the fact that she owned and proudly rode a pink Harley. Who did that shit? If *this* had to be done, Venus was the only one he trusted to do it.

With her on the way, he continued to listen to the four chatter inanely. Listened carefully, but they kept spouting the same lies and bluster over and over. The fact none of them turned on the other willingly told him all he needed to know about their consciences. They had none.

Venus slipped quietly into the room and moved to the far corner accompanied by Andy, a tall, slender man who'd been working the bar tonight. New Kid was also there. Beast had wanted him there for another reason, but it was just as well he was here for this. With his brothers and sisters in the room to witness and give guidance where needed, Beast felt free to start.

Instead of confronting any of his guests outright, he simply turned to the screen behind them. "Let's watch a movie," he said in a mock-cheerful voice. "I think you'll find this very interesting." He gave them a grin that was probably more like a sneer. "Sorry I'm all out of popcorn, but I think you'll be fine without it."

Ripper had loaded everything up in chronological order, each step from beginning to the very bitter end on full display. Beast had previewed it briefly, but it still disturbed him at what he'd found. What they were all about to witness.

"Keep in mind, we did all this very quickly and were only able to get video from today. Ripper has done some digging, though, and we'll review the rest of it after the little movie is done." Beast pressed play on his remote and sat back to watch. He positioned himself where he could see both the screen and the faces of the participants. It was very important for him to see their faces. Their eyes. He had to note every subtle reaction if he was going to make a fair decision.

It started off at the gym that morning. Debbie got there about ten minutes before Jeremy, Ben, and Greg. Once the men entered and signed in, the four met for several minutes. It was easy to tell by watching they knew each other. The way she waved the men over the second she spotted them and their easy return greeting told they had a familiarity with one another. Debbie had handed Jeremy her phone and he'd passed it around to the other two, all of them grinning and punching each other playfully as they discussed whatever it was the woman was showing them.

Debbie had gone over to the treadmill and began a slow jog until Fleur had entered about half an hour later. The men had congregated near some of the leg machines, not really doing anything, but keeping a close watch on the door. Once Fleur greeted Debbie, the two women jogged on the treadmill for another ten minutes before Debbie had urged Fleur to the weight bench where she'd attempted to bench press the weight bar and Beast had intervened.

They all went about their business for another hour or so, Debbie moving Fleur from one machine to another, seemingly at random. After that, Fleur and Debbie left together. Ten minutes later, Debbie had entered again and met the guys one last time. They'd smiled and nodded several times before Jeremy had taken a thick envelope from his gym bag and handed it to Debbie. The cuts had gone through at fast forward except the important parts, the time stamp proving the time of day and its passage. The whole thing was something Ripper had put together on the fly in order for Beast to confront everyone with.

The next cut was from the club earlier that evening. Ben had approached the bar near the entrance and made a hand-off to the bartender, the very same man Venus had brought with her, a point that had hit Beast hard the first time he saw it. Another envelope, though this one contained more than money. Something they all saw as the bartender pulled out a small vial a few minutes later. Thank goodness Ripper was super paranoid and had cameras all over the fucking place, because it took several different angles to see everything so it wasn't speculation. The next part was something else that had Beast ready to beat the living fuck out of someone very specific. It was bad enough Andy had betrayed them, but this was something altogether different.

They watched as Fleur was ushered into the club, then later shoved up against the bar by none other than fucking New Kid where Fleur ordered her drink -- water, from the audio. Darrin made a sound but was quickly hushed when Grease backhanded him none too gently. Andy had dumped the contents of the vial into the glass of ice water he handed Fleur. She'd made a face but continued to drink at Andy's encouragement. The video went on up until the moment Beast had burst into the room, again most of it at fast forward until something important happened.

When the three young men started protesting how that was all edited to make them look bad and Debbie protested right along with them, Beast held up his hand for silence. Then he clicked on a few other files, putting them on display on the big screen.

Group text messages from Debbie to Jeremy, Ben, and Greg, along with several separate text messages between Ben and Andy and New Kid were there for them all to see. Details on payment and expectations were almost too much for Beast, but he kept his control by sheer force of will. There would be time enough later to lose his mind. This had not only happened on his watch, but right under his fucking nose, using the club's territory as well as a member of his own security team. A man he'd hand-picked for the job. A man he'd intended on bringing to Cain as a prospective employee of ExFil, which meant he'd have likely be a prospect in either Salvation's Bane or Bones at some point. He was going to have to talk to Thorn about this, and it wasn't going to be pretty.

As bad as all that was, he'd saved what he considered the worst for last. Text messages between Debbie and Fleur establishing they'd known each other since high school. How Fleur had never thought to have such a strong friendship with Debbie because Debbie had been part of the "in" crowd while Fleur had been a nerdy band geek. She'd devoted her time to studying either music or academics, planning on going to college as a physics major before her parents had died in a car crash. Debbie had understood her loneliness since her parents had basically shipped her off to Palm Springs to get her out of their hair. She'd invited Fleur to live with her rent free if she tutored her in her college classes.

The short of it? Debbie had lured Fleur to Florida from Tennessee. The text messages with the Hay brothers and Kinson had started the same fucking day Fleur agreed to move to Palm Springs.

Chapter Three

"Not really sure there's much to add to what we've seen," Beast remarked. "But if any of you have something to add -- beyond the assertions none of you had ever seen Fleur before or that you didn't conspire to... put her in a bad situation -- I'd very much like to hear it."

Kinson looked scared and ashamed, but said nothing. Jeremy crossed his arms over his chest, still defiant.

"That's all bullshit. You made that to make us look bad so you could get money from our old man. Well, it ain't gonna work. We'll sue you --" He was cut off when Ripper stepped forward and punched him in the nose with a quick jab. Jeremy yelped and covered his nose as blood poured. His brother, sitting beside him, quickly scooted over in an effort not to get blood on him.

"Hey! You can't do that!" Ben apparently wasn't the brightest bulb in the box because Ripper was still hovering close. Ben's nose met the same fate as his brother's.

"Gideon," Darrin started, holding out a hand as if to try and calm the big man down. "We can talk about this. It's not what it looks like, I swear."

"Oh, really, New Kid?" Beast rose so fast his chair tumbled backward. "Because it looks like you took a payout to sacrifice that girl to three sadistic pricks for torture and rape." He gave Darrin a stare he wished would have put the other man six feet under. "Please. Enlighten me to what this *actually* was."

Darrin looked to Venus, who had a neutral expression on her face as she buffed her bright pink nails on her vest. The vest was the same bright pink.

Her nails looked to be sharp as daggers. Beast knew she'd used them as weapons on more than one occasion, and God help everyone if she broke a nail doing it.

"Well... it... we were just..." he stammered, sweat beginning to bead on his forehead and upper lip.

"Yeah," Beast finally interrupted. "You were just." He looked to Debbie then. The woman looked... bored. "You know you're in a world a' shit. Right?"

She shrugged. "Whatever." She probably thought her mommy and daddy would get her out of this. Probably knew none of the men there would touch her like they had Jeremy and Ben and thought she was in the clear.

Beast focused on Kinson next. "Well?" The boy shook his head, not meeting Beast's gaze. "Little lesson here, son. When you jump off a fuckin' cliff because your friends do, you're just as dead as they are." That got the young man to whimper in fear, a single tear sliding down his cheek. Beast had no doubt it was more for his present situation than for any remorse he had about what they'd done to Fleur.

"What was in the fuckin' vial, Jeremy?" When the other man didn't answer, he looked to the other Hay brother. Finally, he focused on Kinson. "Well?"

"J-just a little Georgia Home Boy." Kinson glanced at his buddies, who gave him angry looks. Jeremy shook his head as if exasperated with Greg.

Gamma-Hydroxybutyrate -- GHB, a date rape drug. Beast clenched his fists. "That all? If you hold out on this, you get to deal with me, and I won't be as gentle as my associates."

Greg nodded vigorously. "That's it. I-I got it."

Again, Beast had to grit his teeth. He pulled out his phone and called Doc. "GHB. They say that's it, but I'm not sure how accurate it is."

Doc was as calm as ever when he replied. "I'm treating her with fluids and other supportive measures. She's resting comfortably at the moment. She'll need someone to watch over her for twelve hours or so. I prefer twenty-four, but if she's not still showing negative side effects, twelve should be fine."

"I'll take care of it once I've seen to this fuckin' mess."

"Want me to take her back to the clubhouse?"

Beast thought about it. Did he? Yes. "Take her to my room and get her settled. Assuming she's ready to be moved. If not, I'll do it when this is done."

"She's comfortable here. Just didn't think she'd want to wake up in the club."

"Good thinking. If you need help, take anyone you need and move her. Make it happen, Doc."

"On it, brother."

Once Beast had hung up the call, he turned back to Jeremy, Ben, and Greg. "Gentlemen, you've got two choices. The easy way where I call the DA, turn over all the security tapes surrounding this matter, and you plead guilty to whatever charges she brings. Or the hard way, where I beat the living fuck outta you. Ain't sayin' you'll get out of this without a beating of some kind, but it will go far easier if you agree to take the guilty plea and the jail time that goes with it. Also, you might keep in mind that, if you fight any of the charges, if your let your daddies and mommies try to get your sentence reduced or the charges dropped, you'll get the beatin' at the first mention of it and it you might not survive said beatin' intact." That was when Greg Kinson began to cry. Then to *sob*.

"I'll do whatever you tell me to!" he cried. "I'll plead guilty and go to jail. Just please don't hurt me!"

"Damn straight you'll do your time," Beast agreed. "But you'll take your beatin' like a man. You earned it." Greg cried all the harder, dropping to the floor and begging. Beast simply jerked his head, and Lock lifted Greg by his upper arms and shoved him out the door. He'd take the kid to the basement and deliver a good thrashing before getting Doc to treat the worst of it. Once they were finished with the Hay brothers -- and Beast hoped to hell the boys took the hard way he'd mentioned -- Ripper would fill in the DA. Thankfully, he knew the woman personally and could handle the situation even if all three were in bad shape when they got to jail.

"How about you two? Don't suppose you want the easy way, too?"

"You won't hurt us," Jeremy scoffed through his bloody hand. Tears streamed down his face to mingle with the blood leaving streaks of dark red down his face and neck. "When my dad sees me --"

Beast was the one to strike him this time. A hard, backhanded blow that sent his head snapping back. It was meant both as an insult and a casual show of his considerable strength. Though he'd hit Jeremy hard, it was just a fraction of what he was prepared to do to the boy if he didn't cooperate.

"Won't hurt you. Right." He gestured to Jeremy's face. "All evidence to the contrary." Beast smirked. "Be very sure you understand what you're getting into, Jeremy. If you choose the hard way, I'll be the one administering your punishment, and I don't go easy on men who hurt women or children."

"Fuck you!" Jeremy spat, blood hitting the floor at Beast's feat. "When my dad's through, we'll fucking *own* this place!"

"Yeah. You said that before." Beast knew it was time to show the little motherfuckers he meant business. He leaned down to rest his fists on either side of Jeremy's hips and put his face barely an inch from the other man's. "What you're missing is the part where I beat you into a fuckin' coma and no one fuckin' knows what happened to you. Think I can't do it? Take the hard way. I'm just itching to prove I can."

Finally, *finally*, the situation got through to Jeremy. His eyes widened and he shook his head. Ben whimpered beside him, but Beast kept his gaze focused on the older brother. He knew he was intimidating. He worked hard to make sure he looked intimidating. Like now. Instead of his usual suit and tie, he had on dress slacks, but a black A-shirt that showed off his powerful shoulders and arms. The Hay brothers might be in good shape, but they had more of an athletic build. Beast was, quite simply, a beast.

"Fine," Ben said quickly. "We'll do whatever you tell us to." Jeremy said nothing, just kept his wide eyes focused on Beast's.

"So, your brother is the more intelligent of the two of you. That's good. Grease, take Ben here down to join his friend. Me and his brother got some more talkin' to do. Might want to tell Doc to be ready when I'm done. Assumin' there's anything left of the little motherfucker."

"Wait!" Ben cried. "Jeremy's coming with me!"

Beast still didn't break his stare with the older Hay brother. "He's not agreed to that. Far as I can tell he's insisting on doin' things the hard way. Thank God."

"Jeremy, tell him! He'll fucking kill you, man! Can't you see that?"

Jeremy seemed unable to say anything. His jaw was slack, and a single tear trickled down his face. Beast smelled the distinct, sharp sour smell of urine as the boy wet himself. Beast wasn't about to take pity on him.

"Well? What's it gonna be? The easy way, or the hard way? Choice is yours."

Jeremy swallowed before finally answering in a voice so soft Beast wouldn't have heard it if he hadn't been so close. "E-easy."

"What's that? Didn't hear you."

"Easy way," he repeated a little louder.

Beast stayed there a few moments longer before pushing himself up and slowly straightening to his full height. He jerked his head, indicating he was to go with Grease. Normally, he'd have sent another man with Grease, but he doubted either one of them would put up much of a fight. Anything they'd had left in them fled the moment Jeremy pissed his pants.

"So, that leaves little Miss Debbie," Beast said, turning back to the woman. She wrinkled her nose delicately at the strong smell of urine.

"None of that proves anything. Anyone could have gotten my phone, and who knows what was said at the gym. You're not going to intimidate me into a confession." She grinned at him. "Call the police and have them take me in. I'll be out before morning."

"You get the same choices as your friends, which is really more than I should give you. You lured Fleur here, making her think you were her friend. This wasn't some spur-of-the-moment thing. It was a deliberate act. A planned attack on an innocent young woman you led to believe you thought of as a friend.

You betrayed her trust and put her in danger all while pretending to offer a safe home and a job to help her find her own way after her life had gone to hell."

Debbie shrugged, crossing her legs. At any other time, Beast might have been distracted by those long legs she displayed to their best advantage under the micro mini skirt. Now, it just annoyed him that she thought he could be that easily diverted.

Fucking bitch.

"Look," Debbie said, sitting back, her hand tracing the edge of her bandeau top just over her breasts. "I'm sure we can work something out. Fleur is fine. She wasn't hurt and she's safe now. No harm, no foul."

Beast didn't say a word. Just held her gaze steadily. She continued to stroke the skin just above her top in a seductive manner. The woman was really beautiful, and she knew it. Creamy skin, plump, ruby lips, a lush, womanly figure, and golden hair that was shiny and silky and gleaming under the office lights. She was exactly the type of woman he'd normally go for except for two things. First she was despicable, deviant, with no moral compass whatsoever. Beast had done some pretty horrible things in his lifetime, but he'd always followed his own sense of right and wrong. This woman followed the dollar and the thrill. Nothing else. Second, when he thought about sex with a woman, it wasn't a sleek blonde he was seeing. It was a curly-headed pixie who was in no shape mentally or physically to take on a man like him.

Goddamn. He was so fucked.

"Are you done?" He was tired of this game. He had other things to take care of. Like Fleur.

Debbie merely shrugged one smooth, elegant shoulder. "Fine. Whatever. Just call the police and be done with it."

"Police wasn't one of your options." He crossed his arms over his chest, trying to look bored when he was annoyed as fuck and pissed as hell. "Easy way. Hard way. It's not that difficult."

She gave a little delicate snort. "You're not going to beat me." She waved her hand dismissively. "Just call the police. Or better yet, call your DA buddy. I know my rights. I'll still be out by morning."

"I left you for last intentionally." Beast raised an arm and beckoned Venus to them. "I'd like to introduce you to Venus. She's someone I trust, but she has a... questionable background." Venus gave Debbie a superior grin like she was really looking forward to what was about to happen. "I'm entrusting Venus with whatever happens next. I don't deal out punishment to women because I'm too fuckin' big and strong. I could do more damage than I intend. Venus here has no such problems. Not because she's not lethal. Just because she's more normal in size."

Venus snorted just like Beast knew she would. Of all the members of Salvation's Bane, Venus was probably the most lethal. In all respects. Because of her looks, people tended to underestimate her. It was usually their last mistake.

"Pretty *myshka*." Venus trailed a finger down Debbie's cheek leaving behind a thin scratch where her fingernail cut into the tender flesh. Her Russian accent was heavy. Her nails were so sharp, Debbie either didn't register the impossibly thin cut, or thought Venus had just touched her with those nails. After all, a lot of women sported them. They looked sharp. No expectation they'd actually be razor sharp. "You and I shall have such fun." Venus's voice was silky smooth and purred like a cat.

Finally, Debbie looked like she realized the scope of her situation. "Y-you won't do anything." Her voice shook slightly but she did manage to only look a little nervous.

"Can and will," Venus said with a grin. "I only need know if you choose easy way or hard way."

Debbie looked from Venus to Beast and back a couple of times, as if judging how much was an act and how much was them trying to cow her. Beast could have answered that question, but he doubted the girl would believe him. Sure enough, Debbie found her bravado and put it back in full force. "Consider your bluff called." She stood up and stabbed Beast in the chest with her finger. "I want my lawyer."

Venus glanced at him. "I take it she choose hard way?" She tsked several times, clicking her tongue. "I so hate to mess up pretty face." She smiled brightly. "I just have to find other ways to cause pain."

"Take her below," Beast said. "Let her watch the brothers punish her friends and know they're getting off easy compared to what she'll be getting." He glanced at Debbie, feeling a bit of the tension drain from him. Venus would take care of this. Take the bitch to the very edge and have her begging for death before it was done, then not give it to her. "Make sure she suffers."

"Oh, that you can be sure, brother," Venus said with a sneer toward Debbie. "My *myshka* here is about to get lesson she'll never forget." She shrugged. "Unless I break something inside her pretty little head. She looks fragile."

"You don't scare me," Debbie said, lifting her chin.

Venus casually lashed out, much like a cat, with those razor-like fingernails, leaving three gouges on the left side of Debbie's face. The girl yelped and clapped her hand over her cheek. When it came back wet with blood, she actually screamed.

"Now you see, *myshka*. Unfortunately for you, revelation came too late. You are mine now." She shoved the woman out the door, taking her to the basement to join the others. No one would hear them scream. No one would find them until Beast was good and ready. As promised, the three men would go to jail. Debbie might make it out alive. If she did, she'd likely wish she hadn't.

Beast picked up his phone and sent a text to Tobias, one of his security people. When the club needed a mess cleaned, Tobias was their man. Beast had a big fucking mess he needed cleaned. And the pissants in the basement and the girl were only the beginning.

His gaze focused on the bartender and the man he'd intended to mentor. Beast decided that was what pissed him off the most. He'd misjudged the kid's character horribly.

"Can we go?" Darrin actually looked hopeful, even though, having witnessed everything so far, he had to know he was in deep shit.

Beast didn't answer. Didn't look at the kid. He couldn't. If he did, he was afraid he'd kill the little motherfucker.

A couple minutes later, Tobias knocked on the door before opening it slowly.

"You needed me, Boss?"

"Yeah. Take these two to the clubhouse. I sent Thorn some information. I haven't gotten a text from him so I'm guessing he's not seen it yet. Tell him to make sure he's with Havoc when he reviews it. It's something both the president and vice president need to see together."

"I take it you didn't send it to Havoc?"

Beast just snorted. "That son of a bitch never answers a text message. He figures if it's not worth a call, it's not worth his time."

"Fucker," Tobias chuckled. "Any other instructions?"

"Yeah. Make sure they're as uncomfortable as possible until Thorn decides what to do. I'll be along shortly. Got something to take care of first."

Tobias turned to New Kid and the bartender. "All right, you little bastards. Come with me. And by all means. Try to escape." Tobias might not know what was going on, but he'd been around long enough to know an order like the one Beast had given him didn't bode well for the two men.

Beast felt nothing but satisfaction. But how would his little Fleur regard him when she found out?

* * *

Fleur's back was on *fire*. She lay on her side and hugged a pillow to her. She barely put her head on another pillow because the feeling of smothering was still too fresh in her mind.

"I can give you something to help with the pain and to help you sleep," Doc said. "You'll be much more comfortable."

"Tylenol and Motrin," she said.

"Something stronger," he urged. "You need to sleep to heal."

"Tylenol and Motrin are all I need. Thank you." She didn't want to lose her wits about her ever again.

"I appreciate all you've done for me but I really need to go."

"You should really wait until Beast -- err, Gideon -- gets back." Doc gave her a worried look. "He intended to get you out of here himself. Take you back to the clubhouse so we could make sure you were good through the night. The stuff they hit you with was pretty potent." He turned away from her and went to a sink across the room and washed his hands. He'd put some antibiotic cream and another cream that soothed the sting on her back with gloves, but, apparently, the guy was a real healthcare worker. Showed in his hand hygiene and use of protective gear, too. "You may not feel much of the effects of the drug right now, but if you get up and move around you could still get dizzy. It's usually best if you take it easy for twenty-four hours or so."

"I'm good," Fleur said. She really wasn't, but she didn't want to stay with strange men one second longer than she had to.

"Is your car outside?" Doc's question should have been casual, but she got the feeling it was anything but.

"I came with Debbie. If you could just get me a cab I can go home and get my car."

Doc put his hands on his hips. "Once Gideon gets back, he'll see you get wherever you need to go."

"Gideon," she said. "You mean Beast?"

"You know him then?"

"Not exactly. I've seen him at the gym a few times. Everyone calls him Beast. It fits."

Doc smiled at her. "I guess it does. Anyway, you're not in any shape right now to go anywhere other than to sleep. The sooner you give in and just sleep, the better you're going to feel."

She knew he was speaking the truth because her body was telling her the same damned thing. "I don't... I'm afraid to sleep."

Doc nodded solemnly. "Because you don't feel safe with all these strangers and no one familiar around you. Understandable." He sat in a chair next to the cot where she lay. "But let me give you something to consider. Gideon and his team called me in to care for you. Whether it was for your safety or to prevent them from getting sued doesn't really matter. They still brought you help with the goal of making sure you were going to be OK. If any of us were going to hurt you, no one would have gone to this trouble to make sure you were out of the situation you were in."

When he put it that way, Fleur felt silly not doing what he told her. "I'm sorry," she said, not looking at him. "Nothing like this has ever happened to me before, but I'm used to being on my own. I guess I just feel safer not relying on anyone right now."

"I understand that, too. I'm just asking you give us all a chance. Especially right now when you're still not feeling well. After that -- tomorrow -- you can reevaluate. But right now, you need someone watching over you. I wouldn't feel comfortable letting you drive, and I'm not sure how much help your friend, Debbie, will be."

"Not much," she muttered. "I'd ask you to take me to a hospital, but I can't afford it. Even if I did, there'd probably be questions I don't want to answer."

"Money isn't a problem if you want to go to the hospital," Doc said without hesitation. "You want to go? Just say the word, and I'll make sure you're well taken care of. But, yes, there would likely be questions. None you have to answer, but I doubt you'd be able to stand your ground with that many people on you about it, no matter how gentle they were."

"I take it Gideon got the men who did this." Fleur didn't like that she sounded so vulnerable. She'd learned after her parents had died that people took advantage of you if you looked weak.

"Gideon has it all under control. Yes."

"I guess I'll just wait then," she said. "You're right. I do feel like shit, and I don't think it's a good idea to go to Debbie's."

"Good. Rest. I can still give you something stronger for pain. It would double as a sedative to help you sleep."

"No. Whatever you put on my back helped. I think I'll rest easily enough."

He gave her a slight smile. "And you won't sleep too deeply."

Fleur didn't bother denying it.

Doc looked like he was about to say more, but the door opened and Gideon entered the room. She knew they called him Beast. Right now, he looked the part. Fleur shrank back, sitting up and pulling her knees to her chest defensively. She couldn't help herself.

"Whoa there girl," he said, taking a step back. "I ain't gonna hurt ya. You know that."

"Ease up, big guy," Doc said. "She's good, but this hasn't been easy on her."

"Fuck," the big man muttered. He cleared his throat and gave a slight smile before sitting on the edge of the cot where she lay. "Doc says you need someone watchin' over you for a little while. Now, I know you've been living with your friend, Debbie, but you can't go back there right now. Tomorrow, me and a couple of the boys will take you there to get your stuff, but now's not the time."

"All my things are there. I can't just leave them."

"Why not? It's just one night. Besides, Debbie won't be there for a while. All your stuff will be safe."

"Is she OK? She didn't get hurt too, did she?" Much as she hated herself in that moment, she almost hoped Gideon would say she had been hurt just so Fleur could spare herself the pain of knowing her friend betrayed her.

He sighed heavily. "No. She's not OK, but not because she got hurt like you did. She's not OK because she helped those guys hurt you."

Even though she'd known it was coming, actually hearing it confirmed nearly gutted Fleur. Over the months she'd lived with Debbie, Fleur had come to really consider her a close friend. "Guess my judgment in people seriously sucks," she muttered, trying her best not to lose it.

"We'll discuss that later," Gideon said. "Right now, we need to get you to the clubhouse and to a room where you can rest comfortably."

"Why do they call you Beast?" The second she asked the question, Fleur wished she hadn't.

He snorted. "Cause I'm fuckin' big."

"Yeah. I guess you are. Is that the only reason?"

He cocked his head as if thinking about it for a second. "I'm mean."

Doc barked out a sharp laugh. "You got that right."

Gideon gave Doc a sidelong glance. "But not to you. I'm a pussycat to you." That made her giggle. Which was apparently what he was going for. "There. See? I'm not so bad. Now. Can I take you back to the clubhouse so you can sleep off the rest of that drug?"

What did she really have to lose? Doc was right. If he'd wanted to hurt her, he'd have done it already. "Yes."

"How bad does your back hurt? I don't want you uncomfortable."

"Not bad. Between the Tylenol and the cream Doc put on it earlier, it doesn't hurt at all right now."

Gideon looked up to Doc. "Was she in bad shape?"

"Not too bad. There were a few thin cuts, but it was mostly welts. She should be fine in a day or two. Sore tomorrow."

"OK then, Sunshine," Gideon said. "Let's get you to bed."

He lifted her gently and cradled her against his chest. For some reason, Fleur felt the need to inhale. Deeply. Taking his scent inside her. There was a slight sour tang of sweat, but not unpleasant. Kind of like how a lemon smelled sour, but not in a bad way. Underneath that was a woodsy, earthy scent. And a faint trace of gasoline. All man.

Gideon carried her down the hall and out the back. She'd been afraid he would take her through the club, and she wasn't certain she could have faced that.

"Relax, Sunshine," he soothed. "I'll get you into Doc's vehicle here and we'll take you back to the clubhouse."

"Doc's going with us?"

"Yes. I want him close in case you need help."

"I'm only going to be there until tomorrow," she said. "I hardly think it's worth the effort."

"Worry about that later," he said. And another red flag went up. She thought about making him discuss it now, but what was the point? Nothing was going to get solved tonight anyway. She had nowhere else to stay and none of her possessions. She'd taken some money with her, but not a lot. Any money she'd made had usually been in the form of odd jobs for cash, so everything she had was at Debbie's beach house. Yeah. Definitely something to worry about when her head was clearer. Once the vehicle started moving, her head spun every time she glimpsed the streetlights whizzing by during the drive.

She and Gideon sat in the back seat while Doc drove them. When she groaned her protest of the speed, Gideon hooked his arm around her and pulled her head to his big thigh.

"Close your eyes." He stroked her hair, massaging her scalp. "We'll be there in just a couple of minutes and you can get out of the car."

"Just a little motion sick," she whimpered. "My head spins sometimes."

"I know." He continued to stroke her hair, the gesture almost tender, if somewhat awkward.

Once the vehicle came to a halt, Gideon opened the door and hauled her out, once again cradling her in his arms. It was natural for her to rest her head on his shoulder, but when she realized she'd slid her arms around his neck, she jerked them back. Thankfully, he said nothing. Just carried her through what was, presumably, the clubhouse. Doc went ahead of him, opening doors and fielding questions, mostly with "none of your business." No one seemed to take offense or even look flustered. Some chuckled and clapped Gideon on the back or patted him on the shoulder. One or two patted her head gently. Strangely, she didn't feel threatened. She was tired, though. Tired beyond belief.

Finally, they entered a little room on the second floor. Fleur had a vague perception of it, but her eyelids were so heavy she couldn't process it all. Tomorrow. She'd worry about it tomorrow.

Chapter Four

Lightning splayed across the sky, lighting the room through the open windows. The scent of rain was heavy in the air. A few seconds later a clap of thunder sounded in the distance. Beast sat in the dark watching the bed where his little pixie lay asleep like the dead. Doc had said she'd need to sleep off the drug, but the way Fleur had protested Beast had thought maybe she wasn't feeling it. Apparently, she was.

He'd had time to reflect on everything that had transpired that night. It wasn't over yet. There was still the fucking bartender and New Kid to deal with. The only thing he'd heard back from Thorn was a one-word message. "OK." The president hadn't sought him out, nor had the vice president. Until they did, he wasn't moving from Fleur's side. Mainly because, if he did, he'd make his way to the basement where he knew the men were being held and he'd kill the fucking sons of bitches. Slowly.

"Ohhh." A faint groan came from Fleur.

"Hey you," Beast said, leaning over to brush one chestnut-colored curl from her forehead. The stubborn thing fell right back without even a moment's hesitation. "How you feelin'?"

"Like I got run over by a train." There was a pause. "And like a cat shit in my mouth," she muttered, not moving a muscle.

Beast grunted. "Not surprised. How's your back?"

She groaned before sitting up, moving her body slightly as if testing the waters. "Not too bad. Sore. Not unbearable." She looked down at herself, then up at him. There was no fear in her eyes, and she seemed to be aware of herself. "This is not my shirt."

"No. It's not."

When he said nothing else, she pulled up the covers and looked underneath before laying them back on her lap. "Not my boxers, either."

"Nope." Again, she seemed to wait for further explanation. When he offered none, she crossed her arms over her chest. "You wanna explain that?"

"Didn't think your dress would be comfortable, so I put you in something that was." She continued to stare at him. "Promise I didn't look at you." Which was a bold-faced lie and she knew it.

She snorted. "I just bet you didn't. What time is it?"

"Five in the morning."

"So I've not been sleeping that long."

"No. But you slept like the dead. Willing to bet you need more."

"Can't argue with you there." She groaned and swung those shapely legs of hers over the side of the bed.

"Not the best idea for you to get up yet."

"Well, it's either I get up or you're going to have to change the sheets. I gotta pee, big guy."

For such a tiny little thing she sure could be a spitfire. "I'll help you. Can't have you fallin' on my watch."

"Park it, big guy. You're not helping me to the bathroom."

He raised an eyebrow. "Keep it up and I'll carry you *and* stay in there with you."

Her eyes narrowed. "If you think you can bully me, think again. I will totally piss this bed full before I'll let that happen. Once a fucking night is enough."

That pulled him up short. "Didn't mean to scare you," he muttered. "I just --"

"You didn't scare me. You tried to go all dominant and shit. I get that's probably your personality, big as you are, but I'm not into it. I don't respond to it. Especially not after this mess. Debbie makes me doubt myself and I get shy, which is why I ended up at that stupid club in the first place. I let her push me around. Not happening again."

"Fuck," Beast muttered. "I'm... uh..." He cleared his throat. "I didn't intend to boss you around." He never apologized as a rule. Apologizing meant admitting he was wrong, and he never second-guessed himself. His decisions kept his club -- his family -- safe. "Well, not much, anyway."

She stood gingerly, taking it slow. Beast tensed up, not wanting to ignore her wishes but needing to make sure she didn't fall. "Right. Very convincing, big guy."

Her trek to the bathroom was uneventful, thank God, but Beast practically held his breath the entire time. Why did he even give a fuck? She was the one being stubborn. If she fell it was on her. Except he knew it would hurt him worse than it would hurt her.

"You should go back to sleep," he said, trying not to sound too bossy.

She glared at him. "I should get a motel room, but it's five in the morning. Rest assured that tomorrow I will."

"Fleur, look. I'm just trying to help you. It was a rough night, and I've still got things to take care of. Fuckin' New Kid and the fuckin' bartender have still got to be dealt with. It would be much better if you stayed here with the club until all that's gone away."

"The club. You mean the Playground? I thought we were someplace else?"

"We are. Remember?"

"I thought I did," she muttered.

"I'm the enforcer to Salvation's Bane, an MC here in Palm Beach. We own the Playground as well as a couple strip joints. You're at our clubhouse. Which means as long as you're here, you're under our protection. Which means, you follow my rules."

"How did 'our protection' turn into 'your rules?'"

"I'm the enforcer. I make the rules. As for protection, no one comes into our clubhouse and harasses our people. The entire club would fight to the death to protect anyone under our roof."

"Sounds a bit farfetched."

"It's not. Just go back to sleep. In the morning we'll sort it all out."

She sat on the bed and sighed. "Look. Thanks for everything you did. If you hadn't stormed into that room…"

"I did. That's my job." He knew he sounded gruff, but he had no idea how to handle this. He wasn't smooth with women. They flocked to him because of his size and the fact he was a biker. It wasn't that he wanted to fuck this girl, but he'd hoped to at least make a positive impression.

OK. Who was he kidding? He wanted to fuck her. Bad. Awful as it was, he kept seeing her naked body in his mind. Only, instead of writhing on the bed in pain as that fuckhead beat her with a whip, he wanted her writhing atop his body in ecstasy as he fucked her until they both passed out. And he could fuck for a long fucking time.

"I just want you to know I'm aware of how much trouble I was in and that you're the one who got me out. I appreciate it."

"So you understand I just want you safe. Right?"

"I know where you're going with this, Beast. I get you." She tucked her legs back under the covers and curled onto her side before looking up at him again. "I'll stay until you tell me it's safe. You'll have to clue me in to the rules, though. Because I have no clue how I should behave in an MC clubhouse." Her brows furrowed. "Do you even say it that way? Is it a motorcycle club clubhouse?"

His own chuckle surprised Beast. He wasn't the kind of man who laughed much. "The only rule you need to worry about is to do what I tell you. Beyond that, there aren't many rules. Don't betray the club. Don't talk about anything you see here unless it's with me. That's it. The girls will probably test you, but that's normal."

"Test me?"

"Oh yeah. They got Vicious's ol' lady drunk at the first party she went to."

"That doesn't sound too bad."

"Well, once her inhibitions were gone, she put on a show like no one had ever seen. And we own two strip clubs."

"Wow. Was she pissed?"

He shrugged. "Don't know what she said to Vicious in private, but I can tell you it backfired mightily on the girls. They all got laid, but every single man in the club had visions of Lucy in his head when they fucked, I can tell you that."

She opened her mouth then closed it. Tried again. "I have no idea what to say to that."

He snorted. "Not much to say. Everyone had a good time and Vicious learned a thing or two about his ol' lady. Mainly that she's an exhibitionist."

"Holy shit!"

That got a chuckle out of him. Again, it startled him that the sound came so easily. It made his chest feel funny, too. OK, so it wasn't the sound of his laughter that got him. It was the woman in front of him. She made him do it so easily. Almost casually. Every time he did it, he could see her lips twitch. Most of the time, her smile followed. And it was a glorious smile. Fucking *glorious*! Just like the sunshine he'd nicknamed her.

"Yeah. That's what we said. They tend to not be discreet about fuckin'. Vicious has always been up for a good time, but I think he's met his match in Lucy."

"I think I better sleep on this. You know I'm probably not going to do anything like that while I'm here. Right?"

"Sunshine, no one expects you to. Join in the fun, watch, or don't participate in any way. Stay for the food until you see it's goin' in a way you are uncomfortable with. No one judges."

She yawned and stretched, pulling his shirt tight over her tits before she adjusted it absently. Thing nearly swallowed her whole, but she'd gotten tangled settling into bed. "What about you? You judging me for what happened in the club?"

That hit him like she'd slapped him. "Sunshine, none of that was your fault."

"I didn't have to walk in there. I could have said 'no' to Debbie. I willingly went into a BDSM club, knowing what went on there." She shook her head slightly. "More precisely, I *thought* I knew what went on, but that's not the point."

"Then what is? 'Cause, I gotta tell ya, I'm not likin' where you're goin' with this." Did she really think he'd take advantage of her just because she was in a place like that? "I work there, honey. I'm there every fuckin' night it's open. I've seen lots of women come and go. Literally. In all senses of the word. All different shapes, sizes, colors, and sexual orientation. They come there for even more different reasons. Some want to fuck anything moving anywhere they can. Others want to find a Dom who can care for their needs, not all of them sexual in nature. Then there are the ones who are just curious. They come in wanting to watch and fantasize. I think you fall into the latter category, though, I bet I could make you want to try at least some of the shit goin' on in there."

"In your dreams, big guy." She yawned again. "That's not me."

"Whatever you say, Sunshine."

He sat back in the chair he'd pulled near the bed and sprawled out. It wasn't the most comfortable place in the world, but he didn't want to leave her alone until Doc said it was OK. The longer he sat there, the more uncomfortable it got. And not because of the chair. Picturing Fleur at one of the club's wild and rowdy parties was getting him hard. Maybe she'd participate, maybe she wouldn't. But she'd watch. She'd be there. He'd just bet he could coax her behind a palm tree or something. If not, he'd still get to enjoy watching her watch others.

Fuck.

"Gideon?" That sleepy, sultry note to her voice was the nail in his coffin. His cock was sprung like a fucking teenager. Barely suppressing his frustrated groan, he sat up a little straighter.

"You all right, Sunshine?"

"Uh, yeah. I'm fine. I just... well, that chair can't be comfortable. Why not go on to your room? I promise I won't get up by myself. You've done enough for now."

"This is my room. And I'm not leavin' you by yourself. Just go back to sleep."

There was another long silence. Then, "Beast." Her tone brooked no nonsense, a bit of a dominant tone to it when he was certain that wasn't her core personality. He also noticed she used his street name, not his given name. "Just get in the fucking bed, will you?"

"Snippy little thing, huh?"

"I'm not lying here while you're in that stupid chair like a dumbass. There's plenty of room in here for both of us."

"Not afraid I'll take advantage?"

"Oh, I'm sure you'll take advantage. But I'm not in a position to be taken advantage of by you, and you're not the kind of guy to push it."

He stood and crossed to the bed. Instead of going around to the other side where there was more room and he wouldn't crowd her, he slipped in close to her small body. "You sure about that?" He took her little hand, his big one wrapping completely around her wrist with room to spare, and pulled it to his crotch. "'Cause I ain't sure my own Goddamned self."

Instead of pulling away, she wrapped those slim fingers around his cock through his jeans. "Absolutely," she answered. Did she sound a little breathless? "If that was the kind of man you were, you wouldn't have rescued me from those creeps in the first place."

Beast let go of her wrist but covered her hand with his, pressing it against his dick so he could move a little and have at least some of the friction he wanted. "You're gonna be the fuckin' death of me, woman."

"Don't want to kill you," she purred. "If I did, I wouldn't get to decide if I wanted to experience what you've got down there."

"Oh, you ain't decided?" Was she playing with him? And why did he like it so fucking much?

"I'm still a little high, Gideon. But I'm not going to lie. I think I might want you, and I have no idea why. I'm not an innocent, but this isn't me." She frowned a little. "At least, it's not who I've been since I had to grow up. Now, I'm wondering what partying would be like as an adult."

"Bane can certainly give you the full experience, if you want it."

"Not the club, Beast. You. I can't process the whole club. That's just too much. But I might be willing to stick with you for a while to see what it's like."

"Good idea, Sunshine," he said, thrusting against her hand once more before pushing it away and turning her over. He spooned her close, making sure to wedge his hard dick between her cheeks as much as he could, giving a good, hard thrust for good measure. She lay on his arm and he curled it around her, his forearm pressed tightly against her breasts, his hand stroking her arm. His other hand rested on her hip, and he desperately wanted to stroke it over her ass.

She shivered in his arms. Good. She wasn't unaffected. Then she wiggled against him -- just a little -- and shivered again.

"You good? Not scared of me, right?"

"N-no."

"Horny?"

"You could say that," she said with a nervous chuckle. "I've got a rough, ruggedly handsome man in my bed with an impressive-feeling dick between my ass cheeks. It's enough to make any woman horny."

"Can't say I'm not glad to hear that," he admitted.

She stretched, thrusting out her chest as she curled an arm around his neck, hissing out a little breath. Beast wanted nothing more than to cup those breasts of hers in his big palms but didn't dare. Anything that happened tonight was going to be her doing. And he wasn't fucking her, much as he wanted to. Her admitting she was still buzzed negated that idea. Not that he wouldn't enjoy fucking her when she'd been drinking -- drunk sex could be good sex -- but not for their first time. And not when she hadn't given him express permission *before* she'd gotten drunk. All that made him a better man than he fucking wanted to be.

"Touch me, Beast," she whispered.

"You want my hands on you?"

"Desperately."

"You're gonna have to put them where you want them, Sunshine. You're still buzzin' from the GHB, and I've done all I'm willing to do on my own."

"Even if I told you I wanted to?"

"Especially if you told me you wanted to. Anything you want, you're gonna have to do on your own, and it stops before my cock gets close to your pussy."

"Oh, God," she whimpered.

Again, he found himself chuckling. "You like me talkin' dirty to you?"

"Yes. I love dirty talk."

"That how your other men get you off?" The thought of her with another man sent his hackles rising. A new experience for him since he could give a good Goddamn how many lovers a woman had before him as long as she could satisfy *him*.

"No," she answered softly. "Never had anyone who wanted to."

"Can't imagine a man not wanting to make his woman wild for him. What kinda dumbasses you been fuckin'?"

She stiffened. "The kind who aren't bikers or in charge of BDSM clubs," she snapped. "Maybe you should leave."

"Hit a nerve?"

"Just because I've not had a guy talk dirty to me doesn't mean I need it to have a good time."

"Relax, there Sunshine. I was just messin' with you." There was that damned chuckle he wasn't used to.

"Bastard," she muttered.

Fleur was still for a long time, and Beast thought she might have drifted off to sleep, but then she shivered again, wiggling her ass and driving his cock deeper between her cheeks. "Beast?" Her voice was soft, as if testing to see if he was still awake.

"What is it, Sunshine?"

She took a deep, shuddering breath. Then moved his hand under her shirt to cup her breast.

Reflexively, Beast squeezed, kneading her tit. He was gentle at first, then she whimpered and thrust her chest at him, tightening her grip on his hand, urging him to squeeze harder. He obliged her happily. His lips found her neck, and he trailed his tongue along the skin there. Fleur threaded her fingers through his hair and pulled him tighter to her.

"Still horny?"

"More horny than angry," she clarified.

He nipped her neck gently. "I didn't mean no offense," he said. "It's just that, as far as I'm concerned, the wilder I can make a woman in my bed, the better off we both are. Any man not smart enough to try it at least once is a dumbass as far as I'm concerned. If you've never had a man talk dirty to you, wanna tell me how you know you like it?"

"You mean besides me liking it when you did it?"

"Sunshine, I haven't begun talkin' dirty to you. I simply asked if you were horny."

"You said you'd stop before your cock got near my pussy."

"I did." God, this wasn't good. Or it was. "My dick is so fuckin' hard, Sunshine. You made it that way, you know."

"I can feel it twitching between my cheeks," she whispered. "Is it as big as it feels?"

"You touched it with your hand. Couldn't you tell?"

"Uh, no. It was through your jeans." She glanced over her shoulder at him. The moonlight through the window shown directly into her eyes. Those silver-green orbs seemed to glitter, mesmerizing him.

"You want in my pants, baby, all you gotta do is say the word. I'm willin' to let you explore."

When Fleur turned over, pushing Beast to his back, he thought he might cream his jeans right there. More than anything he wanted to shove them over his hips and free his dick. He imagined her hair bunching like silk through his fingers as he forced her head to his crotch before stuffing his cock into her mouth. Instead, he lay as still as he could, watching her intently.

Her hands slid under his shirt and bunched it up over his chest. She ran her soft palms over the muscles of his chest and abs. Beast couldn't prevent his growl, or the way his muscles jumped at her touch.

When she sat up, he finished taking off his shirt then rested his arms behind his head. It was the only fucking way he was going to keep them off her.

"Since you already gave permission, I'm not giving you a chance to back out," she said, grinning down at him as she reached for the button to his jeans.

"You don't see me stoppin' you, do you?"

It was almost embarrassing how fast his dick sprang free when she pulled at his boxers. She didn't immediately touch him, though. Her hands went back to shaping his chest and abdomen. His biceps where they bunched in his effort to keep them behind his head.

"You can touch me, you know," she said softly. "I'm not going to hold it against you."

"Sunshine, if I touch you now, I ain't stoppin'."

"Who said I'd want you to stop?"

"Done told you. Ain't happenin' tonight."

"Are you always so stubborn? I'm practically throwing myself at you here. Most men would take what I offered and ask questions later."

"I ain't most men, Sunshine. I give you my word, it's as good as done."

"What if I did… this?" She shimmied out of her shorts and lifted one creamy thigh to swing it over his hips, straddling him. Once settled, she whipped her shirt over her head, baring those glorious tits.

"Fuckin' Goddamn," he bit out. His hands shot to the tops of her thighs, his fingers biting deep.

She settled herself over him, pressing her pussy against his dick so it was trapped between his belly and her wet heat. With a subtle roll of her hips, she rocked over him, making his dick wet with her little cunt.

"Still want to keep your dick away from my pussy?"

"Never did," he said. "But I'm still not fuckin' you tonight."

Fleur draped herself over him, resting her head on his chest as she rocked over him in a slow, sensual side. She didn't say anything else, but she whimpered constantly.

This was fucking torture! "You know that shit they drugged you with is probably what's makin' you horny, right?" He had to point it out, otherwise he'd feel like an ass. Much as he wanted her -- and he *really* wanted her -- he absolutely would not take advantage of her. Hell, just climbing into her bed had been questionable. She might have wanted it, but he could have stayed on his side instead of crowding her.

"Does it really matter if the end result is the same?" Her breath fanned across his chest, a heated enticement.

"You'll regret this in the morning, Sunshine. Just... aww, fuck..." She hit just the perfect spot. If he shifted just that little bit, he'd be inside her.

"I'm so close," she whispered. "Please don't make me get up now. I need... I need to finish."

"If I thought you didn't need it, I wouldn't be in this fuckin' position." Beast knew he was grinding his teeth and gripping her hips too fucking tight. She might even have bruises later. More bruises to mar her lovely skin. It was that thought alone that dulled the ache in his cock long enough for him to get control. He was not going to be the cause of more pain to her. He took a deep breath, then gently urged her to move faster. "Do what you need, Sunshine," he rasped. "Can you get off this way?"

"I -- I think so."

"What do you need?"

"Your dick inside me?"

"Not happenin', Sunshine."

Fleur reached between them. The second her hand circled his cock he knew what she was doing. Beast shoved one of his big arms under hers, batting her arm out and away from their bodies.

"I said, not happenin'. Ain't goin' there tonight."

"But --"

"Only 'butt' there's gonna be is yours. When I blister the fire out of it with my hand."

"Oh, God!" She twisted her hips, tensing up and pressing herself tight against him. "Please," she whimpered. "I need to come, Beast. Can I just... I need it in me, Beast."

"You want my cock, Sunshine? You beggin' so sweetly just for my big dick?"

"I do! I am! Please!"

He flipped them over so he pinned her with his larger frame. "Said I ain't fuckin' you, but I'll make you come so hard you soak me with it."

Fleur wrapped her legs around his waist, lifting herself as much as he could, tilting her hips and writhing beneath him. In like fashion, Beast wrapped his arms around Fleur, holding her to him. Her nipples stabbed his chest, sweat making them move over his skin in a silky glide. He wanted to taste them, to suck until she screamed. Right there, he made a vow.

"I swear to you, Fleur," he whispered by her ear. "Before you leave this clubhouse, whenever that is, I'm gonna suck those luscious tits of yours, eat that juicy pussy, and fuck you blind in every hole I can fit my dick into."

"Beast!" she screamed, her body shuddering beneath his. She'd come, but he wasn't satisfied yet.

"Gonna sink my cock into your pussy, Sunshine. Then I'm gonna fuck that pretty little ass of yours." She squirmed under him, and he began to move with her, sliding his cock between her lips with ease. "God, you're soaked. I think you like the idea of lettin' me have you. Any way I want, Sunshine. Gonna fuck you so fuckin' good." Stroke. "Want you comin' around my dick until I come deep inside this luscious, little body of yours."

Her scream was the sweetest music. Her pussy quivering around the length of his cock just about sent him over the edge himself. Fleur clung to him, sweat sheening her skin and making her slide against him.

Beast slowed his pace, letting her come down as gently as he could. He stroked her damp hair from her face before placing a gentle kiss on her chin and nibbling until she moaned for him.

"Feel better, Sunshine?"

"Beast," she sighed. Fleur was completely limp, her arms draped around him but not clutching him like she had been. He rolled them over so she was back on top of him. No way he was letting her move. Felt too fucking good.

"Sleep, girl. Got a big day ahead of us tomorrow."

Chapter Five

Fleur woke with a start. Sitting straight up in the bed, gasping for breath, she struggled to remember everything that had happened the previous evening. Seconds later, it all came back in a rush, and she wished she could forget.

Groaning, she put her head in her hands. "Fuuuuuuck."

"Good morning, Sunshine."

Gideon, or rather Beast, entered the room with a sack and a cup in his hand. He tossed her the sack and set the cup on the nightstand. "Brought you some dinner," he said. The gruff note in his voice wasn't unpleasant. Fleur got the impression this was probably the closest he'd ever gotten to bringing a woman breakfast -- or dinner -- in bed.

"Smells good." It did. She hadn't eaten the night before, too nervous about going to the stupid club, and she was famished.

"You feeling OK? Doc said you might be a little groggy or, at the very least, hung over."

She opened the sack and pulled out a cheeseburger and fries, then took a pull from the straw in the cup. Coke. She took a bite before replying with her mouth full. "Too soon to tell. Right now, I'm just hungry."

Beast grunted, turning to go. Then he stopped, looking back over his shoulder. "Your clothes are on the chair." He pointed to where he'd been sitting the night before. Before she'd insisted he crawl in bed with her. *Oh, my God!* "If you feel up to it, dress and come downstairs to the common room. Thorn wants to talk with you."

"Fine. Let me eat, then I'll shower and be on down."

Was it her imagination, or did his nostrils just flare? Like the thought of her in the shower turned him on. She glanced down below the waist, but he was turned away from her too much for her to see if there was a bulge at his crotch. *Shit.*

"If you feel dizzy, call out. I'll be outside in the hall."

"You're gonna just stand outside the room? Waiting?"

Beast shrugged. "Ain't stayin' in here with you. You need me, you call, I'll come running. Otherwise, I'll be out here. Respecting your privacy."

OK. That was a hard shut-down. Like she needed this kind of complication anyway. She sighed and stood carefully. The room didn't spin, and she didn't feel like she wanted to throw up. Taking another bite of her burger, Fleur crossed to the chair and checked out the duds. Not hers, but she thought they'd fit well enough. No panties. And a short skirt. Marvelous.

"Nice sense of humor," she grumbled to herself.

After she finished her food, Fleur showered. She took her time, enjoying the hot water after the punishing night and the hours she'd slept. Her body was stiff and sore, and she just wanted to… what? She couldn't go home. She didn't *have* a home. She'd sold everything she had to move here. Granted, she hadn't had much because she'd needed to use the money from the sale of her parents' house to pay off the mortgage, and the sale from one of their cars to pay off her vehicle. That had left her with a little money and a car. And by little, she meant *very* little. Now that she had nowhere to stay, and no job, she wasn't sure what she was going to do. She probably had enough money saved back for a month in a cheap motel or something, but that was it.

She found a toothbrush still in the pack on the sink. Thank God, too, because she seriously needed it. Dressing was a delight. The shirt skirt was *very* short. With no panties... yeah. More marvelous. Looking in the mirror, she turned every way she could, trying to see how she could move without flashing everyone. Impossible.

Frustrated, she threw caution to the wind and found Beast's closet. Jackpot. She found a long-sleeved flannel shirt which she tied around her waist. It covered her ass, as long as she was careful, and the tied sleeves hung down long enough in front to cover her. Problem solved, and fuck whatever bitches picked out the clothing for her and didn't give her panties. If they didn't have some still in the clubhouse, they should have given her a longer fucking skirt.

Deciding she was as presentable as she could be with no make-up and wet hair, Fleur opened the door to face Beast. The man was just gorgeous. *Fuck.* Tattoos. Muscles. A strong jaw and high cheekbones. With shaggy blond hair and a short beard, he was mouthwatering. A flashback from the previous night hit her like a punch to the gut. Or a tickle to her clit. It was all she could do not to whimper, knowing she was bare under that stupid skirt and he'd have access to her any time he wanted. Did he realize? What was she thinking? Of course he realized.

His gaze was hot on her as it roamed over her from top to bottom. The muscles in his jaw clenched and unclenched, and he looked stern and more than a little displeased.

"What?" she asked.

"That's not much of an outfit."

"Well, don't blame me. I added the shirt -- otherwise everyone in the place would get a show."

"Fuckin' bitches," he muttered. "Come on." Beast snagged her hand and led her to the common room where there was a gaggle of bikers and nearly as many women. Beast looked around as if searching for someone in particular.

"Hey, Beast." A busty redhead sidled up to him, draping herself over him like she owned him. "I thought you'd never come join the party."

"Not a party, Mercedes. Thought you left."

She shrugged, pouting. "It's still boring at home." Then she gave him a man-eating smile. "I like it here better. Don't you want to go have some fun with me? I've got everything set up just the way you like it. You can even play with my ass this time if you want." The woman purred, standing on her tiptoes to lick his neck.

Fleur twisted out of his grasp. If he was taking this woman somewhere to fuck her, she didn't want to know anything about it.

"Fleur! Don't you take one more step!" She'd never been one to respond to commands. Peer pressure? Intimidation? Maybe. Probably. But bullying? No. Not her thing. But when Beast bit out his command, she did exactly what he told her to. She turned back to face him, clenching her fists at her sides.

"What is it, Beast?" Fleur asked the question calmly, though she was anything but calm.

"Do not go anywhere without me. Understand?"

"Well, I'm not hanging out with you while you bone Red here. I'm actually going to just head out. I need to go apartment hunting anyway."

"I said," he bit out between clenched teeth, "stay. Put."

"Fine." Fleur turned on her heel and stalked to a nearby vacant chair and sank into it, ever mindful of her state of undress.

"Fuck," Beast muttered. That was when he was approached by another man. This one tall, with hair as black as coal, heavily muscled. Like three quarters of the men there, he was built like a tank. "Thorn," Beast said. Beast actually looked relieved. "I thought Mercedes had left the clubhouse."

"I did too." The man looked at the redhead. She moved from Beast to Thorn quickly enough, giving the other man even more attention than she had Beast, rubbing her ample chest against him provocatively.

"Beast doesn't seem to want to play with me," she said. "You're always up for it, though, ain't you, Thorn?"

"Not now, Mercedes. You need to have a talk with Vicious about your expectations here."

Mercedes actually pouted again. Did the woman have no shame? "He's no fun since he found that woman."

"Watch your mouth, girl. That woman is his ol' lady. She has a place of respect in the club that you better never forget." Thorn sounded harsh and most definitely displeased, something Mercedes seemed to either be oblivious to or simply ignored.

"She's not one of us, Thorn. She don't belong here. Vicious was in my bed before he was in hers."

"Yeah, well he's in hers last. As to her not being one of us? She's more like us than you are. She can't go home to her rich daddy whenever she decides she wants a new pair of shoes that cost more than a car." He grabbed her by the upper arms and put her a little bit away from both him and Beast. "You need to go home. Now. And don't you come back. Understand me? You're not welcome here any longer."

At first, Mercedes looked amused, like Thorn was just kidding her and she was waiting for the other shoe to drop. Then, when he just kept staring at her, her look morphed into stunned shock. "Not welcome? I've done everything anyone asked of me! I can't help it my daddy's rich! What the fuck, Thorn?"

"I don't have to explain myself to you, Mercedes. I'm the president. I decide who stays and who goes. Second, you've never done anything except what you wanted to do. Which usually involves sex. While all the men have appreciated your adventurous spirit, you cause more trouble than you're worth. You keep the other girls in an uproar all the time, and that's not good for anyone." He crossed his arms over his chest. "Pack your shit. Get out. You have an hour before I'm having you escorted out."

"You'll regret this, Thorn. You and your whole motherfucking club!"

Thorn went from casual to intimidating in a heartbeat. "You don't threaten my club, girl." He closed the distance between them just as quickly and wrapped his big hand around the woman's throat. It didn't look like an easy grip. "I'll let it go this one time. That's it. Just remember. You threaten the club, you answer to me. I'm not a gentle man, and I have no qualms about hurting a woman if she earns it. Threatening my family is a capital offense here. Get me?"

Mercedes looked like she didn't know whether to be scared or turned on. Thorn realized it, too. He shoved her away from him and called out to one of the guys in the club. "Tobias!"

"Right here, brother." Tobias was across the room, but since the place had gone quiet when Mercedes got her bluff called, everyone was listening attentively.

"Get her off the property. Now. She does not get to collect her things, and if she doesn't have her car keys with her, drop her at the nearest bus stop and have her car towed. I want her out. Now."

"All over it." Tobias took Mercedes's arm and pulled her after him.

"I want my stuff, Thorn! You can't keep it!"

He didn't bother answering her. He inhaled through his nose and exhaled through his mouth. "If she shows back up here, I swear I'll kill her."

"Might want to think about that one, Prez. You know she'll be back." Beast stood there, arms at his sides, and waited until Tobias had Mercedes out the door before he relaxed even a little.

Thorn nodded to Fleur. "You talked to her about this?"

"Talked to me about what?" Fleur wasn't sitting there and letting the two men talk about her like they were the adults in the room and she a naughty child.

Thorn turned to her, addressing her for the first time. "The men in our employ who were part of the team who plotted to drug and rape you are in the basement. The other four have been taken care of, but we're still trying to decide what to do with these two."

"Why would Beast talk to me about that?"

"Because he thought you might want a say in what happened to them."

"I didn't have a say in the others."

"That's because they were going to jail. These two… not so much."

Fleur just stared at him for several long minutes, her mind not really processing what he was saying. If they weren't going to jail, then what? Finally, she just shrugged and shook her head. "I have no idea what you mean."

"It's best if we talk about this downstairs," Beast said, glancing around. While no one in Salvation's Bane would rat them out, especially on a matter like this, the less the club as a whole knew about things like this, the more deniability they all had. If anyone took the fall for punishments dealt out by Bane, it would be Beast. He was the enforcer. That was part of his job.

"What am I going to see down there?" Fleur got the distinct feeling whatever had happened so far was probably not the most civil of occurrences. No one had alluded to such, but there was a very violent vibe coming from both Thorn and Beast. It was like the two men were strung so tight they were about to snap. Funny. She'd never thought about bikers caring about who they hurt, so she didn't think it was their conscience bothering them for beating up someone. She thought it might just be the fact that the men were employed by them. "Is this because they betrayed you in some way?"

"Absolutely," Thorn said immediately. "They were hired by the club to work on club property. They betrayed the trust we put in them, so they aren't getting out of this. What they did was just about the worst thing they could have done."

"I see," Fleur said. Then she sighed. "Well, I didn't get a say in what happened to the men who flogged me. I guess if you're giving me this opportunity I should at least investigate and hear you out."

"You understand," Beast said, "that by going with us down there, seeing what's going on and what we're gonna do to these fucks, if you go to the police with it, you'll be guilty of the same crime. Right?"

"This is the part where I should run screaming. Except I want to know what's going to happen to the assholes who sold me out. I honestly don't care what you do to them. If they've done it once, they've done it more than once, and they'll keep doing it until someone stops them." She stood as gracefully as she could considering part of her bare ass was on the chair. "After that, can I please go? I've got shit to do. Like finding a place to sleep tonight."

Beast reached for her, grabbing her hand once more as he dragged her after him. "We'll discuss that later. Right now, I want this done."

Beast had a look on his face like he thought he was going to hell. She had no doubt he'd done a lot of bad things in his life, but why did Fleur get the feeling he considered this worse?

"I'm going to tell you now, before we go in there. People are gonna die tonight. No doubt about it. The only question is how." He urged her on. "I have no qualms about it. Would gladly do it myself, no matter how grisly. I just hate dragging you down to this basement with me."

"Then why do it?" Fleur got the feeling there was way more to this than she realized.

"Because you belong with us," Beast said. The conviction in his voice was unmistakable.

"And you know this... how? I've been here less than twenty-four hours and have been asleep most of the time."

"I just know. Besides. Where're you gonna go? You have no home. No family. You certainly can't stay at Debbie's. I'm giving you a chance to put down roots. Start over. All you have to do is take it."

She stared at him a long moment before speaking. Beast liked that. She considered her words carefully. "Looks like you're making that decision for me whether I like it or not."

Beast didn't even have the good grace to look embarrassed. "You need someone to help you make decisions. Clearly, you're no good on your own."

A flare of anger and hurt shot through her. Before she'd realized it, Fleur had taken a step forward and swung her hand. Beast merely jerked back, avoiding the blow. Instead of being angry she'd tried to hit him, he chuckled. "I can see baiting you is going to be a party in itself."

"Bastard," she muttered.

"I was teasing you."

"Yeah, well, it's too soon for that. Especially now."

He sobered. "I'm not the best at the social thing," he said. "My job is to protect. I'm suspicious of everyone, and I never get close to anyone not in the club. It's not... safe."

Fleur narrowed her eyes, studying him closely. "That's why you're so upset about this. These men were part of Salvation's Bane."

"Not exactly, but close. I had intended to recommend New Kid be a prospect. Was putting in a good word with our boss at a paramilitary company most of us work for so he'd hire the kid. The bartender, not so much, but he was still hired by me."

"You know, having me as part of Salvation's Bane doesn't mean you can trust me." Fleur had to point out the obvious. Beast was probably flying on blind instinct right now. He was obviously the controlling type, and something like this would seriously shake his confidence.

He gave her an impatient look. "That's not why I want you here."

When he didn't elaborate, Fleur prompted him. "So... why *do* you want me here?"

Beast just shrugged and continued on.

"I'm not stupid," she said softly, hoping he was the only one who heard. "If I do this, if I go with you to see this, I'll be tying myself to Salvation's Bane forever. Thorn won't want me leaving until he's satisfied I won't betray you." He didn't answer her. Just opened the door to the basement and ushered her inside.

Once Fleur moved ahead of him, Beast locked the door with the deadbolt, then followed her. At the bottom of the stairs was another, heavier door which he also locked. This one had a double deadbolt.

Fleur stopped, watching him intently. "Paranoid much?"

"You're being allowed down here because this is directly related to you. No one is allowed down here unless there is a very good reason."

"And you're just letting me walk in?" When Beast opened his mouth, Fleur held up her hand. "I got what you said before. What I don't get is, if you won't even let your club down here, why are you letting an outsider?"

"Just accept you get a say in what happens to these bastards," Beast said, snagging her hand again and leading her down the dark hallway into a dimly lit room. The only light hung over the heads of the two men tied to chairs. She recognized the bartender and gave an involuntary shiver, trying to twist her hand out of Beast's. He was having none of it, his grip tightening. The other man, she didn't recognize.

Wait... was he the man who'd pulled her out of line and brought her straight into the club?

The second she had a clear path, she took three steps in their direction. Beast snaked an arm around her waist, halting her forward progress so she spat, hitting the younger looking of the two men in the chest. "You bastard!" The outburst surprised her. As a rule she wasn't prone to bursts of temper, but seeing those two, recognizing them, and knowing how they'd set her up to be raped and tortured just kind of snapped something inside her.

"I'm sorry, Fleur," the young man pleaded. "I'm really, really sorry! I didn't think they'd hurt you! Debbie said you liked stuff like that but just needed something to relax. I was only trying to help! You've got to believe me!"

"Are you fucking kidding me?" She shrugged Beast off, advancing on the man again. "You didn't think they'd hurt me? And you just took Debbie's word that this was what I wanted? If that's true, why not approach me? Why not tell me what you were doing? Ask me if it got me hot to be a little out of control? Ask me if that was what I wanted?" She spat again, this time hitting his face. Then once again for good measure. "I have no idea what they're going to do to you, but you deserve everything they do and more!"

"Don't you get it, you stupid cunt?" The man strained against the bonds holding him to the chair. "They're gonna fuckin' *kill us*!"

Beast growled, but Thorn put a restraining hand on his shoulder.

Fleur's immediate reaction was to deny it, but she had a feeling the man was right. She closed her eyes and took several calming breaths. She needed to think, to choose her next words carefully. All eyes were on her, she knew it. So, how did she feel about this? Could she actually stand there and watch this? Could she even acknowledge it was going to happen?

"Beast said you were hired by the club to work in their establishment," she asked the bartender. "Is that right?"

"Yeah. So?" The bartender was belligerent, seeming not to care about his fate. Maybe he was just blustering, trying to deny the club any pleasure in killing him.

Fleur looked around her. The only people in the basement were Beast, Thorn, and two other men. She addressed the two men she didn't know. "I'm Fleur Durand. I don't think I've had the pleasure of meeting the two of you."

It was Thorn who answered for them. "Tobias and Ripper. Ripper's our intel guy."

"What does Tobias do?"

Thorn shrugged. "He's always here on club business. Especially when there is a security issue involved."

"In other words, not my business."

Thorn shrugged.

The breather was what Fleur needed to calm down and think rationally. Did these men deserve to die? She couldn't make that moral judgment.

"What did they tell you when you were hired on?"

The bartender answered. "To keep my fuckin' nose clean. I've never been in trouble, and I've worked for these motherfuckers for three damned years!"

"You know," Ripper said softly. "I've had several hours to go over all the security tapes."

"Yeah. So?"

"So, I pulled every single feed from every single shift either of you worked."

That was the point the bartender broke down and started sobbing. "I don't want to die," he whimpered.

"Wow," Fleur said. "I thought you were a big strong man. Why you crying now?"

"I don't want to die!"

"You think I wanted to get drugged, beaten, and raped?" She jerked her head at Ripper. "I'm guessing I'm not the first girl you've done this to. Why should they give you mercy when you didn't give those other girls mercy? Or me?"

"But you got away," he whined, snot dripping steadily.

"Are you actually using that to plead your case?" Fleur had no idea why she felt the compulsion to do this. She was surprised the men hadn't stopped her questions already.

The man cringed. "Just please don't let them kill me. I'll do anything! Please!"

The emotions roiling inside Fleur were so overwhelming, she thought she'd be sick. Anger. Fear. Surprise… Hate. She hated these two men for what they'd done to her.

"How could you do this to another person? Either of you?"

The bartender snorted. "Just another bitch to me. You walk in there with your skimpy little outfit -- like now. Little cock tease. Then you cry foul when someone touches you. You want the attention, or you wouldn't dress that way."

Beast lunged for the man but Thorn got there first, backhanding the man with a vicious strength. The man toppled over, still tied to the chair. His head hit the concrete floor with a sickening thud. For several moments, Fleur thought the blow might have killed him, but then he groaned, his eyes fluttering a few times before closing.

"Pick him up," Thorn ordered. Ripper and Tobias readily obeyed. "Wake him up." Tobias poured a bottle of water over the bartender's head until the man sputtered and opened his eyes once more.

When he looked like he might have his wits back about him, Thorn crouched down in front of him. "That one's for disrespecting the young lady," he said softly. "You've got a long list of transgressions to pay for. Whether or not you have to pay for all of them will depend on your conduct while Fleur is here." The bartender gasped for breath, still reeling from the head trauma.

"How many women have you two sold out?" Fleur was surprised her voice sounded as calm as it did. Neither man said anything. The bartender was still stunned, and the other one was sobbing like a baby.

"Does it really matter?" Ripper spoke softly. "They did it once, and I found text messages they were planning on doing it again."

Fleur turned to Beast. "You were responsible for hiring them."

Beast grunted. "I was."

"The others involved -- Debbie, and the three guys. They get treated differently because you -- the club -- weren't responsible for them." Fleur wasn't sure where she was going with this, but she was beginning to understand the graveness of the situation.

"Correct."

She took in a shuddering breath. "I get it. You gave them your trust, and they betrayed you. Hurt people you were supposed to look out for."

"We can't have our own people involved in something like this. Not only because they hurt innocent people, but they put the club in danger. Salvation's Bane is family to all of us. You don't put your family in danger. It's no secret we do things that aren't exactly legal. We can't have anyone here coming under that kind of scrutiny."

"We were never part... of your... precious family," the bartender gasped. He was getting more and more control.

"But you were taken in by them," Fleur insisted, finally getting it. "They trusted you. Gave you a job. Paid you well." She looked at the other one. "If Beast made you part of security, he had to have trusted you."

"He still can trust me," he pleaded. "It was a stupid mistake."

"One you made over and over," Thorn said. "Until you got caught."

"One more thing," Fleur said, turning to Beast. "You're the enforcer. The guy in charge of enforcing the rules."

Beast put back his shoulders, obviously proud of his job. "I am."

"Say you fuck up," she said, not liking it when he stiffened. She didn't like putting him on the spot, but this was something she had to know. "You fuck up, and someone gets hurt because of it. Like this situation. What if someone gets killed? Or maybe it's just the excuse the cops are looking to investigate the club more closely. I'm assuming you have some less-than-savory dealings?"

Beast shrugged but said nothing.

"So, the cops start looking. What happens then?"

It was Thorn who answered. Fleur didn't take her eyes off Beast as the president spoke. "As enforcer, it's Beast's job to prevent that from happening. If he fails in his duty, there are measures in place that would lead any investigation to Beast. He'd take the responsibility." There was a beat of silence. "And pay the consequences."

Fleur's stomach turned over, threatening to empty its contents. She knew what was coming and couldn't blame them. Maybe it was the intimacy she'd shared with Beast the night before. Maybe it was because he was big and had proven he'd protect her. Fuck. Maybe Fleur just like the way he smelled. All she knew was she didn't want to be without him. Not now. He hadn't promised her anything other than sex before she left them, but it didn't matter. Knowing he was the kind of man who protected his entire club with his life was… something. If she was part of that circle, would he protect her as fiercely? Also, could she really blame him or Salvation's Bane in general for disposing of the two predators? They destroyed lives. For money. For the thrill. For whatever reason they came up with to justify their actions, they still hurt people.

Fleur wrapped her arms around his waist and buried her face in his chest. "I don't want to be here when…" She trailed off, unable to say it. "I understand, but I don't want to witness it in case I get asked." She looked up at Beast. "I'm a terrible liar. I can talk my way around anything I've seen so far, but not if…"

"At least you're honest about it. That's all I ask." Beast jerked his head to the left. A second later, he let her go and a heavy hand settled on her shoulder.

"Come on, Fleur," Ripper said. "I'll take you back to Beast's room. Do you mind waiting for him there?"

She didn't trust herself to speak. She'd reached her limit. "No," she whispered, then looked up at Beast. "Will I see you tonight?"

"You will. Give me an hour."

She nodded. Then, on impulse, Fleur stood on her tiptoes and curled her arms around his neck. She pulled him down to her and kissed him. It started out gentle enough, but Beast took control quickly. Those wonderfully big arms wrapped around her so tight she thought she might break. She loved it. The feeling of safety was matched only by the heady lust she felt when he thrust his tongue inside her mouth once and lapped at hers. Then he squeezed her once before setting her back firmly on her feet.

"Go, Sunshine," he murmured. "We'll talk later."

She nodded and went with Ripper back upstairs. Back to Beast's room. Could she face him when he came to her? Would he even come to her first? And what was going to happen in the meantime?

No. She didn't want to know. Not now. She wasn't squeamish, but if Beast took his job as seriously as it seemed he did, then this would take something out of him. If he needed to share, she'd see to it he did. After all, it was the least she could do since he was in this situation because he'd rescued her.

Chapter Six

Death for the two men hadn't been easy. Or swift. It wasn't because Beast enjoyed that sort of thing, either. He intended to send a message, both to those involved who were still living -- if beaten to bloody pulps -- and to any of their other employees who thought to dishonor or betray the club in any way. All of them knew Salvation's Bane owned the three clubs. They had to know running illegal side businesses that could in any way be traced back to the club would not be tolerated. Tobias would make the bodies disappear, but there would be untraceable pictures of the men taken and discreetly shown to a select few of their employees. Ripper would take care of any digital footprints they left, just as Tobias would take care of the bodies.

By the time he stood in front of the door to his room, it was nearly two in the morning. Far sooner than those fucks deserved. Truth was, he just wanted to get back to Fleur. She wasn't his, but he wanted her to be. As far as the club was concerned, she was. Especially after what had happened in the basement. She'd pegged him solid. No woman in his life had ever taken the time to look deeper than his body and tats. Or his club. Even with word spreading about him and Fleur, a couple of the club girls wouldn't back off. If anything, they'd become more aggressive. Probably because no self-respecting club girl could stand to back down from a challenge.

Mercedes was one of them. She should never have been allowed back in. Probably convinced some prospect or one of the patched members had said she could come back. Once in, no one had paid enough attention to her to kick her back out. She'd been through the entire club, him included. She was a good enough lay, but not a woman he cared to fuck twice. She was looking to get her claws into someone, and that someone wasn't him. The other woman was Topaz. The woman was harmless enough, but she liked to cause chaos. Likely she was showing interest in Beast simply because Mercedes did.

Quietly, so he didn't wake Fleur, he opened the door and slipped inside.

"Gideon?" Fleur's sweet voice drifted from across the room at the big picture window where there was a window seat. As the moonlight spilled through the pane, casting a silvery glow, he could see she'd made a nest of blankets and pillows. She'd curled up there to rest as she stared outside through the glass.

"You should be in bed." His gruff reply didn't seem to be the right thing to say, but it was all he had.

"I wanted to be awake when you came back." Fleur slid gracefully to the floor and walked toward him. Her hips moved from side to side, an enticement he had no business giving in to. She reached up and brushed a lock of damp hair off his forehead. "Did you bathe?"

"Ran through the shower." Beast knew he didn't sound good, but how to tell her how much blood there had been? The basement stank of it. He was surprised he didn't still smell like it.

"Will you let me hold you tonight?"

He blinked down at her in confusion. "I don't... what?"

She smiled. "Everyone needs a little TLC from time to time. I'd say this is one of those times." She gave him a worried frown. "There are so many shadows in your eyes, Gideon. I hate that I added to them."

"Not you, Sunshine," he said. "Never you." There was no way to resist what she was offering. As before when she'd kissed him downstairs, Beast bent down to wrap his arms around her. This time, he lifted her, taking her to the bed and stretching out on top of her. "This is a do-or-die moment, Sunshine," he said in a husky whisper. "Not going to deny I want you. But it's not a fling. Not scratching an itch. You take me on now, you take me on until I say it's over. You stay here with me and Salvation's Bane. You figure out how to fit in here and make a home for yourself until I'm ready for you to leave. Just understand, I'm in control. You don't get to leave unless I say. You get me?"

She smiled a little serene smile. "Not really. At least not the why of it. I understand what you're saying, though. I let you have my body, you're keeping it until…" She swallowed whatever she had been about to say and amended her sentence, "… for a while. Until you say you're done."

"That might not be for a long while, Fleur. Make sure you're ready to make that much of a commitment."

"I'm willing to try," she said. "It's not like I have many any other options. Besides. You've proven your club might be a little shady in some areas, but it's for the right reasons. If hurting people who prey on others is wrong, then I'm just not a good girl. I have zero problems with your club."

"You have no idea what other activities we participate in."

"Don't get me wrong, Beast."

Beast was coming to realize she thought of him as two separate people. Gideon and Beast. Where he thought of himself as the biker, the warrior, Beast, she saw something different. Because when she called him

Beast, it was all about the rough and dangerous persona he tried to project to everyone around him. When she called him Gideon, she was trying to get through to the man beneath. Well, good luck to her with that. He didn't even know who that man was anymore.

"I know there were a multitude of reasons for what happened last night and today. Some were strictly a security issue, but there were some things that weren't. You wanted rid of the threat to your family. Your club."

"You," he whispered.

Fleur blinked several times before acknowledging him. "Me." Clearing her throat, she continued. "I don't believe for a second anything you do is for the purpose of harming others, especially not women or children. Anything else doesn't bother me in the least." She grinned. "I still don't want to know. I wasn't kidding when I said I was a terrible liar."

"Works for me," Beast said, then claimed her mouth once again.

God, she was heaven! There was no other way to describe it. Kissing her was a revelation. Like nothing he'd done before meant anything to him, where just Fleur's kisses meant *everything*.

He shivered, the totality of what he was doing hitting him like a boulder smashing down a wooded mountain. He threaded his fingers through her hair, tightening his fist and pulling her head back. She gave out a little shocked cry, but what was shining in her eyes wasn't fear or pain. It was lust.

"This is your last chance, Sunshine. Tell me to fuck off. Tell me not to touch you."

"Not going to happen, Gideon," she said. "I want you so bad I'm willing to give this a shot."

"Not a shot, baby. You're all in or you're not."

"Until you say it's over."

"Until I say it's over."

"Another woman ends it, Beast." She met his gaze boldly, recognizing the biker in him. The roughneck. "I don't share."

"I'd kill any man you fuck other than me," he countered.

She smiled. "Then I think we're in agreement. Now, shut up and fuck me."

He took her mouth again. Aggressive and primal. This had been building in him since he'd first touched her intimately the night before. She responded so sweetly to him, taking all he had to give her and demanding more. His kind of lover.

He found her breast with his mouth, his fist still clutched tightly in her hair. She tunneled her fingers through his hair and pulled just as hard as he pulled hers. The bite was delicious to Beast. He growled against her chest and bit down sharply on one nipple. Fleur let out a cry, wrapping her legs around his torso.

"Fuck yeah, you taste good, Sunshine."

"Suck me," she whimpered. "Suck my tits."

"Such a naughty little girl," he growled again. "Do you need a spanking while I fuck you?"

She arched her back, offering herself to him again. Again, he bit down on her nipple. "Beast!"

"That's it, baby. You like it rough, don't you?"

"More! Give me more!"

He continued to kiss, nip, and suck every inch of Fleur's skin he could manage. She'd have little marks all over her body before he was done. There would be no doubt who she'd had in her bed. Beast intended for everyone in the fucking club to know it had been him.

Finally, when he could wait no longer to taste her, Beast shoved her up the bed and settled himself between her legs. She tried to urge him back up her body, but he was having none of it.

"I'll fuck you when I'm good and Goddamned ready. Not a second before, Fleur. You're mine to do with as I please!"

"Bastard!" she shouted. "I need you to fuck me!"

"And I need to eat this beautiful, wet little pussy. Guess which one of us is gonna win that battle, Sunshine?" She screamed at the same time he snarled before covering her pussy with his mouth in a tight suction.

Every pull, every drop of honey she gave him was like a drug. Beast doubted he'd ever get enough of her. He loved every single sound she made, the way her body broke out in a sweat when he turned her on, the way she responded to every single thing he did to her. This was... heaven. Beast had never known he was missing so much. Sex had always been good, but nothing like this.

Fleur's cries grew louder and louder, her body tensing beneath his. Beast thrust one finger deep within her, and she screamed, thrusting her pelvis at him.

"Oh, God! Oh, God! Beast!"

"You like that?"

"Yes!"

"Want my cock?"

"So much!"

"Good."

Beast had all he could stand. He was taking her hard and fast, not giving her a chance to change her mind. His next thought was to just plunge into her and worry about it later, but he couldn't do that. Even though every second pained him, Beast crawled up her body and reached for the nightstand drawer to pull out a condom. He hadn't intended to use one, but he just couldn't do it without having a serious discussion with her first. Once he went inside her bare, he never intended to have anything separating them again.

Rolling the condom took precious seconds he didn't want to waste, but finally, he was ready. Bracing himself on stiffened arms above Fleur, Beast found her entrance with the tip of his cock and thrust hard.

She was *impossibly* tight! He tried to halt his movements. Give her time to adjust. But Fleur was having none of it.

"Goddammit, Beast! MOVE!"

"Fuck! I don't want to hurt you, Sunshine."

"Fuck it," she bit out and shoved at him. Beast was afraid he was hurting her, cutting off her air or something, but when he pushed up, she heaved. He rolled to his back. The next thing he knew, Fleur was straddling his hips and impaling herself on his length.

"God! Fuck!" Beast gripped her hips, trying to slow her movements, but she was persistent, slapping his hands away.

Then he looked up at her.

She looked... *magnificent*...

Desire and lust morphed into some kind of euphoric high. Her expression was one of dazed confusion, as if she couldn't believe what she was feeling. Beast knew he certainly felt that way. Her hips snapped over him in a quick little slide, creating the most maddening sensations. How he hadn't come was beyond Beast, but he was doing everything in his power to hold off. Not until she came first. No matter what.

She stretched her body back, placing her hands on his thighs. The position not only thrust her breasts up, but drew his gaze down her body to the place where they joined. Never had the sight of his cock in a woman's pussy thrilled him more than it did now. Fleur's body was a perfect, erotic counterpoint to her movements. She was small, but curvy and lush in all the right places.

Beast sat up, wrapping his arms around her waist and pulling her against his chest. She wrapped her arms around his neck and continued to rock, fucking him. It wasn't enough. He quickly flipped her over to her back and scooted up just that little bit...

Then started a hard, driving rhythm into her body. Fierce, bold shoves forced his cock ever deeper until she was crying out with each thrust, each time his cock hit inside her as far as it could go.

Faster and faster he went, yelling until he was hoarse. He fucked her. And fucked her.

"Gonna fill you with my come. Gonna fuck the shit outta you!"

"Yes! Yes! Do it! Come in me, Beast!"

Had he not already put on the condom, had he not already protected her as best he could, Beast would have lost himself in the moment. With her words, he thrust as deep as he could go and did exactly what she begged him to do. She screamed even louder than him, and her cunt milked his cock.

Beast felt like he'd run a marathon. His heart pounded, and he could barely catch his breath. Sweat streamed from his face to drip on her neck. Fleur didn't seem to mind, though. She clung to him, her tongue darting out to lap at his shoulder several times before he finally realized he might be crushing her.

Beast rolled to the side, taking her with him. "Are you OK, Sunshine? God! Did I hurt you?"

"No," she breathed, snuggling into his chest. "I'm more than OK."

"Just rest a minute," he said, inanely. What else was there to say? The best sex of his life had left him ill prepared for the words she probably needed. So he settled on holding her instead.

The second he slipped out of her, he pulled free the condom and knotted it. He wadded some tissue around it and dropped it into the waste basket by the bed. Fleur still clung to him, not moving other than to dig her little fingers into the skin of his chest.

And, God help him, nothing in his life had ever felt more right.

Chapter Seven

The next two months were the best of Fleur's life. She had loved her parents very much and their passing had devastated her, but they had been loners. They'd lived on a small farm in rural Tennessee with no neighbors for more than ten miles in any direction. The only social interaction she'd had was at school or on the Internet with her friends from school. College was supposed to be her big breakout. She was smart, hardworking, and accepting of different cultures and ways of thinking. She had been looking forward to the whole experience. Since she lived in Tennessee, even though she was poor, hard work had gained her acceptance at Vanderbilt University on a partial scholarship. The remainder of her tuition and board had been provided by the financial aid she'd gotten from the school based on her parents' income. She'd thought life couldn't possibly get any better. She would be studying physics and astrophysics at one of the most prestigious universities in the country and, in the process, she'd be opening up a whole new world of social interaction.

She still wanted to go to college, but what she was experiencing here with Salvation's Bane -- and Beast -- was so far beyond her imagining. Beast was the most fantastic and inventive lover she'd ever been with. He took her anywhere and anytime he felt like it, pushing her boundaries, but never so much that she regretted anything they did. He was always there to support her when the club girls got too aggressive and made sure none of the men got handsy. It happened, occasionally, that a few of them would try to dance with her at a party or would pull her into their laps, but Beast was always there to shut it down. The other men would laugh at him unmercifully. She noticed they only did it when he was looking or where he could hear, though. All of it made her suspect any interest they showed in her was merely to get a rise out of Beast.

Which was the only downside to an otherwise glorious time. Where did she stand with Beast? Outside of them having sex or sleeping together, he wouldn't get near her. There was no small talk, no talk of the future, no discussion as to what he wanted from her other than sex. She'd agreed to that, but now she wanted some definite idea as to what was going on between them. She wanted to get her life back on track. School. Making a home for herself. All the things adults did. Right now, she kind of felt like a kid living in her parents' basement. It wasn't like that exactly, but she had no rent, no real responsibilities. Her chores consisted of cooking and cleaning, but nothing heavy. She mostly did it for lack of something else to do. Of course, when Beast got wind of that, he simply had more sex with her. He didn't seem to want her working or getting too comfortable around the club girls, but wasn't able to offer an alternative for her.

Which was another thing. Fleur didn't know the first thing about MCs. She knew enough to know they skirted the edge of the law sometimes, but there was a whole other culture about them she had barely scratched the surface of. With Beast not letting her around the club girls much, the only thing she could do was search the Internet.

As if thinking about him had conjured him up, Beast walked through the door of their room. "Hey there, Sunshine." His demeanor in private was so at odds with his behavior with the club it was hard to reconcile one with the other. When he was like this, in their room where no one could see or hear, she thought of that personality as Gideon. Otherwise, he really was Beast.

"Hey, yourself. I wasn't expecting you back from your run until late this evening." It was still daylight, if barely. The men usually didn't get back to the clubhouse until well after midnight.

He took off his club colors -- the jacket he wore with the club patch on it and his designation -- and carefully hung it in the closet. "You complaining?"

She pretended to think about it. Secretly, she was already getting wet for him. "Hmm... depends."

"Oh, yeah? On what?"

"On whether or not you plan on showering." She wrinkled her nose. "You smell like gas."

He grinned at her. "Definitely plan on showering." He stalked toward her, shedding his T-shirt as he went. "And you're comin' with me."

Fleur squealed as Gideon bent down and scooped her up into his arms. It always thrilled her when he did that. The casual show of strength wasn't something she'd ever get tired of. He carried her to the bathroom before setting her on her feet and whipping the tank top from her body. She'd figured that would be the first thing he'd do so she hadn't worn a bra. As always, his gaze fastened hungrily on her tits. He actually licked his lips before lowering his head and latching on to one nipple.

"Mmmm..." His rumble went straight through her, vibrating her insides deliciously. "Love these tits. Fuckin' perfect."

His big arms looped around her, holding her tightly to him. Fleur wound her arms around his head, encouraging him to continue. She loved the way he did that. Beast was always wrapping himself around her protectively. Possessively. The idea of both appealed to her on a purely feminine level. Having a man so brutally handsome, capable of protecting her and keeping her, was a heady feeling.

"Strip," he commanded. He tossed his boots, socks, and jeans in the corner. No underwear. She giggled, loving that about him.

"How in the world you manage to ride a bike without chafing your balls is beyond me." She laughed.

"'Cause I'm a tough motherfucker," he groused. "Now strip and get in the fuckin' shower. Gonna give you a good seeing-to."

Fleur didn't resist, just did as he said. It didn't take long for Beast to adjust the water, then she was in his arms, kissing him as the water beat down on both of them.

Every time he kissed her it was like a possession. There was no doubt in her mind he was in complete control. She was his and very much suspected she always would be. She wasn't as certain of him being hers, though. He was as biker. A man used to having women whenever he wanted. So far, he'd stayed true to her. As far as she knew, there hadn't been even a whisper of him with another woman. She'd seen for herself the club girls trying to hook up with him, but he'd always shut it down. Never once since this had started had he slept anywhere other than with her.

Fleur was taking it at face value, but the longer things remained uncemented between them, the more she felt like he was growing used to the situation. If a man like Beast got complacent in a relationship, it was doomed.

Then he set her on a ledge in the shower and her mind refused to dwell on the "what ifs" that usually plagued her. All she could think about was that he was about to put his mouth on her pussy, and she wanted it more than she wanted to breathe.

* * *

Beast knew Fleur was starting to get antsy. He'd seen her looking into schools, requesting transcripts and test results be sent to places like the Florida Institute of Technology in Melbourne. That was almost two hours away! Why would she do that? And what was she studying? He'd known she was intelligent, but this wasn't something he'd foreseen. So he'd done what any other self-respecting enforcer would do. He had Ripper investigate. Should be getting that information soon. For now, he'd do the only thing he knew how to do. He was going to keep her happy and satisfied. And fuck her brains out every chance he got.

Her pussy was the sweetest he'd ever tasted. She creamed so wonderfully for him. Every time he went down on her he was amazed anew at how wet she got. His little Fleur was always ready for him.

Now, she spread her legs wide and reached for him as he lowered his mouth to her bare pussy and sucked. Her sharp cry echoed around them, and Beast thought he'd give anything in the world to always hear that sound when he was pleasuring her.

Hands on the bench to brace herself, Fleur rocked her pelvis up and down as he ate her out. The little sounds she made fueled his lust like nothing else could. She was a woman being pleasured. *His* woman. He growled and sucked hard at her pussy, drawing out her honey before moving to suck her clit.

Beast licked and sucked, never letting her fall over the edge. It was one of his favorite things to do with her.

"Beast," she gasped after one particularly close call, "I need to come!"

"No," he bit out. "Not 'til I say."

"Oh, my God!" She screamed as he thrust two fingers inside her, pumping them, fucking her like he wanted to do with his cock. "Oh, my God! Do that!"

"Oh, Sunshine. I'm not nearly done with you yet. I'm gonna drive you fuckin' crazy before I'm done with you."

"You already are! Please don't stop!"

He added a third finger, moving slowly, twisting his hand to get in farther. "Gonna fuck you in a minute. Gonna ram my cock so far in your tight little cunt you'll never get me out."

"Yes," she panted. "Do that. I want your cock inside me. Your come. I want it all!"

He chuckled, aware he sounded more sinister than amused. "You're gonna get it, too, Sunshine. Gonna come inside you. Maybe put a baby there. You'll have my baby growing inside you, and everyone will know who you belong to."

He could see the startled look in her eyes try to shine through the glazed lust and be defeated. "Yes," she breathed. "I want you to put a baby in me, Beast. I want your come. And your baby."

God, those words affected him! He'd never even contemplated it before, but now the thought was almost like a compulsion. *Come inside her. Get her pregnant. Keep her.* Over and over those words echoed inside his head.

He shook his head hard, trying to clear it. He had to have his wits about him. Had to keep control. It scared him how easily she could reduce him to the Beast he was named. Mindless. When he fucked Fleur, sometimes there was nothing he could think about other than the pleasure of being inside her.

When he removed his fingers from her pussy, she actually sobbed, grabbing his wrist to shove them back in.

"No!" Fleur responded to his sharp command, going still. "Keep those legs spread wide," he said, giving the inside of one thigh a sharp smack for emphasis. "Scoot to the edge of the shelf." She did without hesitation. He hooked his arms around her thighs and pulled her even farther, but she didn't protest. He sucked and lapped at her pussy for a little longer, reluctant to leave her as well as needing to drive her as high as he could.

Finally, when she was sobbing and begging him to fuck her, he thrust two fingers inside her again, pumping several times before retreating. Much as he wanted her pregnant with his child, it was something he needed to discuss with her outside of sex. Much as he wanted to just do it, it wouldn't be fair to her. Though he was a heartbeat away from saying to hell with her choices and taking her at her word in the heat of the moment. He didn't warn her. Instead, he slipped the tip of his wet finger inside her little anus.

For several seconds Fleur froze. Beast wanted to watch his finger disappear inside her, but had to watch her face for signs of discomfort. Eyes wide in shock, glazed over with lust, she stared at him. Her mouth made an "O" of surprise. Then she started trembling.

"Easy," he murmured, petting her thigh before sinking his finger farther, pulling out, then all the way in.

"Holy shit," she gasped. "Holy shit!"

"Push out against me," he said. "Slow and gentle."

"Wha -- what are you doing?"

He shook his head hard to try to clear it a little more, to explain what he was doing. "Changed my mind. I told you I was gonna fuck you in every hole I could fit my dick into. Makin' good on my promise."

She shivered in his arms. Beast added a second finger, scissoring his fingers slightly to stretch her open.

"Beast," she whimpered. He got the feeling she meant to say something more, but she shook her head slightly and did as he told her. She pressed out against him as he'd instructed.

"That's it, Sunshine," he praised. "Your little ass is gonna be so fuckin' tight around my fuckin' cock. I'm gonna stick it in, then fuck you hard. When I'm ready, I'm gonna come inside you, filling your ass with my sticky come. You think you can take that, baby?"

"I -- I don't... Beast!" She gasped when he smacked the inside of the other thigh.

"Answer me, Goddamnit!"

"Yes! Yes! Whatever you want! I'm yours!"

"That's right. You're mine. Mine to do with as I please. I'll fuck you hard, and you'll love every second of it, won't you?"

"I will!"

"You will." He pumped his fingers several more times, watching her carefully. Much as he wanted this, he didn't want her hurt. He might pretend not to give a good goddamn, but he would rather cut off his own dick than hurt her this way. For her, he could be patient. He could get her worked up so that any discomfort she might have would only amplify her pleasure. Right now, she was on the verge and Beast knew it.

He'd placed a bottle of oil-based lube in the shower for just such an occasion. It would be gentle for her but stand up against the water as long as he was careful. He'd adjusted the sprays in the shower days before, making sure he could control where they hit. The water sprayed all around them, but not directly on them. When he was ready to clean her, it would be easy but not in his way right now.

Beast liberally rubbed the lube on his cock, stroking himself several times to make sure he was as slick as he could be. Then he worked some around Fleur's puckered ass, painting the inside with his finger. Satisfied things would move as easily as they could, he stood before her, giving his cock a few last strokes. That was when he realized his hands were shaking.

"You ready, Sunshine?"

Fleur opened her mouth to say something, but almost immediately closed it. Beast noticed she trembled beneath his touch. Probably a combination of fear and lust.

"I need the words, Fleur," he said. "If you're not ready for this, I'm not doing it. Period."

"I -- I'm scared," she admitted. "But I want this. I want to have you in every way I can."

He placed the head of his cock at her back entrance. "Last chance, Sunshine."

"Do it," she hissed. "Do it!"

Beast eased the head into her. The look of surprise on her face made him pause. She turned her head and her gaze clung to his.

"Talk to me, Sunshine."

"I -- it doesn't hurt," she whispered. "Keep going."

He did as she instructed, easing his cock inside her, stopping ever inch or so to pull back slightly before sliding inside again just that little bit farther. Finally, after several careful thrusts, Beast was seated all the way inside her. He pulled back until just the head was there, then slid back inside again. He did this several times, moving just a little faster. When he pulled all the way out of her, she hissed her displeasure.

"What are you doing?" she demanded.

"Just making sure you're OK."

"I'll tell you when I'm not OK, Beast," she snapped. "Get back inside!"

Beast let out a strangled chuckle. "Don't get snippy with me. I'll take care of you."

"Unh!" Fleur reached for him, guiding his cock back to her ass. She braced her feet on the edge once again and used the leverage to force his dick back inside her.

"Fleur! Fuck!" The sensations were overwhelming. She moved on him as much as he moved inside her. She was impossibly tight. Her ass clamped down on him every now and then so that he just knew she was going to make him come before he was ready. To distract her, he washed his hands, making sure he was completely clean, then shoved two fingers inside her pussy while he tried his damnedest to hold still. Just a few seconds. He had to prolong this. Couldn't come before she did.

"Oh my God! Yes! Do that!" she screamed, wiggling on his cock. Her thighs were spread as wide as she could go. Then she hooked her hands behind her knees and brought her legs up near her shoulders. "Fuck me, Beast! Oh, God! Fuck me!"

He inserted a third finger in her while he began a slow glide in and out of her ass. He could feel his cock with his fingers moving inside her through the thin layers of tissue. It was erotic as fuck. "Feel good, Sunshine? You like me fucking your little ass?"

"I love it," she gasped, her breath coming in little pants now. Her pussy was drenching him with her creamy honey. As it dripped down, it eased the way for his cock even more. Beast picked up his pace as he stroked her clit with his thumb.

"So fuckin' tight," he bit out. "*So fuckin' tight!*"

"Faster," she pleaded, rocking against him as much as she could.

Beast complied, beginning a hard, driving surge that jarred her body as he buried himself as deep as he could go. He kept his fingers inside her as long as he could. When she urged him faster still, he removed them to grip her hips and fuck her harder and faster.

When she came, Beast thought she might truly squeeze his cock in two. The pressure was indescribable. The ability to hold his seed nil. With a mighty shove and a roar to the ceiling so loud his ears rang with it, Beast emptied himself inside Fleur, filling her with his come as he held her tightly to him. He didn't want even an inch of space between his skin and hers. Her legs wrapped around his waist tightly as she continued to come around him.

Once it was over, Beast thought his legs might give out on him. He had no idea how he managed to keep from sinking to the floor of the shower in a heap. He still held Fleur tightly, kissing her neck and stroking damp hair from her face. She hadn't said a word, but she clung to him just as tightly, her breathing still ragged.

He washed her gently, then himself. Turning off the water he snagged towels and wrapped her in one while he quickly dried himself so he could spend extra time on her. She hadn't moved, still sitting on the ledge, her legs spread and a dazed expression on her face.

Beast lifted her gently and carried her to his bed. He tossed the damp towel aside before pulling her against his chest, urging her to rest there. She gave one long, shuddering sigh, then was still. Beast watched her carefully. He'd exhausted her, for which he was exceedingly proud, but something seemed a little off to him. He had no idea what, but it was something he needed to talk to her about the second they woke. For now, he was nearly as wiped as she obviously was.

Feeling happier than he could remember being in a very long time, knowing he'd taken her in every way he possibly could so far, Beast wanted to thump his chest. Fleur was his. He'd gotten her to agree to it when she'd thought it was temporary, but now, well. He knew he'd never let her go. Their temporary situation was about to become permanent. He just had a couple things to take care of, and then it was as good as done.

* * *

Fleur woke to an empty bed. Beast was gone. She sighed. Hadn't he said that before she left the club he'd have her in every hole he could fit his dick into? It was still dark, but her phone said it was five in the morning, so last night had been it. He'd taken her in every way he could. It was his room, but he was gone. Was that her cue to leave? He'd talked about wanting her pregnant with his baby, but was that all dirty talk? Meant to arouse her?

And why did it fucking hurt so much? God! There was a sick feeling in her stomach that wouldn't be denied. Last night had been special for her. She'd allowed herself to be stripped bare. Allowed Beast to take her in a way she'd never imagined letting anyone do. It had been intimate. Personal. And, Goddammit, it had meant something to her!

She'd known this day would come. Her time with Beast had lasted longer than she'd first thought it would. It's just that the sex had been so wonderful, she'd hoped he'd give her a few more days. Explore what they'd shared. It obviously wasn't his first time in that department. Maybe that was just his way of saying goodbye. She could take the hint.

It didn't take long to pack her backpack. What few things she'd managed to get back from Debbie's were meager. She'd retrieved everything that mattered to her and a few items of clothing. She'd actually left most of her clothing because she hadn't wanted to be in that house a second longer than she'd had to. Knowing all she knew now, the place gave her the creeps.

Getting out of the clubhouse proved easier than she'd thought. If there was anyone guarding the driveway entrance to the Salvation's Bane compound, she didn't see them. She actually didn't meet anyone on her way out. Her car was parked just inside the compound next to a few of the prospects' bikes. She hadn't parked there last time she'd driven it. Now she had to wonder if that was because Beast was giving her another hint. Until they'd proven their worth, prospects weren't actual members of the club. Neither were club girls, but most of them stuck around once they were there. She had no idea how other clubs worked, but this club seemed to make sure all the club girls were protected at all times. Their rooms were in between the members' rooms so there was always a line of defense before anyone could get to one of them. Their vehicles -- bikes or cars -- were hidden so no one girl could be pinned down as being there at any given time unless she wanted to.

But Fleur... well. She was parked right out there in the open. Sure, it could be because she was due an oil change, because her car was usually parked with the other girls', but for some reason this just seemed telling. Like she was temporary. Just like with Debbie. Fleur's parents had loved her, but they were gone. The funny thing was, she'd never felt more alone in her life than she did in this moment. Debbie hadn't done as much with her betrayal. The loss of her parents had devastated her, but she'd known she could do it on her own. She'd known it would be hard, but she'd known she could do it. She'd just needed a plan.

Leaving Beast, knowing it was what he wanted her to do, nearly gutted her. Maybe he'd only wanted her because of the whole she-was-in-danger thing. Beast was over-the-top protective. Fleur had no doubt that was why he'd been chosen to be the club's enforcer. Now that she was safe, he'd lost interest. It made sense, in a way. He'd be looking for the next woman who needed his help. Being saddled with her would make that job more difficult.

Fleur climbed in her car and took off. She'd planned on looking into the Florida Institute of Technology in Melbourne. It was only a couple hours' drive from Palm Springs. She could drive there, secure lodging with her meager savings, then contact admissions. They should have had time to get her transcripts and test scores. She'd also been in touch with her advisor at Vanderbilt, explaining what had happened and why her situation had changed. The woman had been beyond understanding and sweet about the whole thing. She'd even offered to write her a letter of recommendation to whichever university she ended up at. That was what she should have done in the first place. The idea of hooking up with a classmate had been so appealing she'd lost sight of her future. She was going to be an astrophysicist. It was time she got to it.

Fleur was about an hour into her drive when her phone rang. Not recognizing the number, she started to ignore it, but something changed her mind.

"Hello?"

"This is Miles at JFK Medical Center in Lake Worth. Is this Fleur Durand?" The male voice on the other end of the phone was pleasant and professional.

"Yes." What in the world?

"We have a patient named Debbie Johnson who's requested we call you for her. Are you able to come to the hospital?"

"I -- Well, I'm almost in Melbourne. Did she say what was wrong?" Fleur's heart rate sped up. She wasn't certain she could face Debbie. Especially knowing the likely reason why she was in the hospital in the first place. Beast hadn't elaborated on what they'd done to Debbie, but it didn't take a genius to figure it out.

"She just needs a ride home and someone to stay with her for the next twenty-four hours or so."

What did she do? If she told the guy "no," she came across as a bitch who wouldn't help out her friend. If she told him Debbie had set her up to be beaten and raped, she had no doubt the cops would be looking for Fleur soon. If she turned around and went to pick her up in Lake Worth, there was no telling what Debbie would have waiting for her.

"Can I talk to her?" Maybe if she could talk to Debbie directly, she could feel the situation out. Lord knew she couldn't lie worth a damn so there was no use trying to make up something for the guy who'd called her.

"I'm afraid not. She's pretty sedated. One of the reasons she needs someone to stay with her." Cryptic much? Oh, well. If Debbie hadn't given them permission to talk about the situation with her, they wouldn't. This guy's job was to get her to the hospital. She knew that from experience when her parents had been killed.

With a heavy sigh, Fleur pulled the car over to the side of the road. "I'll be there as soon as I can. Understand it will be at least an hour and a half. I was on my way to Melbourne."

"I'm sure she appreciates it, ma'am. Drive safely. Again, my name is Miles. Once you get here mention her name and mine. We'll get you back to her."

"Miles. Got it." She hung up the phone.

Fuck. Double fuck. Oh, well. It was the decent thing to do. She'd take Debbie home, then it would be up to her to find someone to babysit her. Fleur wasn't staying in the house. Wasn't even setting foot in the house. Maybe this was for the best. She'd at least get some closure with the woman she'd thought of as a friend.

It was only a little after nine in the morning when she walked into JFK Medical. Getting back to see Debbie was easy enough. Seeing her... wasn't. The woman had been beaten to within an inch of her life.

"We wanted to admit her, but she refused," the doctor said as he gave Fleur instructions on how to care for Debbie and when to bring her back to the hospital.

"Then that's what you should do," Fleur said. "I can't care for her. This is beyond anything I'm capable of. She needs professional help."

"I agree with you. Unfortunately, we can't keep a patient against their will. She's signed out against medical advice."

"If she's sedated, is she even capable of doing that?"

"She signed the papers before we gave her the second round of pain medicine. She insisted. I insisted on the medicine. Once it wears off, I have a feeling she'll change her mind about being admitted. If for no other reason than for pain control."

"Then why not just tell her there was no one to come get her and let it wear off? She changes her mind, she gets the care she needs, and I don't freak out thinking I could do something to hurt her worse! I can't do this! I'm not qualified!"

"I probably shouldn't tell you everything but, since she insisted she be released into your care, I'm taking it as permission. You need to know the extent of her injuries in order to care for her." He took a seat and indicated Fleur do the same. "Other than a slight concussion, most of what you see is purely external damage. Cosmetic. Provided she doesn't get an infection, she should be fine." He paused, looking at Debbie before continuing. "We're not sure what happened. Someone dropped her off at the ER door and took off. Typically, when we see that type of behavior, there are usually drugs involved. Her tox screen came back clean. Do you have any idea if she was in some kind of trouble?"

This was exactly what Fleur was hoping to avoid. Even that one little "no" she needed to utter would be hard for her.

"Uh, Debbie and I haven't had contact for a couple of months. We had a falling out, I guess you could say." There. That was the strict truth. No lying.

"I see. And you haven't had contact with her since then?"

"No. To be honest, I really don't want to have contact with her now either. I don't want her to be defenseless because no one should ever feel that helpless." Speaking from experience. "But I really think you should just tell her I was unable to take her home. Her parents live in Rockwell, Indiana. I don't have their phone number, but both of them work for Argent Tech. Should be easy enough to get in touch with them through the company." She held her hands up in a gesture of surrender. "I really can't help her. It would be safer for her to be admitted. If she refuses…" She shrugged. "I imagine you're better equipped to deal with that situation. I really am sorry."

"One more thing. It looks like her injuries have happened over several weeks. She's been tortured. She could really use a friend now."

Fleur winced. She couldn't help but feel that was on her, but it didn't change the fact that Debbie had sold her out. Literally.

"Crap," she muttered. "What a mess."

"More so for her," the doctor said. Right.

"I don't mean to be rude," Fleur said as calmly as she could. "But you have no idea what happened between Debbie and me. She set me up to be raped and beaten. I'm really sorry this happened to her, but it looks like maybe she got in trouble when she couldn't deliver." As lies went, Fleur didn't think that was too bad. "Much as I hate this for her, this is close to what she had planned for me." To Fleur's complete and utter horror, a tear escaped her, trickling down her cheek. "She was supposed to be my friend! My parents had just died, and my future was so uncertain. I wasn't sure I could still afford to go to college and didn't even have a place to live. Debbie told me she was my friend. Let me live with her if I'd just move here from Tennessee. I was supposed to tutor her this semester so I could have some income. Then everything just crashed down..."

Fleur couldn't help it. She was sobbing now. All that was upsetting, but what really got her was the fact that, faced with evidence of what Beast had ordered to happen, she still believed in him with every fiber of her being. He was the man she wanted beyond all reason. The man she trusted with her life. With everything that she was. And he was gone.

The floodgates opened and she *sobbed*.

Chapter Eight

When Beast arrived back at his room with his gifts for Fleur, he nearly came unglued when he found that, not only was she not in his bed, but she wasn't even in the Goddamned compound. A quick check of the security cameras told him when she'd gone and which direction. Having Ripper ping her cell phone had told him her location. He had headed in the direction of Melbourne when he'd gotten a call from Ripper telling him she'd turned around. It had taken another hour for him to figure out she'd gone to the hospital in Lake Worth.

Fuck. What was she doing there?

When he'd asked for her at the desk, they'd shown no one listed by her name. How the fuck was he going to find her? He was just about to have Ripper do another ping on her phone when he overheard someone ask if they'd heard of a place called Rockwell, Indiana. That set off alarm bells. He quickly put together what was happening and asked the lady at the desk if there was a Debbie Johnson listed.

Bingo.

Surprisingly, they let him back in the ER easier than he'd have thought and told him what room she was in. That was where he found Fleur, sobbing her heart out. He was just about to enter when a familiar voice stopped him.

"Gideon. Hold up."

"She your patient, Doc?" Not only was Doc a patched member of Salvation's Bane, but a real doctor.

"No. What's going on? I just found out Fleur was in there with Miss Johnson."

"I'm not sure what's going on, but that girl is the one who set Fleur up at the club. Venus was responsible for taking care of her."

"Well, she took care of her, all right. They can't get anything out of Miss Johnson, but believe me, they're trying. Can she identify you?"

"Oh, yeah." Beast shrugged. "I'm not here for her. I'm here for Fleur. Why is Fleur here to begin with?"

"The patient refused to be admitted, but they wouldn't send her home unless someone was with her. She gave Fleur's name and number as someone to call. I'm assuming that's how she ended up here."

"So why's Fleur crying?"

"That I couldn't tell you, brother. Had I known who that girl was, I'd have made sure they didn't call Fleur." Doc looked around, scrubbing the back of his neck as if deciding on what to do next.

"I'm not here to cause you trouble, Doc. This is my mess. I'll take care of it."

"That's what fuckin' bothers me," Doc bit out angrily. He took a deep breath before continuing, drawing Beast away from the main flow of traffic. "Look. You go wait outside. I'll get Fleur and meet you there. You guys can leave, and I'll take care of this."

"No. Like I said. This is my responsibility."

"Well, I'm not leaving you." Doc entered the room with Beast. The other doctor looked up. "Dr. Lyons."

"Dr. Collins," the other guy said. "Everything all right?"

"This is Gideon Leigh. He's here to help Miss Durand."

"Good. Fleur was concerned she would be unable to take care of Ms. Johnson given the severity of her injuries. Perhaps you'd be of assistance?"

"Afraid I don't know much about taking care of injuries," Beast answered. "I was concerned for Fleur. She's upset."

The doctor didn't question how Beast knew Fleur was upset. Probably thought she'd texted him or something. "Yes." He glanced at Fleur then back to Beast. "She was telling me how Miss Johnson had put her in a... rather awkward and difficult position the last time they saw each other. You know about that?"

Beast didn't flinch. "If you're asking if I did this to somehow avenge Fleur, I can assure you I didn't. I'm not in the habit of killing women." He looked at Debbie. "I won't pretend to be sorry, though. I know you're doing your job and part of that includes empathy, but as far as I'm concerned, Debbie deserved what she got. And more."

"You know I'll have to report this. It's not my job to judge you, but I do have to advocate for my patients."

Beast shrugged. "You do what you have to, Doc. I'm not about to hold it against you for doing your job. If Fleur were in this situation, I'd hope you'd do the same for her."

"I take it you know Dr. Collins?"

"I do."

"We've known each other for several years," Doc said. "He's one of my closest friends."

Dr. Lyons looked startled. "Oh. I'm sorry. I had no idea."

"Nothing to apologize for."

"Well, if Dr. Collins vouches for you --"

"No, Doc," Beast cut off the other doctor. "You're doing your job. Who I am or that I know your colleague shouldn't matter. You do what you feel is best for your patient. I'll not stand in your way."

"I appreciate that, Mr. Leigh." He addressed Fleur, who had gone quiet when Beast had entered. She still sniffled occasionally, but otherwise remained silent. "Are you still uncomfortable taking Miss Johnson home?"

"I just don't think it's appropriate under the circumstances. The best thing for her would be to stay here until her parents can come for her. I'm really sorry."

Dr. Lyons stared at her a long time, then finally seemed to come to a decision. "I have to ask, Fleur. You stopped being so upset when Mr. Leigh entered the room. Went almost completely silent, in fact. Are you safe with him? I mean, I was going to call the cops given he knew what happened with you and Miss Johnson. I changed my mind when Dr. Collins was willing to vouch for him, but maybe I need to ask you."

"Gideon found me. If it hadn't been for him…" She shuddered, another little sob breaking free. Tears began to stream down her face again, and her voice shook. "I can't even imagine what would have happened to me. Understand me, Dr. Lyons. I owe Gideon my life. He's been nothing but decent to me since the moment I met him."

Dr. Lyons nodded. "That's all I needed to hear. I'll have our secretary get to work on locating Miss Johnson's parents."

Once he left, Beast squatted down in front of Fleur. "You OK, Sunshine?"

Once again, she crumbled into tears, throwing herself into his arms. Beast held her tightly while she cried. The hospital was no place for this. He needed her back at the clubhouse where he could fix whatever was going on.

"I'm sorry," she sobbed. "I'm so sorry."

"Baby, why are you sorry?"

"For whatever I did to make you want me to leave! I know I'm not that experienced, but I'm trying to learn what you like. I'm trying to fit in with your club."

"Sunshine, what are you talking about? You fit in perfectly with my club. As to pleasing me, I've never been with a woman who pleases me more."

She blinked up at him, those silver-green eyes of hers mesmerizing him. "What?"

"What made you think I didn't want you? Didn't I tell you it wasn't over until I said it was over?"

"Well, yes. You said that, but…"

"And did I tell you it was over?"

"Not in so many words…"

"So why would you think you could just up and leave like this?"

"Because I couldn't just wait around for you to kick me out! I couldn't bear it!"

"Christ," he bit out. He stood, pulling her to her feet with him. "We're leaving."

"But Debbie --"

"Isn't your responsibility. Now, come on."

* * *

Beast put a helmet on Fleur's head before getting on his bike. "Get on," he ordered gruffly.

She'd ridden with him so many times over the last two months. Hell, they'd had sex on the bike more than once. But today, it just seemed like a bitter reminder of everything she was losing. "No, Gideon. I was on my way to Melbourne when the hospital called me. I need to get back on the road."

"Not happening, Sunshine. Get on the fuckin' bike." He didn't raise his voice, but Fleur knew he meant business. The only question was, did she do what he said? Roll over and let him have his way, knowing he was breaking her heart? The thought of leaving him and the thought of staying when he wasn't keeping her was enough to start a fresh flood of tears. Angrily, she batted them away, taking several deep breaths. "Sunshine. Honey." He gently tilted her face up to him. Fleur tried to resist, but he was insistent. Careful, but insistent. "What's this about?"

She huffed, angrier at herself than him. He'd warned her, hadn't he? "Nothing." Pulling away from him, she straddled his bike and strapped her helmet on. "Let's just go. Who's bringing my car?"

"I'll send one of the boys after it later." Now that he had his way, Beast was all business. He climbed on in front of her and started the bike. Then they were off.

As much as Fleur enjoyed the freedom of riding, as much as she enjoyed riding with Beast, this was all a reminder of what she was losing. Well, she didn't want to lose it! They were good together, Goddammit! If he couldn't see that, they why would she even want to waste her time on him? The ride should have mellowed her. Instead it fueled her anger. By the time they got to the clubhouse, she was fighting mad.

Beast turned into the driveway, and the second he shut the machine down, she was off. She yanked the helmet off and threw it on the ground next to the bike and stomped into the clubhouse. She had just made it to the middle of the common room when Beast grabbed her arm and spun her around.

"You wanna tell me what the all-fired fuck is goin' on?"

"What's going on is, I'm leaving. Getting the fuck outta Dodge!"

"Wanna tell me why?"

"I was good to you, Beast! Good *for* you! When we first met, I never thought I'd see you smile or have a real laugh. Over the last few weeks, I've seen you mellow. Maybe not much, but when we're alone I can get you to have tickle fights with me! I never meddle in your business with the club. I never hound you about when you're coming home. I do every little thing you ask of me, and now you're ready to get rid of me?"

Right up until the end, he'd had this mellow look of something like satisfaction on his face, but Fleur had kept going. The second she said that last part, repeating what she'd said at the hospital, he'd frowned. Then he narrowed his eyes, looking around the clubhouse. "You mentioned before you thought I wanted you gone. You tell me what fucker told you that. Was it one of the club girls? Because, let me tell you, if one of them did, she's gone."

At once, every single club girl in the vicinity voiced denial. Loudly.

"No one had to tell me, Beast. *You* told me. Last night in the shower."

He looked at her like she'd grown two heads. "Huh? What the fuck, Fleur? I did no such thing!"

"You told me --" Oh, God, the tears were going to come again. "You told me the first time we had sex that, before I left this clubhouse, you were going to fuck me in every hole you could fit your dick into. Well, you claimed the last hole last night!" Fleur practically wailed the last before bursting into a fresh flood of tears. "I let you fuck me in the ass, and now that's it! We're over!"

Beast looked around him. He absolutely could not believe she was having this conversation with him in the middle of the clubhouse common room. He didn't care, but she would when she realized what she'd just yelled at him. It was everything he could do to keep a straight face.

"Sunshine, I wasn't telling you to leave."

"You said it! Then you were gone this morning! You left me! What else was I supposed to think or do!?" Still yelling. OK. This was way, way off in left field.

As if Thorn had just been waiting for the right moment, he tossed Beast the jacket he'd had made for her, and a tiny box he'd picked up just that morning. The reason for his sudden early departure.

"OK. First of all, I never said I wanted rid of you after we'd, uh... I never said I wanted you gone." He cleared his throat, knowing that, no matter what happened in the next few minutes, she'd still have to deal with all this later. Everyone in the club would tease her about it. For *months*. "Second. I left to pick up some things I had made for you. It was supposed to be a surprise after dinner tonight, but I can see perhaps now is the better time."

She blinked. "Wait. What?"

"Yeah, Sunshine." He held out the jacket to her, spreading it out so she could see the back. *Property of Beast* was emblazoned on the back on rockers top and bottom. When she looked up at him, her eyes still narrowed in irritation, Lucy, Vicious's ol' lady, stepped forward.

"It's not what you think. That's Beast's way of claiming you. Making you his ol' lady." She grinned. "It's a good thing, honey."

It seemed to take Fleur a moment for that to sink in, so Beast took a tentative step toward her, the little box in hand. He opened it and pulled out a ring. Taking her left hand, he slid the ring onto her finger. "The jacket is for me. The ring, for you." Then he got down on one knee. "Fleur. Will you marry me? Be my ol' lady?" She stood there, mouth gaping open. A strangled sound came from her, but she couldn't seem to form a coherent response. Beast grinned. "I'm taking that as a yes."

To the cheers of everyone around, Beast picked Fleur up and swung her around before wrapping his arms tightly around her. "Sunshine," he sighed.

"Oh, Gideon!" This time, the tears were happy tears. She wrapped her arms and legs around him before kissing his face all over. "I'm so sorry. I just thought --"

"That was your first mistake. A woman as smart as you should never try to think like a guy like me. You'll get it wrong every time, because I'm not nearly as intelligent as you are."

"That's not true!" He cut off her protests with a hard kiss before tossing her over his shoulder.

"Listen here, little Miss Astrophysicist. We're gonna get you into Florida Technical Institute and you're gonna find a star and name it after me. Then, you're gonna find twelve more and name them after our kids."

"Twelve!"

He swatted her ass. Hard.

"Yes. Twelve. Then, when our kids start having kids, you're gonna retire. I'll find a peaceful place for us to go camping every year, and you'll show our grandkids where every one of those stars are while we roast marshmallows by the campfire."

"I'm not having twelve kids!"

"Thirteen is an unlucky number."

"Beast!"

The echo of his club's laughter followed them down the hall until he shoved open his door and closed them inside. He set her on her feet then placed his hands on her shoulders. "Look at me, Fleur. Really look at me."

When she did, he could still see the worry lying beneath her adorably dazed and confused expression. "I love you. I know I haven't said it, and I don't show a lot of affection around other members of the club. That stopped tonight. You're my ol' lady. I won't deny I didn't want to get too close to you before, but that was my own insecurities. I was afraid you'd do exactly what you did. You ran. I just had no idea it was because you thought I didn't want you. Stupid of me since I hadn't given you a reason to think otherwise."

He took a breath, aware he was starting to babble. "Anyway. I love you, Fleur. I'll support you in any way I can. I'll protect you and our children with my life."

He closed his eyes against the tears threatening. When did he become such a pussy? "Just..." He swallowed. "Just stay with me, Sunshine."

Finally, *finally*, a smile split her face, once again as bright as the Sunshine he'd named her. "Yes. I'll stay. Gladly!"

Beast brought her in for a kiss. One thing led to another and before he knew it, they were naked in bed, his head between her thighs.

"Oh, God!" Fleur screamed as she gave him more of that honey he'd come to crave.

"More," he growled. "I want more!"

Her breath came in ragged little pants, sweat glistening off her skin. "I love you, Gideon," she panted. "I love you so much!"

"That's my girl," he said as he crawled up her body. He entered her in one swift movement. She cried out and wrapped her legs around him, digging her heels into his ass.

"Oh, God! Oh, God!"

"So fuckin' tight! Don't think I'll ever get used to this!"

"Fuck me, Beast. Oh, Jesus, fuck me hard!"

He did. Slamming into her over and over until they were both on the verge. Her little pussy gripped him until he saw stars with the effort to hold back. When she screamed, he let himself go. With a roar to the ceiling, Beast came inside her with one hot, creamy spurt after another. In his life, nothing had ever felt so right. His woman. In his bed. His seed inside her.

"I came inside you," he murmured, wondering how she'd take it. It was a shit move on his part, but he didn't fucking care. He was doing everything he fucking could to tie her to him.

"Yeah," she said, sounding supremely satisfied. "You certainly did."

"You're not mad?"

"Well, you are doing the right thing. You know, putting a ring on my finger and everything. It was bound to happen eventually."

He chuckled. "Yeah. I guess it was." He kissed her mouth gently, taking his time and savoring her sweetness. "We good? You're not going to run again, are you?"

"No." Then she frowned. "But what about Debbie? Won't she come after you?"

"I doubt it. Once I figured out what was going on, I texted Venus. Her response was cryptic, but she indicated there was nothing to worry about." He shrugged. "I trust my people. If she says it's good, then it's good."

"I was surprised Debbie isn't in jail. I mean, I thought all the guys who did this were in jail."

"The men are. It wasn't likely there was anything Debbie would be charged with to keep her in prison more than a couple years, so I didn't try very hard to get her to agree to plead guilty. I just let Venus do what she does. Debbie isn't in jail, but if she says there's nothing to worry about with her, Venus has taken care of it in some way. I'll trust her."

"Well, if you do then I do, too. I'll have to remember to thank her."

"Oh, I think the little show in the common room was thanks enough. I haven't heard Venus laugh like that in years."

At the mention of the episode just a few minutes earlier, Fleur groaned. "Don't remind me. That's not going away. Is it?"

"Not likely."

She shrugged. "Oh, well. I guess I'll have to learn to live with it."

"If by *it* you mean *me*, then I don't think you'll have anything to worry about. I'm a beast when it comes to protecting my woman. You want it shut down, I'll take care of it."

Fleur laughed. "No. It's to my advantage, really. Now every club girl here knows there's not a single thing I won't let you do to me. There's not a fucking thing any of them can lure you to bed with."

"Only you have that power, Sunshine."

"I love you," she said, kissing him once again.

"I love you, too, Sunshine. I love you, too."

Marteeka Karland

Erotic romance author by night, emergency room tech/clerk by day, Marteeka Karland works really hard to drive everyone in her life completely and totally nuts. She has been creating stories from her warped imagination since she was in the third grade. Her love of writing blossomed throughout her teenage years until it developed into the totally unorthodox and irreverent style her English teachers tried so hard to rid her of.

Marteeka at Changeling: changelingpress.com/marteeka-karland-a-39

Changeling Press E-Books

More Sci-Fi, Fantasy, Paranormal, and BDSM adventures available in e-book format for immediate download at ChangelingPress.com -- Werewolves, Vampires, Dragons, Shapeshifters and more -- Erotic Tales from the edge of your imagination.

What are E-Books?

E-books, or electronic books, are books designed to be read in digital format -- on your desktop or laptop computer, notebook, tablet, Smart Phone, or any electronic e-book reader.

Where can I get Changeling Press E-Books?

Changeling Press e-books are available at ChangelingPress.com, Amazon, Apple Books, Barnes & Noble, and Kobo/Walmart.

ChangelingPress.com

Printed in Great Britain
by Amazon